TALK TO ME

TALK TO ME

ZOE AMOS

SAPPHIRE BOOKS

SALINAS, CALIFORNIA

Talk to Me
Zoe Amos
Copyright © 2021
All rights reserved.

ISBN - 978-1-952270-20-8

This is a work of fiction - names, characters, places, and incidents are the product of the author's imagination or are used fictitiously. Any resemblance to actual persons living or dead, business, events or locales is entirely coincidental.

All rights reserved. No part of this publication may be reproduced, distributed, or transmitted in any form or by any means, including photocopying, recording, or other electronic or mechanical methods, without written permission of the publisher.

Editor - Heather Flournoy
Book Design - LJ Reynolds
Cover Design - Fineline Design

Sapphire Books Publishing, LLC
P.O. Box 8142
Salinas, CA 93912
www.sapphirebooks.com

Printed in the United States of America
First Edition - March 2021

This and other Sapphire Books titles can be found at
www.sapphirebooks.com

Acknowledgment

Thank you to my initial readers: Julia Carson, Cecelia Davidson, Jade Elk, Greg Evans, and D.M. Starfield, who provided feedback on early versions of the manuscript. Your viewpoints enabled me to appreciate my characters and storyline from new perspectives. To Lois Winsen, thank you for your keen eye, insight, and the first edit. You showed me how to be a better writer.

Later in the revision process, my beta readers stepped up with invaluable feedback that I used to make needed changes. Thanks go to Sharon Bohannon, Mary Ann Horton, Eunice Parisi-Carew, Jane Ripley, and Judy Stojsavljevic. My sincere thanks go to my editor, Heather Flournoy, for providing the smoothing touches necessary to reach the finish line.

All of you provided various stages of support. You have my gratitude for the time you spent and the interest you showed in my work.

Chapter One

Radio. It's good company—at the beach, in your car, or no place special at all. News, talk, music, even the ads sound like trusted friends, a voice that informs and entertains with reassuring familiarity. There's comfort in knowing it's there, and right now I needed it in a way I had never considered.

I found solace in listening to the radio, and lately it filled the lonely spaces in my head. Lively music crowded out sad thoughts and the recitation of recent events that flashed strobe-like through my mind. Since leaving home, the radio had become my companion. That shred of synchronicity gave me hope as I sat in the lobby at KZSD AM 780, "San Diego's Community Connection."

As the traffic report droned in the background, I examined the employment application in front of me. The form was shorter than the online versions I dealt with the day before. The anonymity of clicking "Submit" left me feeling undistinguished from any other seeker, and I hoped showing up in person would give me an edge. I carefully printed my name and new address, yet the information looked as if it belonged to someone else. Phone number—*damn*. In a moment of carelessness, I had dropped my cell phone and it was taking forever to get it fixed. Explaining the problem to interviewers made me feel inept, and as it was, I didn't have much work experience. Here I was, over forty with two almost grown kids and a soon-to-be ex-husband, forced to make calls from borrowed phones to follow up on job prospects. If someone would take a chance on me, I could dispense with these painful phone interviews and get on with my life.

Repetitive monotony from the endless parade of job applications caused the words to blur. Rather than fill in all the blank spaces, I decided to wing it and slid my freshly printed resume into the folded form. It was five minutes after eleven. As I waited, I glanced around the room, which was unremarkable in its plainness. I had expected a radio station to be more glamorous, even though the position of administrative assistant was not.

My attire was as businesslike as I could put together—a patch-pocket jacket over a flower-print dress. I remembered when I had made this outfit. Had it been more than a year since I picked out the material and stitched it together? Though not long ago, the luncheons and school conferences I had worn it to were the farthest thing from my mind. My pre-interview jitters were evident as I swung my foot around in circles, and I could feel my skin dampen where my legs touched. I needed relief from the heat, but rather than risk looking unprofessional by removing my jacket, I pushed the hair away from my neck to let in a little air. In the background I could hear the telltale hum of an old air-conditioning system compete with the weather broadcast. What did it matter? San Diego summer days were pretty much alike.

Betty, the office manager, called me in for our interview. I ran my moist palm inconspicuously across my clothing before I shook her hand. Her long nails were painted red, accented at the tips with diagonal ivory lines. As I sat across from her, I curled my fingers inward to hide my unpolished nails. We were separated by the barrier of her desk, a cluttered altar adorned with two generations of family photos, little figurines, and posters featuring Scottish terriers sporting plaid bows. I visualized a more organized placement, the taller frames in ascending order with shorter items in front. It must have taken her many years to accumulate the variety of objects scattered about her workstation. Perhaps these personal reminders of her homelife served to remove her thoughts from her job. She seemed uninterested in me. I guessed she was burned out and not merely tired from the heat. I answered the questions she asked, but her gloomy mood made it hard for me to be perky. Still, I tried my best and remembered to offer an occasional smile. As she set up the computer for a typing test, a dark-haired woman burst through the door.

"When are you going to get me someone who can be trained?" the intruder barked. "Did you hear the last ten minutes of my show? Well, did you?" She dragged her fingers through her long bangs and shot Betty a frenzied look. Then she turned her irate gaze at me. "Who are you? Are you here for a job?" Her piercing stare skewered me to my chair.

Betty sprang to life. "Why would I listen to *your* show? You have some nerve. This is a private interview."

Ignoring Betty, the uninvited woman swept up my resume from the desktop. "You're Claire Larson?" She didn't wait for my reply. "Did Betty tell you I needed someone?"

"Do you need, uh, an office assistant?" I couldn't breathe.

Betty crossed her arms and tapped her foot in double time.

"No, I need..." Our eyes locked. I felt immobile, hotly aware of the wild energy radiating from this spitfire. "I'm Marly." Her tone softened and she extended her hand. Her touch was firm and her grip lingered. "I need someone, someone who's intelligent, who can make quick decisions about a person's true intent. I need a call screener for my show. Hmm, you've got a liberal arts degree, and you've volunteered at several schools."

Betty thrust herself between us as Marly looked over the linen paper detailing my past.

"My kids' schools." I peered around Betty, whose considerable girth looked uncomfortably stuffed into rigid undergarments beneath her double-knit dress.

"I'm conducting this interview," Betty snarled as she snatched the resume from Marly's grip. The neatly arranged words crunched in her fist, and I winced at the sight of her nails—long, blood-red streams against the wounded paper.

Marly acknowledged Betty with a glare. "She'll do. How many other qualified applicants have you kept from me, huh? I want her. You want a job?" Her face brightened as if all had been forgotten between her and Betty. "Returning to work, hmm? I have a feeling about you. You'll see, we'll work together just fine. The pay is the same as the other office work around here, but the hours are better and the job is more interesting. I'll train you myself." There was no hostility when Marly spoke to me, only subtly nuanced desperation.

Before I could respond, Betty chimed in. "I was about to offer her the admin assist position. I'm sure she'll be more comfortable in an office setting than in that cramped booth. Don't you agree, Claire?" she asked, never taking her narrowed eyes off Marly. Her saccharine tone was edged with bitterness and reflected in her sour face.

I was obviously the newest pawn in their ongoing power struggle. My view of Marly was nearly blocked by Betty's body, whose torpedo-shaped bosom was aimed at my head in a manner that threatened war.

I shifted around the ordnance to size up her nemesis and at once felt myself drawn in by the sparkle of Marly's blue eyes. She was shorter than average and had a medium build. The strain on her face had disappeared, replaced by an impish smile. Loose, casual clothing did not hide her girlish figure slightly softened by her thirty-some years. I felt captivated, not only by her magnetic personality and atypical beauty, but by the understanding that I was the spoils of the battle she had won. Here was someone who truly needed me, and I could not say no.

Chapter Two

Marly asked me to start immediately and I agreed. She was too busy to show me around the studios that day and suggested I come in at eight thirty the following morning. "My slot is right after drive time," she explained. "Nine to eleven a.m., Monday through Friday. Studio B."

I felt brave taking a job I knew nothing about, save what I might have glimpsed on old TV sitcoms. Despite that, I suspected I could do no worse than the supposed incompetents who had recently held the position. She seemed confident I would work out fine, and I was determined to prove her right.

I had heard of KZSD. The station aired talk shows relevant to the community at large: real estate investment shows, call-in health forums, and the like. It was a minor player among a large array of stations stretching from one end of the dial to the other with audiences reaching from Los Angeles to Baja, Mexico. Getting the specifics of Marly's show seemed irrelevant at the time; the important thing was she was going to give me a chance. I was not in a position to be too picky.

To make a good impression on my first day of work, I chose my classiest outfit—a black suit worn over a knit mauve shell, set off by a freshwater pearl necklace, matching earrings, and strappy sandals. I carefully applied a tasteful amount of makeup with a hint of color for a finished look. I secured part of my long hair into a topknot held with a fancy clip and let the rest fall in hairspray-managed waves a few inches past my shoulders, striking a balance between formality and San Diego casual. This was an outfit I reserved for special dinners and theater galas, and I felt peculiar wearing it during the daytime. Nonetheless, I had always believed it was better to be overdressed and modestly accept compliments than to bear the indignity of appearing too sloppy.

Unlike a dinner party, I could not arrive fashionably late. I walked into KZSD fifteen minutes early. Not knowing where to report, I explained my situation to the receptionist, who gave me a once-over and stifled a laugh. She pointed the way and shouted a good luck message as if I would truly need it.

A red "ON-AIR" light glowed above the door marked Studio A. Through a large pane of glass, I saw a young man read from a sheet of paper. His body posture—shoulders raised, chest out, back arched—seemed to say, "I'm important!" as he spoke into a microphone propped close to his lips. His workspace was open and neat with a few papers piled off to his left. To his right was digital equipment that reminded me of the expensive audio system Ted and I bought for our son, Jonah, when he graduated high school. Looking at its smooth black surface and sophisticated controls made me recall I never did figure out how to use his five-disc CD player. I wondered if this young man's topic was as high tech as his equipment. Then, it hit me. He was on the radio, right now! Excitement filled me as I watched him speak, realizing his words were being broadcast beyond the hallways of KZSD into radios all across San Diego. A fluttering sensation tickled my stomach like an effervescent soft drink.

With a sense of wonderment, I looked farther down the hall for my destination: Studio B. In a few steps, I was there. This was a larger space than Studio A and similarly enclosed by generous panes of glass that started three feet up from the floor and rose to the ceiling. Inside, the windows were covered in part by mini blinds that had seen better days, their slats crushed and ends broken off as if they had been slammed in a door. Peeking in through the smudged glass, I spotted older electronic equipment covering the tabletops. Row after row of sliding adjustments marked with indecipherable abbreviations and colored lights were visible beneath the litter of cables and headphones. Odd-shaped cassette tapes were scattered about the room. A rack half-full of CDs had tipped onto its side, resting precariously askew. Piles of papers, CDs, and cassettes lay in unorganized heaps on the floor. The butterflies in my stomach rapidly metamorphosed into heartburn as I realized I was about to enter a foreign environment much worse than the mess left in any of my children's bedrooms. A sharp slap to my back caused me to jump forward with an audible exhale.

"Ack! Marly. I mean, good morning," I said as I tried to catch my breath.

"Hey, yourself," she replied as she fingered my lapel. "Dressed for success? Not a bad idea. Find strength where you can, I say."

She unlocked the door and I followed her into Studio B. Marly cleared the way, brushing aside CDs and tapes, then she kicked the door closed with the bottom of her shoe, leaving a dark tread mark. "This is my spot, and for now, you can sit here." She gestured at two stools. My eyes widened. The vinyl seat of my stool had been repaired with a long stripe of duct tape. I gingerly inched my bottom onto the seat and unbuttoned my jacket to allow it to drape smoothly down my back. Marly tossed a few tapes into a corner to expose the full length and breadth of the electronic sound equipment before us. It occurred to me that call screening would not be as simple as answering a phone. What would I possibly do with this confusing maze when I couldn't even set the clock on my microwave? My mouth felt glued shut.

"Don't worry," she said as she touched my arm. "I know it looks difficult, but that's only because you've never done this before. I'm going to walk you through the board op until you get the hang of it."

Board op? I tried to muster a smile. I felt sick and wondered where I'd find the ladies' room.

"Everyone starts out this way, so don't be nervous. You'll see, by the end of the show you'll start to pick it up. Besides, I'll be doing almost everything today. Now, here's our log sheet. It tells us which commercials to play, when to do our PSAs, top-of-the-hour ID, stuff like that."

I nodded, though I had no idea what she was talking about. Her words streamed through my head like elevator music. Part of me was listening, but another part had drifted off to a safer place, reminding me that in a little over two hours the worst of it would be over. If this ridiculous exercise wasn't going to work out, I could quit. I could take the office position if it was still available. Or, I could get through this experience and hopefully laugh about it one day.

Marly gathered a handful of the odd-shaped cassette tapes, "carts" she called them, and set them aside. She helped me position my "cans"—headphones, that is—and sat to my left where she had full access to the operations board. She tested the sound level on her mic and our cans, and then adjusted the levels of the incoming drive time show finishing up in Studio A. As she prepared, I could see she was more organized than her surroundings indicated. She told me to remain quiet.

A few passers-by walked down the hall outside our booth, but no one entered our space or even peered in. She fine-tuned several knobs and sliders on the equipment before us that I thought resembled spaceship controls in a 1950s B movie. I held my breath as if preparing for blastoff, and I could hear my heart beat in my ears, the increasing rhythm amplified by the cans.

The top-of-the-hour ID finished playing. Poised at attention and assuming a familiar grace, she spoke. "Good morning, you lazy butts. I'm Marly Minestrone, and this is *Gayline!*"

Chapter Three

Gayline? As in "gay"? What had I walked into? I gulped down a knot in my throat.

"Today on *Gayline*," Marly continued, "we're going to feature music performed by San Diego artists. If you're a loyal listener, you'll recognize some of these groups. This first CD just came in the mail. I listened to it yesterday and hope you'll like it as much as I did. They sent me two copies. The first caller who correctly names the artist wins one. Call me at 555-KZSD."

I listened intently. Marly's voice was rich in timbre, not too high or low. Each word was enunciated clearly, yet her speech flowed naturally. My first shock over, I was now curious about the upcoming music. Marly dialed up the correct track on the CD player and a folksy rhythm played loudly in my ears. I sat bolt upright. Marly sensed my discomfort and adjusted the volume downward.

She turned off her mic, slipped the cans off her head, and gestured for me to do the same. They caught in my hair, loosening my topknot.

"The phone lines are going to start," she said. "You won't hear them ring. You have to watch for the light to start flashing." Marly shifted in her chair left to right. "Shit! Where's the fucking phone?"

I cringed as she flung papers into the air to uncover the tabletop. A blizzard of colorful sails flew around us. I slid off my stool to help look, delicately lifting a few paper piles where a telephone could be hidden. It occurred to me it might be a cell phone or even a deceptive piece of equipment cleverly disguised as something else.

"What's it look like?" I asked.

"A *telephone. Duh.* Aha!" She focused on a point over my left shoulder and lunged my way. I dodged as she blew past me through an unlocked door and into a small adjoining booth I hadn't noticed. A large pane of glass separated us, revealing an equally messy studio. She held up a desk phone as if it were a trophy, unplugged it, and brought it into our room. Starting near the operations board, she traced a wire to its end. When she plugged in the phone, three lights flashed in unison.

"Okay," she said. "This is why I need you. Watch and listen."

She picked up the receiver and punched line one. "*Gayline*...Hi, yes, who?...You're absolutely wrong." Without hanging up the receiver, she deftly pushed the button above line two. "*Gayline*...Jewel? I don't think so." Line one flashed again. She hit line three. "*Gayline*...Yes, uh-huh, yes. Hold on. Here, Clara, take this guy's info."

She shoved the phone at me. The receiver was tacky with grime. Marly turned over a crumpled orange flyer and smoothed out the wrinkles, indicating I should write on the back with a pen she tossed my way. I wrote down the caller's name, address, and phone number, and thanked him for calling before ringing off. She snatched up the note, put her finger to her lips, and prepared to speak. After announcing the winner over the air, she pushed a cart into a black box—the player—using the heel of her hand, slapped a button on the operations board, and adjusted a slider. A commercial played, then another. She put on a different CD and marked the time in her log.

"You gotta be fast, Clara. Those phones can get pretty hairy, but I think you can handle it."

"Claire. It's Claire."

"Okay, Claire, part of your job is answering calls for prizes, which we're doing today because it's easy. But you're going to have to learn how to take calls in that other room and transfer them through the board so the caller and I can talk on the air. You've got another board in there." She gestured with her shoulder to the small unlit room. "That's where you're going to be after you learn this stuff. Think you can do that?"

I nodded despite my total disbelief that I would be able to do any of what was expected of me. How, I wondered, had I managed to end up in this tornado of an environment when a day earlier I could have been at a clean, if ordinary, desk job with co-workers who didn't say the f-word? Marly was calm as she sorted through her next batch of CDs. She had not sworn at me per se, but the rising and falling tension in the room was unnerving. It was not in my nature to be a quitter, especially on this first day of my first job. The squalid room repulsed me, yet I felt an adrenaline rush that excited me and dared me to continue. Rather than make a snap judgment, I felt it best to learn what I could. While administrative-type jobs were common, it was unlikely another opportunity of this sort would come along. I couldn't afford to be thin-skinned at a time when I needed to muster courage. I had never meant to quit my marriage, and the last thing I wanted was for that specter of failure to spill into my new working life because I felt vulnerable.

Playing music during the two-hour show helped steady my nerves. Marly selected long tracks during which she explained the board op equipment and its functions. I enjoyed the new music, different from NPR, what I usually chose to hear at home or in my car. I did answer a few calls, and except for disconnecting one person—well, three actually—I was of some use. Time flew by. At eleven, when her time slot was complete, I was tired. I imagined that in the days ahead when I knew my job better, I would be able to relax in the adjoining booth with the music playing in the background, take calls, and enjoy the repartee between Marly and her call-in guests as they chatted about budding musicians and offered interesting critiques.

After a tuna sandwich and an apple in the employee lunchroom, I returned to find Marly listening to CDs, her feet propped up on the op board. She shut down the equipment and escorted me to her private office, a windowless room barely larger than the walk-in closet at my old home. As I suspected, the interior was post-cyclone—in short, the office version of Studio B with tapes, papers, clothing, and CDs strewn over desktops and file cabinets with more piles of clutter on the floor. Posters with gay and lesbian themes were taped to the wall. My eyes grew large and my jaw clenched involuntarily. Other than her announcement that we were listening to *Gayline*, I had no specific indication of how her show served the gay community, though I assumed some if not all of the musicians we heard were gay. It was unclear to me if Marly was gay, and it would have been impolite to ask. These answers would come soon.

My anxiety rose as I looked at a poster of two clothed women touching in a provocative manner. I felt a mounting urge to ask her, "Are you gay?" I couldn't possibly say those words any more than I could follow up with my own admission: "I only ask because I'm, also, well, you know." No matter her response, it was doubtful I would be able to laugh away my uncomfortable feelings over the coincidence, though with recent advancements, it seemed being gay wasn't such a big deal anymore—at least for some people. For me, the realization was still unsettling. Other than my fling with Crystal, I had only my innate sense that there was another world waiting to be discovered. I had recently come to believe that in my childhood, heterosexuality had been assumed without a second thought as to what might have been a different yet more natural direction. Crystal said she could sense my secret longings by the vibes I emitted. Did Marly have those vibes? I couldn't tell. And what if she could sense those vibes in me? During a break in the show, I mentioned being separated with two kids. She would have no tangible reason to think I was gay.

I sucked air in between my teeth and tried to appear casual as I picked up a magazine with lesbian topics splashed across the cover. Before I could discover the "Seven Sexy Secrets Every Girrrl Should Practice," Marly handed me a long feature article about small radio stations in Southern California. KZSD was mentioned, but her show was not.

When I finished reading, I cleared my throat to get her attention. Marly extended her hand but did not take the article. Instead, she reached for my hair and pulled on strands that had loosened out of place. My freshly polished nails had chipped. She said nothing about my apparel; it wasn't necessary. She wore jeans, casual clogs, and a T-shirt. Her straight dark hair, almost black, was medium-short, a wash-and-wear haircut that did not look especially messy after pulling her cans on and off throughout the show. Beltless jeans fit snugly below her waist. She did not wear makeup. Her ears, dotted with sparkling crystal posts, stood out like two exclamation points on each side of the unforgettable smile that now spread across her face.

"You were fine today," she said. "And tomorrow will be better."

"Thanks. You're being kind."

"I mean it." Her eyes focused on me as if to drive home her point. "My show is very important to me, and I can't make it into what I want without a call screener. I need help. Your help."

I doubted the gravity, but I accepted her words and smiled in return. "Betty asked me to drop by her office to fill out a W-4."

"See you tomorrow?" she asked.

"Yes."

I spent some time wandering the building and eventually arrived at Betty's office. As I drove home, I kept thinking how this was not what I had planned, but then what had become of my plans? We make plans. Life happens anyway.

Chapter Four

The next day at work an otherworldly time warp caught hold of me as minutes dragged one moment and sped by the next. Board op filled me with anxiety. "Nothing is worse than dead air," Marly cautioned. Broadcasting in real time scared me almost as much as finding a job in the first place. I was afraid to adjust the sliders on the board more than minuscule increments for fear I might make a mistake that would inadvertently wreck her show. I could not understand how Marly could be so relaxed. Fortunately, she sat close, guiding my every move.

The first hour of *Gayline* showcased CDs from a woman artist I'd never heard before. Marly took several calls. Actually, I answered the phone while music was playing, and it was decided that a few callers would "go live," meaning to speak with her on the air. These callers were familiar with the music, and the discussions that followed focused on the artist's budding career and upcoming concert dates.

My nervousness did not prevent me from enjoying the show. The music was good, and I got a lift every time I answered the phone. It gave me a sense of importance to take Marly's calls, and the immediacy of our actions was exhilarating. It reminded me of the last play I'd seen at the Old Globe; the actors performing live on stage behaved as if speaking in front of an audience were the most natural thing in the world.

That kind of bravado was beyond me, but being behind the scenes was fun—a bit like Hollywood, with me providing assistance to the busy star.

A more sensible choice in clothing improved my physical comfort—slacks paired with a cotton shirt, and my hair in a ponytail tied with a colorful elastic band that kept it neatly in place. Unfortunately, the extra deodorant I applied after my shower fell short. On the other hand, Marly's tank top revealed a generous patch of dark hair sprouting beneath her arms. It seemed unlikely that I would offend her.

I wanted to fit in to my new situation at KZSD. At some point, I would know my job well enough to move into the adjoining booth. Marly would be relying on me to do everything right and I wanted to do a good job for her. Eager to return to her preferred format of less music and more talk, she compiled a list of regular callers and suggested I put them on the air as much as possible while I got up to speed.

Though she made it look easy, she obviously put a lot of effort into her show. It puzzled me why she had such a hard time finding a suitable call screener. It was true she could be volatile. Not everyone wants to be around that kind of intensity. Some might not have liked the confines of the screener's booth, even though the large pane of glass separating the rooms gave the illusion of open space. At times I had the sense that it was only us in Studio B, but I knew better. The pressure of performing for an unseen audience did not inspire relaxation. During those two hours on the air, time flew by if all went well, or could be excruciatingly slow if we hit a snag. It was disorienting. The combination was exhausting, and I was relieved when eleven o'clock came and the show ended. The time warp over, I was left much to my own devices for the remainder of the afternoon and spent my time reading, strolling the halls, and watching others prepare and perform their own shows in Studios A and C.

After work I picked up my cell phone, made a simple dinner in my apartment, cleaned up, and called the one person with whom I wanted to speak.

"Jennifer? It's Mom. Hi, honey, how are you?"

"Oh, Mom. Okay, I guess," she replied.

"How are high school preparations coming along?"

"Okay."

"Just okay? C'mon, can I get some details?" Jennifer grunted. Why did this have to be so hard? I swallowed and continued. "Well, I have good news. I got a job."

"You did? What?"

I played up on her glimmer of interest. "At a radio station, KZSD AM 780. I'm going to be a call screener."

"KZSD? Really? I know that station. How'd that happen? I thought you were trying to get, like, an office job or something."

"It's a funny story. I started yesterday. It's very different, and I think I'm going to like it, I mean, I do like it. The woman I work for is bright and interesting. And she's nice, well, most of the time. She's definitely intense. She plays music and talks to callers. Have you heard from your brother?"

"Dad talked to Jonah. Hey, Dad. Pick up the phone."

"No, no, honey. I'll call you tomorrow. Love you, bye." I ended the call. Tears filled my eyes. I let them roll lazily down my cheeks where they fell and moistened my shirt.

The stress of the past two days caught up with me. Who was I kidding? The stress of the past weeks. Months! I can't say why I chose to work for Marly when I could have settled on something less chaotic. I was sure returning to work would be difficult. Pressures bore down on me—moving into my own apartment, being without Ted, Jenny's anger, Jonah's indifference, or was it avoidance?

The final breakup with Ted had been a nightmare. All the warm fuzzies from my "Teddy Bear"—gone. An arctic winter set in. I had been thrown out onto the street and chose to live in a hotel for ten days rather than suffer the humiliation of staying on a friend's sofa. Most of my friends were Ted's friends, too, and I couldn't face them—not yet. Finding any apartment without sky-high rent had been a challenge. Moving gave me a sense of purpose. I had not taken much from the house and settled in quickly. Soon I had more free time on my hands than anticipated, gaps with no agenda, unsettling my once orderly life. Where the busywork ended, guilt took over. It was my doing.

I had not been alone since college. Before Ted, my guitar had kept me company. Then for years it stood in a closet collecting dust. I was always too busy driving the kids here and there, tending to anything out of place around the house. There was never a good time to take it out. On impulse, I brought the instrument with me. I sat on the bed and unlatched the worn case. Smells of old wood and lacquer along with the memories they held filled my mind—jamming with friends, setting poetry to music, laughing over silly made-up lyrics.

The tuning pegs creaked as I tightened the slackened strings. I managed a rough rendition of "House of the Rising Sun," the dead strings sounding dull beneath my clumsy fingertips. Surely there were other songs I could remember. I tried using the tortoiseshell pick, but it felt strangely unfamiliar as I swept it across the strings. The reverberation faded away and the silence beyond the notes was more than I could bear. As many times as I had fantasized about playing without interruption, this was not how I wanted it to happen.

Chapter Five

Friday—yes! After three days of work I was ready for a break. The show went pretty much the same as it had for the previous two. I tried my hand at board op under Marly's watchful eye. She tolerated a lower level of sound quality in exchange for my doing the work. It was a trade-off, one that left her free to converse with callers and to flip through music selections without being unduly burdened. I was amused by Marly's sense of humor, and I enjoyed the work even though I felt drained. And to my own amusement, I became interested in learning this strange occupation. My life was on a new track. Unlike Marly, it was too soon to say if this was any sort of career position. I was relieved to learn something new and completely different. It was a break from thinking about my problems.

In the studio after our lunch break, Marly and I spent the afternoon reviewing the basic tasks ahead of me. The equipment was easier to use than I had feared. It was fairly low tech, especially in comparison with the newer equipment in Studio A. Interpreting the log, answering phones, patching through callers, playing commercials and CDs were all starting to make sense in relation to one another. On the air my transitions were rough. The extra practice was helpful.

At five o'clock, I called Jenny from the studio. We agreed that I would pick her up for dinner and an evening at the mall for back-to-school shopping. Over burgers and fries, she relaxed a bit and told me about her upcoming high school schedule. It was her sophomore year, a welcome trade up from lowly freshman status. Being a teen comes with its own angst, and I felt guilty about contributing to that by leaving home, a situation that could make things worse before they got better. The neutral environment of the mall was a good place to connect. With the family broken up I felt a greater responsibility to keep communication lines open. I had lost so much ground with my daughter these past few months, and my absence from our home made my insides twist. Somehow the mundane realities of life had turned into anxieties from which I could not escape. Acting the part seemed the best recourse.

"When do you think you'd like to see my new place?" I asked bravely. "You can't put it off forever."

"Yeah, I know. I don't feel ready. It's weird that you're not home with me and Dad. Jonah's away at the university, and I never thought I'd say I miss him, but I do, my big bro. You haven't said much about your job. How's it going?"

"Marly says I'm picking it up pretty fast. We'll be returning to the regular format next week—more callers, less music."

Jennifer put down her curly fry and leaned forward. "Marly? You're on Marly's show?"

"Yes. Do you know it?"

"Oh. My. God! Mom, how could you?" Jennifer pulled back from me with a look of abject horror. "Haven't you done enough already?"

"I don't understand. What's the problem?"

"Are you trying to ruin my life? You can't work for her. My friends can't know you're working for

Marly. You have to quit before it's too late."

"Don't be ridiculous. I like my new job. People call in and talk about music."

"Mom, don't pretend you don't know."

"Jenny, tell me what's wrong." Trembling through her layered clothing, my sweet girl was near tears. Her mouth quivered as she spoke. "How could you not know?" she squeaked.

A silent shudder passed through me that awakened the one lingering question I had not broached with Marly: the gay aspect. At this point, I knew at least some of the music she played was performed or written by gay artists. Caller comments, same-sex lyrics, and promotional mailers had cleared up that question. In general, the content did not contain anything I found objectionable, even the occasional rap song. In fact, the pleasant melodies were a lot better than some of the hard rock, hip-hop, and techno that pounded out of passing cars. Still, Jennifer's strong reaction had me worried. I had raised her to embrace diversity in others.

"You don't know, do you?"

I shook my head.

"*Gayline*, Mom." She emphasized in a harsh whisper so others near us wouldn't hear. "It's a gay show. Marly is so beyond gay. She's a shock jock, a raving lesbian. She says things. She does things on the radio. She's totally nutso—couldn't you tell?"

My gaping stare must have convinced her I did not know all the intricacies of the show, its host, nor the implications of my staying on the job.

"The kids at school make fun of her. They call her 'The Loony Lesbie.' If anyone finds out you're working for her, I'm dead! They're going to think you're crazy, too. I'll never be able to go back to school. I'm so embarrassed."

Jennifer tented her mouth with her hands and ran out of the restaurant. I tossed a twenty onto the table and ran after her. I caught a glimpse as she rounded a corner. She ducked into a locked service doorway and I caught up to her. I grabbed her arm. She pulled it back.

"I didn't know," I pleaded. "The show hasn't been like that at all."

"Yeah, right. Mom, I don't get you. You're not 'Mom' anymore."

Jenny burst into tears and turned toward the brick wall, her face buried in the crook of her arm. Her body heaved with bellowing sobs. I was too stunned to speak, too afraid to touch her, yet more afraid if I didn't reach out I would lose her forever. I clutched her shoulder. To my astonishment, she spun toward me and threw her arms around my neck. I cried with her, even though I was aware other shoppers could see our dramatic display. I didn't care. What was important to me was that despite the circumstances of my life, which seemed to be getting worse instead of better, Jennifer still needed and loved me. I *was* still Mom.

Chapter Six

Over the weekend I couldn't stop thinking about how Jennifer described *Gayline*. I wish I had seen or heard for myself the outrageous behavior she claimed was in store. Part of me could imagine Marly going beyond the pale; her edgy humor was glib and irreverent. Had I merely glimpsed the tip of the iceberg? If so, would there be a titanic collision? Would I be among the casualties? I didn't want to embarrass Jennifer, but I also recognized that being a parent of a teenager was itself sufficient cause.

I had left the home I loved and returned to the working world reluctantly. On the other hand, I had been presented with an unusual opportunity. Being in the studio was a kick. Marly needed me and made an effort to tell me that what I did helped manage her show. To quit for no real reason would be unfair to her. I had to find out if Jenny was being truthful or manipulatively dramatic.

I had never imagined working as a radio call screener, and the first few days went well enough. Being a planner by nature, I believed you created your own fate when you made the effort, unlike my sister, Deena, who always believed things happened for a reason. I called Deena in Minnesota to tell her about the job.

"It's meant to be," she said.

"You're so predictable. I knew you'd say that."

"Then you must have wanted to hear it."

"Come on, Deena. I have serious doubts about this. What if I'm making another mistake?"

"We all have doubts," she replied. "That doesn't mean the decision is wrong. Also, I think you have to separate doubt about this job from your own insecurities."

I frequently looked to her for guidance, even though we didn't always agree. She was five years older, a huge difference when we were kids. I remember watching in awe when she touched the back of her knees with a drop of Chanel No. 5 or added Vaseline to her mascara tube. In quiet moments, she shared the mysteries behind these and other grown-up secrets our mother never revealed. It was obvious my sister knew more about the ways of the world, and as time passed, I never stopped wanting and valuing her opinion.

When Monday morning arrived, I turned off my alarm and staggered to the bathroom where I fastened my hair atop my head. I slowly woke myself in the shower by rubbing soapy bubbles in sleepy circles across my body. After I rinsed, my fingers found their way back to the cleansed folds between my legs. Using a light pressure, I felt renewed dreaminess as I lazily slid my middle finger back and forth, inside and around. Warm water spray beat on my back and wet the exposed underside of my hair. Leaning forward, I reached in deeper. While caressing my breasts, I pretended it was not I doing the touching, but someone else—a mystery lover who made me climax in a prolonged shudder.

Wrapped in soft terry, I plodded to the kitchen, poured bottled water into a Pyrex measuring cup, and tore away the protective paper surrounding an individual tea bag. As I waited for the water to boil, the microwave hummed in tune with the dreamy sensation lingering in my body, yet my head felt crowded with thoughts all shouting to be recognized. Today could be my last day at the station if Jenny's warnings were justified.

I arrived at Studio B with cautious trepidation. I tried not to let my nervousness show when I greeted Marly. We reviewed the show log. Marly was focused. She pulled out music we could use in a pinch and reminded me that taking phone calls would be our primary objective. I was not ready to be in the adjoining booth by myself and was astonished when she suggested I go in there. This new development jolted me awake as if I had downed a triple espresso.

I took the music, the commercial carts, and other needed items into the glassed-in booth and reluctantly closed the door. Our practice session the previous week seemed cold and unfamiliar as I looked over the operations board. The telephone was back in place. I took time to straighten up the small room, stacking unused carts and piling papers of unknown importance onto the floor to be sorted later. Repositioning my microphone several times, I set up the board so that Marly could hear me through her cans and also through the speakers in her room. After consulting the log, I placed the first two carts in the cart machine and lined up the others nearby in the order in which they would be heard. Two commercials were missing and there was no time to find them.

"Good morning, San Diego," she began after the top-of-the-hour ID. "Moaning Marly here, your lover girl if you're lucky tonight. Call me if we haven't done it yet. I like to be in touch with my girrrrlfriends out there, if you get my drift. Talk to me."

It was starting. Jennifer was right! I grimaced and swallowed hard. The light on line one flashed, demanding my attention like an incessant two-year-old. Marly joked about last week's format and I tried to hear both her conversation and the one I attempted to have as I picked up the first phone line.

"*Gayline.*" My voice cracked. "Ahem. Excuse me. Hello?"

"Lemme talk to Marly," a man snarled.

His tone threw me off kilter. "Who's calling and what is the nature of your call?" I asked, remembering my script.

"Cut the polite crap, you stupid dyke. Just gimme Marly."

I glared at the phone receiver, disgusted at the offensive words it transmitted, and then looked at Marly before realizing I had already lost the thread of her conversation. I wasn't sure if she wanted a caller, and how could I know if this man was the right one to put on the air? Would she welcome his antagonism, or would she reprimand me later for putting her in the hot seat? Other lines blinked. I put the first caller on hold and pressed line two, where a woman pleasantly answered my questions. Marly held up her hand, fingers together, her sign for me to pause. She tapped her watch and seemed to be finishing her thought. I looked at the wall clock. It did not show the correct time.

"We'll take calls after this break," she said.

I pushed a button on the cart machine and a commercial began. The sound levels looked good. I opened up my mic so Marly could hear me.

"There's a woman on line two," I said. "And—"

Marly flew at her board controls and switched off her mic. My voice had been broadcast inadvertently during the commercial.

Blood surged upward in my body. I felt prickling at the back of my neck and a cold sweat formed across my forehead. "I'm sorry, I'm sorry," I cried into my mic. Marly pointed at the phone. "Line two," I said. "Geri wants to talk about an upcoming songfest."

Marly gave me the okay sign and pointed at the cart machine. The first commercial was finishing. I pressed another button to play the second commercial, took out the first cart, and replaced it with the next in line. My shirt stuck to my back, making it uncomfortable to move. Tears welled up in my eyes. I rubbed my nose, took a breath, and concentrated on the phones. As the commercial came to an end, Marly sat taller and turned on her mic.

"We have a new call screener here at *Gayline*. Her name is Claire, a lovely wench if I ever did see one. She'll be taking your calls, and since she's new, be sure to give her a hard time. Okay, Claire, let's take our first caller."

I was horrified. Countless listeners had heard my name and knew I was in the booth making mistakes. Would they all assume I was gay? My mind blanked. I lost track of what I was doing. The phone! Which line was the correct one? Mass confusion. Ack! My wet eyelashes stuck together. Through the blur I glanced up at Marly, who gave me the victory sign. She pushed her two fingers at me and mouthed a word. I got the message and put through the caller on line two.

"Hi, Geri, are you there?"

"Hey, Marly."

A deep sigh of relief passed my lips. To my utter despair and embarrassment, the sound came over the air. I flicked off my mic.

"Geri, I think Claire likes you. She's breathing heavy in here."

And so it went for a full two hours.

Chapter Seven

By the end of the show I felt I had slogged through a primeval jungle, a densely filled tropical nightmare infested with threatening creatures and poisonous viny plants that strangled and sapped my body of strength. Overheated, overwhelmed, exhausted both mentally and physically, my head spun as I tried to reorient myself. I had hacked my way through the last two hours and was ready to collapse. I had no energy left to cry.

"Good job!" Marly exclaimed as she took off her cans. "Let's go."

I opened the door that led to her booth and followed her out into the hall. My legs and feet felt like they were filled with buckshot. Zombie-like, I shuffled along a step behind, leaving my intangible foes in the strange world of Studio B. Marly carried a pile of papers that she spilled onto her desk as we entered her office.

"Hey girlfriend, you look like you need a pee break." She shooed me off.

I wandered into the women's room where someone I vaguely recognized stared into the mirror. Her skin looked wan and clammy as if a recent high fever had broken. Strings of hair stuck to her forehead and temples. Her lipstick was uneven and her eye makeup smeared. I ran water until it warmed and washed my face with pink liquid soap from the wall dispenser. I blotted with the brown paper towels, taking care to not let the rough surface scratch my skin. The damp towels felt refreshing as I ran them into my shirt and under my arms. The face in the mirror still needed improvement. I used moistened toilet paper to remove the vestiges of smudged eyeliner and tried to reshape my brows. I wiped my mouth one last time and reapplied lipstick. After brushing out my hair, I felt a little better. I stopped at a drinking fountain on the way back to Marly's office and paused in the hall. What would I say to her? There was too much to think about and no time to straighten out my jumbled thoughts.

"Better?" she asked, not waiting for a reply. "I want you to hear something. We got a few phone messages while we were on the air." I sat down to listen.

"Marly, it's Angus. Tell your new bitch not to cut me off." *Beep.*

"Hi, it's me. I'm so glad you're back to your regular show. You have so much courage. Don't ever let those guys run you off the air. We need you. You go girl." *Beep.*

"Hey, Marly, it's Carlos. Love our new Condom-Mania commercial. Thanks so much. You know I'd be lost without you. No one else wants my advertising. You provide a real service to the community. Love ya." *Beep.*

"Marly, it's Yin-Yang. Sorry I couldn't call in today. That airhead who went on about grandparents' rights had me fuming. He obviously did a shitty job with his own kid and now he's trying to make up for it by usurping the rights of other parents. And being gay does not make you an unfit parent." *Beep.*

"Hello, Marly? Glover Hayes. My sources tell me you've got another girl in training. Be sure to tell her to patch me through." *Beep.*

"This is Ivy O'Neal. We're having a prayer meeting next Thursday night at our church. We'll be discussing how to help folks like you. Of course you may come. Jesus welcomes sinners back into the fold if they are truly repentant. We know you can change and we'll be praying for you." *Beep.*

Marly laughed. "Ever hear of Ivy O'Neal?"

"Isn't she the one who's always getting arrested outside abortion clinics?"

"Yep. Never stops trying to convert me, as if her church cared at all about my civil rights. Let her pray all she wants. She's a thorn in my side—one minute preaching tolerance and the next calling me the devil incarnate."

I could recall my own preacher's words, "Love the sinner, hate the sin." I had never been a real "churchy" type, and though I could have switched congregations, I decided to quietly drop out a few years ago.

"Anyway," Marly continued, "Yin-Yang is one of my best callers. Whenever she calls—or maybe it's a he, no one's ever been able to figure it out—put them on. Whoever it is, they don't want us to know because they want to get the message across without any gender bias."

"Okay. What about Glover Hayes? Why does that name sound familiar?"

"Does *The Glover Hayes Show* ring a bell? Glover's got a top-rated talk show on AM 780. He's so in love with himself and his voice, his own show isn't enough. He's got to be on mine, too. He's a right-wing moron, which makes for good radio, so be sure to put him on. As for Angus, you did the right thing by shutting him out. After a while you'll get to know the voices of the regulars and those who make good radio.

"Listen, my primary objective for *Gayline* is to provide a service to the community. Some of our advertisers are denied access on other shows. We don't always air opinions that are mainstream for our demographic. In addition to being gender non-conforming, Yin-Yang can be politically incorrect, but not in the way you might think. It reminds our listeners that the LGBTQ community comes from a wide range of backgrounds and beliefs. We're just regular working folks, moms and dads, volunteers and so on, except for the one thing that everybody seems to focus on, our sexuality. Oh, and which bathroom we use. Then, boom! Everything else we are and do is of little consequence.

"Of course it's all in the name of entertainment." Marly's eyes sparkled as if she were letting me in on a secret. "I say things to get a rise out of my audience, to get them to call in. Some people think that's really who I am, but it's an act, an on-air persona. I don't always say what I personally believe, like at the beginning of the show when I made those remarks about you, well, don't take that stuff seriously, okay? I'm not trying to harass you."

"Oh, okay," I mumbled. "I won't take it personally."

"Good. You're not homophobic or anything, are you?"

"No."

"Good. You look tired, Claire. Why don't you take a long lunch? Go home and change if you want and we'll meet back here around one."

As I left the studio, I wondered if I would ever come back.

Chapter Eight

A vague recollection of my morning shower flitted through my brain as I stepped into the stall once again. Massaging my head with fragrant shampoo helped loosen the residual tension I had carried with me out of Studio B. As I rinsed away the remnants from trudging through the jungle of radio operations, I gathered my thoughts. Did I or did I not wish to continue at the station, and why?

I unwrapped the towel from my head, stepped into the kitchen, and stood in front of the open refrigerator until my bare feet felt cool, eventually deciding on a chicken salad sandwich. I ate, the food tasteless in my mouth, as I mulled over my options. Life's choices are full of positives and negatives, opportunities and sacrifices. I drew a line down a sheet of paper and wrote two lists. Cons: demanding work/exhausting; know nothing about radio; is this what I want to do?; first, not only, opportunity—something better out there?; Jennifer wants me to quit; reputation—not comfortable being associated with Marly/being an out lesbian; might not do a good job; unsure about opportunity for advancement; messy work environment; she probably thinks I'm a slow learner. Pros: different kind of work; fun, crazy, frenetic atmosphere; lively; makes me forget my problems; have to find own way; station close to home; learning about radio; feel important; Marly friendly, good person/teacher; needs me, says I'm doing okay, makes me laugh; lesbian—could learn a lot from her about being gay; I may need her/get unknown benefits; think I like her, those eyes!

No! Did I really write that? I crunched the list into a ball and stuffed it into the basket beneath the sink, cleaned up, fixed my hair, and drove back to the station.

Marly was laughing into the phone when I arrived at her office. She rang off and commented on the sundress I had put on. I realized I had been silently staring into her eyes, so luscious and seductive, like round blueberries rimmed with dark lashes. I blushed and turned away to hide my thoughts. I had no idea what to say.

She broke the silence. "I taped our show—thought you might like to listen to it. I know you don't think you did a very good job this morning, but when you hear it, you'll change your mind."

I readily agreed. This was a good stall tactic—two hours in which to arrive at a final decision to stay or go. I got as comfortable as I could in the extra office chair and focused on a far-off object out in the hall. She dropped a cassette tape into a beat-up boom box, which rested askew atop a paper stack.

"Can you believe I still have to use this old stuff? The GM won't update Studio B because if I wanted to, I could work out of Studio A or C and they have all the updated equipment. But I like having my own space. Everything works. It's just old."

She started the tape. The top-of-the-hour ID played and Marly's voice greeted her listeners. I scrunched up my face as I listened to the beginning of the show. There was my voice against the backdrop of a commercial. It was not as pronounced as I thought it would be. In fact, I could barely make it out. The commercial played on as if the mistake never happened. Hearing myself sigh into the mic followed by Marly's joke embarrassed me a second time. I fanned myself with a flimsy magazine.

"It was funny," she said in defense. "I bet the audience liked it."

During the next two hours, Marly pointed out gaps of dead air, callers who were disconnected or misnamed, varied sound levels, and other rough spots. She did not seem perturbed by these imperfections, which made me feel less self-conscious. Maybe she was sincere, and I had done a decent job. There were extended portions of the show I did not remember at all. Callers frequently remarked on how thankful they were for *Gayline*. Others called in with helpful information or told funny stories. I was amazed to hear opinions expressed on what it was like to be gay and how that related to everyday life. I had no idea such a show existed in San Diego, and I wanted to hear it again.

When the tape ended, she said, "See, Claire, you were just fine."

"Thanks, I guess."

"You don't believe it. You'll see. In time you'll get more confident. The first days are the hardest, but I can tell you're a quick study. By the end of today's show you were already getting the hang of it."

"Um, that could be." This was no time for timidity. I needed to summon up my inner strength to make a decision. I was rested now and feeling alert. Energy coiled around my solar plexus, whirling and growing by the second. *Decide! Decide!*

"I've got some suggestions that will make your life easier at the board tomorrow. You just need to be a little more organized."

Look who was calling the kettle black. I had always been organized to the point where Ted and the kids used to tease me. At home, it provided a sense of comfort to know where everything was located. It made for ease of living. In Studio B, I needed to have some basis from which to get organized, to be organized. Like kundalini rising, I could feel my bundled energy surge up through my body and release as I blurted out my thoughts. "Organized? Your studio is a mess. And this office—it's a dump!" I slapped my hand over my mouth. I had no right to insult or tell her what to do with her studio space. I felt out of control. "I am so sorry."

"No, you're right," she said without a hint of irritation. "We've got the rest of the afternoon to get the studio into shape. Come on."

We walked to Studio B and I entered the small adjoining booth where I had blundered my way through the morning show. "If you don't mind," I said. "I want to start with my workspace. Is there a wastebasket?"

Marly laughed. "You mean a dumpster. I'll go find some trash bags."

Many of the flyers lying about the floor were outdated—trash. Unopened mail from various churches—trash. Unopened mail with CDs inside—keep. Pens with no ink, old magazines, a stained Tinky Winky doll with its head torn off—trash. We played unmarked carts and noted their length. She showed me how to bulk erase the carts for future recording. Marly selected music, lively tunes that helped the time go by. In fact, she was good company. At four, she had a pizza delivered to our booth. As the debris disappeared and the floor reappeared, I had a sense of accomplishment. While sorting, we found several forms and a script used by a former call screener, a sign that someone else had tried to make sense of the madness bouncing between the two small rooms. Before we left, we tied up three large black garbage bags and set them in the hallway. There were still a few piles, but at least they contained similar items. The countertop next to the operations board was cleared off, and I laid out my organizational materials in preparation for the next day's show. I made a mental note to bring in appropriate office supplies.

We did not clean up Marly's side. It was getting late and I felt it would be intrusive to suggest we tamper with her space. "Now, you're not going to let the overflow from your part of the studio get into mine, are you?" I was afraid I sounded territorial.

"Ha! Claire, you crack me up. When are you coming to my house to clean?"

Outside the building, the foggy marine layer drifting in from the ocean felt damp and cool on my bare arms. Picturing Marly's house and the disaster it must be gave me the shivers. I tried to rub out my goose bumps. Committing to work the next day also made me tremble, or was it the thought of seeing her?

Chapter Nine

When I walked into my booth the next day, seeing uncluttered countertops made me feel I was getting a fresh start. I removed paper towels and cleaning spray from my canvas bag and gave the surface a thorough wipe down. The grimy board was in need of a good scrub, but for the moment I did what I could. Ditto for the telephone and the glass that separated the two rooms. I took out a newly purchased notebook, markers, and other writing instruments, and lined them up in a neat row. After replacing the old batteries from the wall clock, I reset it according to my watch, which I had already set to the radio station earlier that morning. Today I promised myself I would be ready for whatever was thrown my way. My racing heart apparently had not gotten the message, for when I spotted Marly down the hall, its pace quickened. I tossed the cleaner back into the bag and stashed it out of the way. I waved as she neared.

"Hey, Claire," she said. "How did you get in here?"

"It was open."

"Damn, I must have forgotten to lock up last night. You know we have to be super careful," she said. "There are people out there...I'll get you a key."

Was she paranoid, I wondered, or was something else going on?

"What's this?" She smirked as she picked up

my ruler. "Did you used to be a school marm, or something? Will there be a test later? Ooh, rap those knuckles." She mockingly went for my knuckles and I flinched. My face reddened.

"Do you think you could go easy on me today? I'm really trying."

"Yeah, sure. Why don't you practice your stuff?"

Marly handed me a copy of the daily log, turned on her heel, and went to her side of the booth. She dumped the contents from an old backpack onto the counter and busied herself by reading some papers. I felt awkward. Communicating with Marly was confusing. One moment she was all business, the next she was cracking jokes and making insults about whatever popped into her head. I didn't know if I had put her off, but chose to believe I was the one being overly sensitive.

While we were waiting to go on the air, I reviewed the process of cueing up music and carts we would use later in the show. I made little labels to mark which slider controlled which piece of equipment. Then I arranged the work area with the phone to my left. That way I could control the board with my right hand, answer the phone with my left, and take notes with my right. Every few minutes I caught a glimpse of the time. *Whew. Calm down. Each day will be easier than the last.* I gnawed my lower lip. Line one lit up.

"We're on in three minutes," Marly said.

"There's already a call. What should I do?" *Stupid question!*

"Use your script," Marly answered matter-of-factly. She closed the door between the two rooms.

Panic from the overwhelming feelings of my incompetency experienced the day before flooded back. I watched the phone light blink as precious seconds ticked away in half-time to my pulse. A prickling sensation crowned my head and the room began to swirl. I sat still, yet I could feel my body waver. I gripped the edge of the counter as if it were the gunwale of a pitching boat. Through my seasick eyes, I caught a glimpse of Marly taking the cans off her head. She entered my booth. I shrank back as she approached. Thinking she must want access to my board, I slipped off my stool to give her space, yet she continued to come at me. In defense, I drew my forearms up close to my chest.

She put her arms around me and whispered in my ear, her words serene and steady. "It's going to be okay, Claire. You can do this. I have faith in you. You're a smart woman and you'll get the hang of this. Don't worry about making mistakes because you're going to make mistakes and we'll get over them. When there's a mistake, we move on. Don't draw attention to it and it's like it never happened."

I was stiff with panic, yet oddly aware of the clean scent of her hair as I took in one shallow breath after another. She gave me a prolonged hug that squeezed my arms against my breasts. After she released me, I stood there staring as she picked up my cans and placed them on her head. The top-of-the-hour ID was ending.

"Good morning, you crab scratchers! You're listening to *Gayline*. Take your hands out of your pants, turn up your hearing aids, and let's get crackin'. I'm your hostess, Marly Mostaccioli. Speaking of lice, we're going to start off with a fun song about bugs and then I'll take your calls."

The bug song was slated for later in the show.

I remembered which CD it was on because of the dancing cartoon cockroaches that decorated its cover. With unexpected clarity, I quickly separated the CD from its case, popped it into the player, and cued up the right track. Marly joked about *las cucarachas* jitterbugging through our studio. When she saw I was ready, she pointed at the "Play" button. I touched it and the song began. She turned off the mic and adjusted the sound level until the bouncing needles on the board fell into the correct range.

"Okay," she said. "Now you can answer the phone." She moved off my stool. "And use those school supplies."

I picked up the phone as Marly went back to her side of the booth. She closed the door between us. I decided to go with the first caller. So I wouldn't forget, I wrote down her name, the phone line she was on, and the subject of her call, then held the paper up to the glass for Marly to see. She gave me the okay sign. I waited until the song was over and patched the call through to her. I heard the next song begin on the CD, so I swept the volume slider down to zero. It was the fastest way to correct the error. It was a small glitch, barely noticeable. Marly and her guest began a dialogue. Adrenaline made me hyper-alert. I rubbed the tension out of my face and rolled my shoulders. Cans in place, I exhaled deeply, expelling as much pent-up energy as I could release, this time with my mic off. We were going to do this. We were making this show work. I could do this. A broad smile crossed my face. *Yes! I am doing this.* I returned my focus to the telephone lines and took the next call. I felt exhilarated.

Chapter Ten

"We've got time for one last call. Hi, Bob, you're on *Gayline*. Talk to me."

"Hi, Marly. I've got a problem. I'm sure you're the only one who can help me."

"Go ahead, Bob."

"I hate to admit this, but I got ripped off. I thought I was buying a TV. Now I'm out a hundred bucks."

"I can tell there's a story here."

"Yeah, see, my friends and I were hanging around Balboa Park near Laurel and Sixth when these two guys came driving by. They said they had a TV for sale. Actually, they had two identical flat screens sitting on the back seat. One was still in the box. I gave him a hundred bucks for the one in the box because it was sealed with tape."

"You knew this was a hot TV, right, Bob?"

"Well, maybe it wasn't."

"And maybe I'm not gay. So, other than you bought a stolen TV, what's the problem?"

"Me and my buddies took it home and opened it up, but the box was full of bricks. I couldn't believe it! So, um, I was wondering if you knew who I could call, you know, to get some kind of satisfaction here."

"Bob, you came to the right person. You have to call L.A. *immediately*."

"I do? What's up in Los Angeles?"

"Not Los Angeles, you dolt. L.A.—as in Loser's Anonymous. You just won a gold medal in the Stupid Olympics. Wow! Next time, take that money and buy a box full of ethics. I'm laughing too hard. I gotta go before I pee my pants. That's it for today. Tune in again next week when Bob plugs his new book, *The Idiot's Guide to Idiocy*. Let's give Boob, I mean Bob, a big hand." Marly clapped loudly. She whooped and barked, then drew her finger across her neck, my sign to cut and go to the commercial.

I started the cart, turned off our mics, and we exploded with laughter. I played the next commercial on our log. As it finished, the sweep-second hand reached twelve and I ran the top-of-the-hour ID. The show was over. I took off my cans and opened the door to our adjoining booths. Marly wiped the sweat from her brow with the sleeve of her T-shirt.

"Whew. I haven't laughed that hard in a long time," I said.

Marly raised her hands over her head and wiggled her fingers in feigned religious fervor. "Thank you, Lord, for Bob. Where would my show be without the Bobs in this world? What a great way to end the week. I can't believe it's Friday."

I had to admire Marly. Working without a script was a tightrope act without a net. The few times I walked through the halls of KZSD I noticed other talk show hosts read from prepared materials, and deejays often read directly from CD liner notes as if to prevent an original thought from creeping into their dialogue. Marly rarely read anything verbatim, choosing instead to paraphrase. It made her sound fresh and knowledgeable. Her unpredictable style had me watching her constantly. We used hand signals to communicate and I held up messages for her to read. Between the verbal and nonverbal communication, we sustained the flow of her program.

I was happy it was Friday; actually, relieved was more like it. Five days earlier I had been paralyzed, frozen in place with debilitating stage fright. All week I made mistakes as Marly said I would. I carried on. New situations arose calling for quick judgment, my best call, sometimes little more than an educated guess or gut feeling about how to respond. Marly provided guidance both during and after the show. Next time, hopefully, I would do the right thing, make the right decision. Each night I took home the air check, a cassette tape of our show. I had to buy a cassette player at a secondhand shop to listen, and as I did, I marveled at how different we sounded than what I remembered happening in the booth. When I turned on the radio at home or in the car, I had a new appreciation for what I heard. I was now part of the behind-the-scenes magic that made it happen. Though overwhelming at times, I was sure this was more interesting than straight office work.

Marly gave me permission to leave midafternoon. It was the beginning of the long Labor Day weekend, for some, anyway. Our station made plans for a remote broadcast on Monday. It didn't matter that it was a holiday—there was airtime to fill. Fortunately, there was no prep work for me. I had only to show up at Balboa Park on Labor Day morning.

To keep busy over the weekend, I decided to hang pictures on my bare apartment walls and buy material for drapes. I missed sewing. At one time, Jenny and I enjoyed wearing identical outfits. We'd pick out the pattern, fabric, and trim. When I finished up the dresses, we'd put them on and I'd take her someplace special where we could show them off. After she entered middle school, she was no longer interested in wearing homemade items. It was more important for her to look like her friends.

I missed Jenny. Acting on impulse, I swung by my house to see if she was there. As I approached the door I reached for the knob and thought better of it. After a quick appearance check, I knocked on the door. I heard her heavy shoes clomping down the stairs.

"Mom." Jenny smiled. "I didn't know you were coming over."

I passed through the doorway and gave her a hug. How odd to feel like a stranger in the home I'd lived in for the past eleven years.

"Are you here by yourself?"

"Don't worry, Dad's not home. It's not even four o'clock."

The living room was filled with clutter. I ignored my impulse to start picking up.

"Want a soda?" she asked.

We took our sodas and sat out on the back patio. Jennifer would be starting school on Tuesday. She told me about her new teachers, and that she and her friend, Amber, were planning to go to the beach on Labor Day.

"Are you doing anything?" she asked me.

"Saturday I'm making drapes. I think a pretty floral chintz will be nice. And I'll buy some decorative hardware, too."

"You could come with us to the beach on Monday."

This was the hard part. Earlier in the week I had

led Jennifer to believe that the radio job was somehow on hold. I rationalized it in my mind by believing I had not yet made a commitment to Marly. I didn't know how to tell her what she did not want to hear, and unlike our phone conversation midweek, I could not circumvent the subject. "I'm working Monday. We're broadcasting from Balboa Park."

She looked confused. "You mean you're doing something else at the radio station?"

"No. I decided to keep the job I had. It's really a lot of fun." My forced cheeriness did not change her dour expression. "I've improved quite a bit this past week. You should hear the tapes from the show."

Jennifer pouted. "When you came to the door you looked so casual, I assumed you weren't working. How can you still be working for Marly? Mom, I thought you were going to quit."

"You wanted me to quit. I decided I didn't want to quit."

"But, Mom, how can you do this? You have to quit!"

"Jennifer, don't talk to me that way. I will make my own decisions based on what I think is the right thing for me to do. I can't quit because you want me to any more than I can move back into this house because I want to." My words surprised me, and Jennifer, too, judging by the light in her eyes.

"Mom, would you? Could you?" She leaned forward and put her hand on my arm. "Can't you and Dad make up before it's too late? You could move back in, and you wouldn't have to work. You guys can work it out. You've done it before."

Her pleading broke my heart. My chest felt constricted, and I found it hard to breathe. I reached for her. She moved onto my lap like an overgrown puppy that no longer realizes its size. Her weight pressed on my thighs, yet holding her provided a familiar comfort. I wrapped my arms around her soft skin and rocked her as if she were still my baby.

"Oh, honey, I wish I could. I wish I could."

"Then do it, Mom. Tell Dad you're sorry and move back in. Please?"

Chapter Eleven

Monday morning I put on a lightweight pair of blue jeans and a dusty-rose-colored T-shirt. Ivory lace appliquéd to the neckline created a peek-a-boo glimpse of my chest without being especially revealing. It was my fanciest T-shirt, but a T-shirt nonetheless. I felt underdressed for work, certainly not dressed for success as Marly had suggested my first day on the job.

Over the weekend, I had spoken with my sister Deena, who encouraged me to find balance in my life. I was glad I had started my sewing project, but for now, the half-sewn drapes lay piled on the living room sofa. I wished I could have finished them without interruption, but I had a more pressing agenda. With that thought in mind, I gulped down the rest of my coffee, jumped in my Volvo wagon, and drove off toward Balboa Park.

I parked at the Navy Hospital and took a shuttle that dropped me off within walking distance of our remote broadcast setup. Rows of booths lined both sides of the street and some were clustered beneath a shady clump of trees. The Labor Day Sun Run, a half-marathon and 5K fun run, would be ending nearby. Scattered groups had laid out blankets in an irregular patchwork and otherwise staked out territory along the open greens parallel to 6th Avenue. A dog galloped past me in a tawny blur, and with a gentle click of his teeth snatched a Frisbee from the air.

I spotted the KZSD van, a large white vehicle with a satellite antenna on top. Next to it was our booth. It had been set up hours before my arrival. First on the morning schedule was Zach and his drive time news show. A huge banner emblazoned with the station name and call letters was prominently displayed twelve feet in the air, held aloft by plastic poles. Heavy cables running from the van to the booth made it appear as if Zach and his equipment were on life support. A small crowd milled nearby in the shade of towering eucalyptus trees. Zach was interviewing an event promoter. I did not see Marly, and wasn't sure what, if anything, I should be doing. I peeked into the van. Sitting inside were two men I didn't know. One of them wore headphones and sat in front of an operations board similar to the ones we used at the station. I smiled and turned my attention to Zach, who questioned his guest about which charities would benefit from the day's events. *Gayline* would not begin for fifty minutes.

To kill time, I wandered around to other booths whose banners advertised a variety of causes. Farthest away were small ethnic food booths emitting the appetizing aromas of German bratwurst, Greek gyros, and Thai chicken on a stick—not exactly my idea of breakfast.

"There you are!" Marly shouted at me. "Where've you been, girlfriend? We've got a show to do."

She squeezed me in a bear hug, an exaggerated gesture as if we had been old friends. Just as quickly she let go. A hint of moisture lingered on my skin where her arms had touched mine. A gentle breeze tickled the fine hair on my forearms and lifted the bangs from Marly's forehead ever so slightly. Her cupid's-bow-shaped lips spread into a seductive wide grin exposing her even, white teeth. I hoped no one in earshot had thought I was actually her girlfriend, yet I had a strong urge to hug her back. Instead, I followed her to the booth. Marly was dressed for the weather in shorts and a tank top. I caught myself staring at her rear where the tight jean material rounded in a curving "W" shape. The day felt warmer.

"You've got it easy today," she said as she turned toward me. "Work the crowd. When someone has anything interesting to say, bring them over to me. If you get started now, we'll be ready when the time comes."

An eclectic assortment of people had assembled in separate groups near our booth. I was not used to approaching strangers and some of them seemed very strange indeed—men wearing black leather jackets and shorts, two women with colorful spiked hair, and teenagers wearing their caps backward with body language that dared me to intrude upon their space. Not feeling especially brave, I approached two average-looking women engaged in conversation with two equally average-looking men. Their talk ended abruptly as I joined them. All eyes were on me in an expectant manner that suggested they thought I would launch into a sales pitch, and in a way, I did.

"Um, hi! I'm looking for people who have something to say." I could hear myself fumbling. "I mean, we're going to be talking to people about the race and everything, and I was wondering if any one of you would be interested in being on the radio."

"I'll talk to Zach," one woman offered.

"Oh, not for his show—for Marly's. She's on

next." I hesitated to state the name of her show.

"HA! You must be kidding." The woman furtively glanced around and peeked at her watch. "We came here to listen to Zach. Come on," she said to her friends. "Let's get going."

The foursome moved on. I felt rejected and alone. Marly was leaning into the doorway of the control van. She would be on soon. I gave the crowd a more discriminating once-over. How could I know who was here for Zach and who would be interested in *Gayline*?

Gathered near a sturdy eucalyptus with peeling bark were three young women. One had a skull tattoo with barbed wire coming out its eyes that encircled her left arm. I did not understand why an otherwise lovely girl would decorate her arm with something permanently unfeminine. Another girl had a series of tiny hoops running up the side of her ear, a fashion trend I had seen before and found more acceptable than hoops through the eyebrow, nose, or lip. Someday, the style would change and at least the holes would close. Despite their age—barely older than Jennifer—I felt intimidated by their looks. I decided the best way to cover my anxiety and dejection from the last group was to be bold and upbeat.

"Excuse me," I said as I strode into their circle. "Would any of you care to be on the radio? We're interested in your comments about today's events."

"Sure," said the girl with the earrings. A round crystal stud embedded above her upper lip flashed in the sunlight. She stubbed out her cigarette on the ground and placed it in a baggie she pulled from her pocket. "Is *Gayline* coming on? Marly's way cool."

"Can I be on, too?" another girl asked. "My

mom's getting chemo for breast cancer. I want to tell people how important it is to be here even if they didn't do the run."

We waited a few feet from Marly and at the appropriate time the young women were allowed to speak into the microphone. I caught myself watching and stepped back into the new crowd that had formed since Zach left. These spectators were here to listen to Marly and I realized finding others to go on the air would now be easier. Were they all gay? I visualized my own image in a mirror and wondered if I looked gay to others.

"I would like to speak with Marly." A tall woman stood before me. She looked vaguely familiar. Her short brown hair was neatly coiffed away from her face revealing yellow plastic button earrings. I guessed she was in her mid- to late-fifties. "I saw you earlier," she said. "You must be Marly's new assistant. Claire, isn't it?" She offered her hand, and shook mine firmly.

"Yes."

"I listen to her show when I can. I considered bringing protesters, but I believe today's message is one we both can agree on. Let her know I'm here, will you? My name is Ivy O'Neal."

Ivy! This was the woman who led the anti-abortion protests I had read about in the paper. I tried not to let my astonishment show. It had never occurred to me Ivy would be a regular listener. She undoubtedly felt a need to keep informed on what she perceived were the evil forces in the city. She leaned around my shoulder and gave Marly an acknowledging nod.

Marly waved her over. "Hey, everybody, we've got a special treat today. Ivy O'Neal has decided to grace our show with her presence. You're looking mighty fine today, Ivy. I wish our listeners could see that fetching outfit you're wearing. You are *hot*. Ouch! What brings you by?"

"Like all the folks today, I am here to support the Labor Day Sun Run and the charities it supports."

"No obscene pictures of bloody fetuses?"

"Our parishioners in Santee personally donated over thirty-two hundred dollars toward today's cause. I'm proud to say we support all life, not just the unborn, but the living in need as well."

"Looking at you, I'm in need right now. Tell me, Ivy, have you adopted any unwanted children lately?"

"Marly, you know I have four children of my own, plus five grandchildren."

"Are you sure they're all yours? Who donated the sperm?"

"I did not come on your show to be insulted. If you—"

"I know some lesbian couples who would be happy to adopt another child, especially if you'll bring the kid over wearing that sexy thing you've got on."

"I want your listeners to know I am wearing long shorts and a T-shirt. Anyone who knows me knows you are making this up."

"Oh, Ivy, I can't help myself any longer. Here, come sit on my lap. Oh, my God! She's not wearing any underwear. Ivy, you can be the mother of my children anytime."

"Ugh! You disgust me. You will answer to the Lord someday, and what will you say then? I thought we would be in agreement here at this charitable event, but I was wrong."

"Like you are about so many things."

Ivy stormed off with long, hurried strides. She

stumbled over a root, and a lanky man I had not noticed earlier reached out and grabbed her arm. The two proceeded onto the green without looking back. Marly began a conversation with a new person who had stood by waiting. I laughed to myself. Secretly I had cheered for Marly, even felt a certain naughty glee at her raunchy spontaneous dialogue. I wished I had her confidence. Being associated with *Gayline* was more than a stretch for me. It amazed me how one moment I could get a thrill from being a part of something so foreign from my previous life and the next feel ashamed of uttering the name of the show. Personally not knowing anyone who would listen to *Gayline* made it easier for me. Besides Ted and the kids, only my sister knew about my being gay. I had not told my parents or the couples with whom Ted and I used to associate. I felt justified in keeping my private life exactly that—private, and I intended to keep it that way. It flashed through my mind that Crystal, my old girlfriend, might listen to the show, but I couldn't conceive of how that might come back to haunt me. No, there was no one who knew about my new life who would know about *Gayline*.

"Mrs. Larson?" It was Amber, my daughter's friend. "I thought that was you."

Chapter Twelve

"Amber! What a surprise. I thought you and Jenny were going to the beach today." I hid my anxiety behind a smile.

"We were, but I canceled. I took a bus to the park instead. Mrs. Larson, can I talk to you about something?"

Whatever it was, I didn't want to hear it. I tried to hide the sense of foreboding that flooded into me. I put her off, blurted something about interviewing crowds, and sent her on her way. Amber wandered off down the row of booths. It pained me to be insensitive, but at that moment, my own self-protection was more important.

During the two-hour show, I had an opportunity to meet some of the regular callers to *Gayline* who had come to support Marly. It was fun to put faces with the names. At eleven o'clock, Marly bowed to a round of applause. Not wanting to assume my duties were complete, I waited for a sign to see if we were done for the day.

"Let's get something to drink," she said.

On the grass in the dappled sunlight beneath the towering old shade trees, we sipped fresh lemonade. I kept an eye out for Amber as I scanned the crowd. Occasionally, friends of Marly's would wave or stop by for a short visit. I rested on my side and slowly let go of my defensive feelings. As I played with a blade of grass, I fantasized that Marly and I were alone in the park. She was lying close next to me. Our bodies fit comfortably together as we spooned with me behind her. I picked a long flimsy blade of grass and imagined twirling it around the curve of her ear, her laughter bright and melodic. She would turn to me, her gorgeous eyes bluer than the Aegean Sea, and we would kiss, lightly, lightly, deeply. I brushed the blade over my lips; its smooth texture quietly aroused me, as did the gesture, so innocent to the casual onlooker.

A lone woman walked toward us. The number 258 was still pinned to her running shirt from the half-marathon. She carried a stack of flyers and handed us each a yellow sheet.

"Thanks," Marly said. "Lourdes, this is Claire. Claire, Lourdes."

"Nice to meet you," I said.

The woman grunted and we shook hands. I looked from the flyer to the woman standing before us. She was rather short and in good physical shape. Her dark hair hung in a thick braid past her waist and I guessed she was Latina. Unfortunately, she had a pronounced underbite. Her jaw thrust forward grotesquely, revealing the curve of her lower teeth. It was hard to look at her, yet I was unable to look away. Lourdes turned her head brusquely and walked on.

"Lourdes is very active in the community." By her tone, I sensed Marly's pointed comment was in direct response to my poor manners.

"I'm sorry," I said. "That was rude of me. It's just, I don't understand why she doesn't do something to, you know, get it fixed. She looks like a piranha."

"Don't you *ever* say that." Like her wit, Marly's anger was sharp and quick. "Lourdes is the best friend the gay community could ask for. We're lucky she works so hard for us, and I'm not going to sit here and listen to you tear her down. She rarely says a word and it's because people like you have been calling her Piranha her whole life. How would you like that for a nickname?"

Her intensity pierced my heart. "I wouldn't. I can't believe I said that. I'm sorry."

"You should be. You think you're Miss Perfect, well, I see through your facade. Don't be so quick to judge. From my vantage point, your life could use some improvement."

I could not hide from the stinging truth of her personal attack. All day I had been petrified others were judging me while I had been guilty of the crime. The blade of grass I had been playing with shredded in my twisting fingers, releasing green ooze. It was apparent to me that I was far out of my comfort zone. Not only was I not my best self, it would certainly help to know who that was.

Jennifer was right. I did not feel like "Mom" anymore. I said and did things out of character. When had I become so judgmental? A new impetuous streak was playing havoc with my analytic side. I couldn't seem to control my impulses. My ordered life had vanished, and I had entered a strange world that left me teetering. Darkness obscured my future and prevented me from seeing where I was going. I feared I would be released into deep space without a lifeline. My mind raced, rocketing out of control. Incurring Marly's wrath ate away at whatever self-confidence I had left. I had lost so much already. I did not want to imperil the new direction my life had taken, yet I questioned if it was an improvement over my old life.

The vagueness of my future made it impossible to focus. I stared at a point in the distance as I struggled to maintain my composure. "Why is it easier to know what I don't want than what I do?" I could feel my frustration mount. "I want to be happy like everyone else," I blurted. "Is that so much to ask?"

Marly turned to me. "What makes you think everyone else is happy?"

The anger was gone from her voice and I had the distinct impression she was speaking personally, from her own heart. Despite her popularity, I was not aware of anyone special in her life and that void was apparent now in her sad glance. I witnessed a glimpse of that same desperation the day we met in the personnel department. We reached toward one another and embraced. As her soft cotton top brushed against my face I burst into tears. My display embarrassed me even more, and I tried to hold back.

"I'm sorry. You must think I'm a hypocrite or a spoiled brat."

"Just let it out," Marly said as she stroked my hair. "That stiff and proper act you put on doesn't fool me. You're never going to get past the pain if you keep it inside. It's okay. I know. I've had my share."

Chapter Thirteen

I hated feeling so vulnerable, especially in front of Marly. And I felt silly for crying like a baby as if that were my only recourse against the unfathomable harshness of my middle-class existence.

"I'm so embarrassed. You must think I'm horrible," I said.

"I think you're hurting. Do you want to tell me about it?"

"No, but I will anyway." I rested my head a bit longer on her shoulder before pulling away and drying my eyes with a tissue I carried in my pocket. It gave me a moment to decide how much I wanted to open up to her. In brief detail, I told her how my marriage had grown increasingly unhappy and that Ted had discovered my affair. I left out the gender of my lover and the fact that she had bolted when our actions had been discovered. Counseling would not change anything. The separation was the first step toward an inevitable divorce, and I was trying to get on with my life. I didn't want to dwell on my problems or discuss my sexual orientation, although a part of me yearned to tell her, "I had a woman lover. Yes, me, little Miss Perfect had an affair." To avoid saying something I would later regret, I shifted the focus. "I guess you've had some bad relationships, too, huh?"

"Yeah, been there, done that. The problem with being a minor celeb is people think they know me because they listen to me spout off for two hours every day. It creates a lot of confusion."

"Are you saying you don't believe what you say on your show?"

"Usually I do, but remember, I say stuff to get a reaction. Do you really believe that I think Ivy O'Neal is a hot babe?"

I laughed. "You haven't found someone who loves you for all the personalities you are. That's too bad. I know you have your sensitive side. If I only heard your on-air persona, I'd think you were a very different person."

"Oh, it's a problem." She snickered. "I'd like to have someone in my life who isn't expecting me to be 'on' all the time. I've got lots of friends. They tell me when I stop looking I'll find someone special. I want to be who I am without having to do a lot of explaining."

I nodded. It sounded like something my sister would say.

"And besides, I need to put my energy into my career right now. I can't be screwing around or I could end up screwing myself."

At work the next day, Marly and I stuck to the basics. Callers rehashed their holiday weekend activities, and I found the conversation easier to follow than in the previous week's shows. As each subsequent day passed, we began to develop a flow both on and off the air. We adjusted our routine to interview a special guest and the variation gave me a new thrill. In general, the work became easier. Despite my continuing errors, I was getting the hang of it after all.

I had felt uncomfortable opening up to Marly during the Labor Day event, but it added a personal quality to our interactions on the job. Acknowledging my inner demons was a challenge I wanted to avoid, but keeping a blind eye would not make them disappear. It was easier to talk superficially about my guilt over what I had done to my family than to face my shortcomings. Admittedly, it was helpful to vent my frustrations to someone who was not judgmental. My sister had told me that any person who engages in finger-pointing ought to do it looking in the mirror, and that included me.

Though I was sorry to hear of Marly's love-life woes, exposing chinks in her granite-walled ego humanized her. Others might believe her to be the unidimensional gutsy on-air persona she cultivated—she had much to gain by projecting a brash facade—yet underneath were remnants of an old injury, a yellowed bruise that still hurt when touched.

Each morning I looked forward to seeing her and hoped she would share other confidences with me. When she spoke of going out, I wondered if she had met someone special. She invited me to go with her and her women friends to a coffeehouse. At first I begged off, thinking her invitations were offered out of politeness. I didn't know if I'd fit in with her friends, and it was easier and more enjoyable to hear about her forays the next morning as we worked together. She persisted, and eventually I accepted.

I'm not sure which fears originally kept me away. If it was being seen with other lesbians, I quickly put that behind me as I realized the other patrons were not paying any attention to us. I thought the women might sit around and talk about being gay—a subject that ultimately would be beyond my comfort level if it came to expressing my own opinions—but that didn't happen either. There was little gay-related talk. Like any conversation, we moved from subject to subject: politics to work to housing to boutiques. It made me realize how narrow my ideas were regarding the so-called "gay lifestyle."

The scope of our intimacy increased each day as Marly and I produced her show, and in her neatened office where we laughed over what had transpired. Aside from occasional errands when I drove around town for one thing or another, we spent an unusual amount of time together in close quarters. I came to appreciate the lingering herbal fragrance from her shampoo. It became as familiar to me as her unconscious mannerisms, which I carefully filed away in an unwritten diary of all the wonderful things that captivated me about her.

As events passed in my life, I related them to her, being careful not to talk on too long or burden her with too many details lest I turn into a babbling idiot in her presence and blow my cover as her secret admirer. I settled into my apartment, spending evenings alone reading, playing the guitar, or pondering what to do about my family. It was easy to converse with Jonah, who was always forthcoming about his activities on campus. Jennifer was unpredictable in her moods and experienced more emotional swings than usual. My separation from her was unbearably necessary, and our loving relationship punctuated by regular visits held us together. Deena continued to challenge me. She pushed me to define a new set of goals now that I was over the first hump at work.

Ted was another story. Every time we got together, whether in person or on the phone, he felt he had to exert some form of superiority, from boasting about our agreed-upon temporary custody of Jennifer to how he was researching the best attorneys in the county. He was the winner; I was the loser. I had hoped things would calm down after I moved out, that his angry explosions would quiet so we could have a dialogue about how to proceed. His mission, it seemed, was to demean me at every turn. If he meant his searing comments toward me then our marriage was little more than a sham, regardless of my sexual orientation. I tried to remember if I had seen this side of him before, yet little came to mind. Ted's hostility facilitated and perpetuated our breakup. He was making it hard to remember why I thought we had a happy marriage for so many years. Of course there had been disagreements, some of them major, but we worked on our problems, put things back together, and for the most part, lived harmoniously. It was our shared goal to create a setting in which our children would mature into productive adults. We made plans for our retirement, though buying a cabin up in Lake Arrowhead had not been spoken of in a long time.

I had begun to pull away in the bedroom before I fully realized my changing sexual feelings, and early on Ted didn't mind. Many times I went along with having sex out of habit or to keep him happy, but he could tell my heart wasn't in it. We hadn't slept together in at least a year when I met Crystal. Somehow she knew I was attracted to women— "gaydar," she called it, the ability to spot other gay women. Was it the vibe I gave off, or was it in the eyes as she suggested? Deena and I have the same eyes and she's not gay. It didn't make sense to me, but my feelings did. I was inexplicably drawn to her and to her bed. At night when everyone was busy with TV, homework, or away at soccer practice, I would sneak into the bedroom and call her. We met secretly for five months.

    One Saturday afternoon, I told Ted I was off to the mall but drove to her house instead. Crystal and I had snuggled a short while when the doorbell rang. She put on her robe, shuffled to the foyer, and opened the door a crack until the chain caught. Ted threw himself at the door with enough strength to rip the security chain from the doorjamb. I could hear Crystal's body thud against the wall.

    "Claire! I know you're in here!"

    "Oh, no! It's Ted. Lock the door!"

    Having already bolted upright in bed at the sound of her shriek, I scrambled to my feet. I reached the flat surface of the bedroom door and leaned into it with my full weight, but a greater power forced it open. I fell back on my bare bottom. Ted stood in the doorway seething, grunting low animal sounds.

    "You bitch. You *bitch*! Get dressed." He picked up a pair of Crystal's shorts and threw them at me. I snatched a corner of the bed sheet and partly covered myself. "Now!"

    In a violent sweep, he backhanded the top of her dresser. Perfume and jewelry crashed to the floor. I cowered, but he grabbed my wrist and yanked me away from the bedside. "What's the matter? My dick not good enough for you anymore? I should fuck you right now. No, I should take you home—like this— and let the kids see what a *whore* their mom is."

    Crystal, who had locked herself in the bathroom with her cell phone, threatened to call 911, but I yelled at her to wait. I yanked my arm free from Ted's grasp. We stood glaring at one another, our breaths competing in mad syncopation. Adrenaline surged through my body and even though I was naked, I felt an unexpected power rising within me. I took a chance at being the first to break eye contact to search for my clothing. As I dressed, I could hear my husband, a usually peaceful man, heaving with each labored breath like a bull ready to charge. When I had finished dressing, he grasped a fistful of my hair close to my head and I let out a small cry. Ted had never made me feel scared, nor had he ever abused me. His grip was strong enough to send a definite message without being too painful. He marched to the front door and pushed me out headfirst. I stumbled forward, but did not fall. He followed me home in his car.

Once there, he told me how his suspicion had escalated the previous month. He checked my email for names he did not recognize, but ultimately he caught us by eavesdropping on our calls. I promised not to see Crystal again. She never called, nor did I.

For the next week, Ted and I could barely look at one another and our conversations were as short as our tempers. I knew I had to make a move; things couldn't continue as they were, and I could not undo my actions any more than Ted could change his response. Everything happened so fast. It was hard for me to imagine getting a divorce, yet I didn't argue when he suggested I move out.

He agreed not to talk about the affair for the sake of the kids—and, I suspected, his own ego—but he insisted they be told the truth about my sexual inclination as the reason for my departure. We called a family meeting. I wanted to do the talking. In short order I was overwhelmed with questions I was unable or unprepared to answer, especially from Jennifer. Our conversation heated to a boil with Ted cursing,

Jonah sitting like a zombie with his mouth half open, me trying to turn down the heat and maintain control by explaining as fast as I could until Jennifer exploded and ran into her room. Jonah spent the rest of the evening in his sister's room with the door locked and the music turned up. Ted berated me until I had enough. I left the house for a long walk and that night I fell asleep on the couch. The next day, we decided to send the kids to see their grandparents in Minnesota so I could pack my things in private. I didn't want to subject them to any further trauma as Ted and I separated out pieces of furniture, items that still seemed out of place in my apartment.

Chapter Fourteen

The transition from summer to autumn had been my favorite time of year back in Minnesota where I grew up. San Diego experienced a gentle transition, but I enjoyed the clear crisp mornings that brought relief from the incessant summer heat. Liquidambar trees slowly turned into a blaze of fiery color: crimson, gold, salmon, and ochre. Fallen leaves, their outer edges curled with dryness, scratched and skittered along sidewalks in the wind much as they did back home. Hillsides, already browned from lack of rain, flattened as tired plants drooped under their own weight. Perhaps the most distinct difference in the change of seasons came with the end of daylight savings time. Evening hours grew short and seemed to disappear altogether into the increasingly cool darkness of the impending winter nights. Most days were still warm and sunny, but the renewed freshness in the air after the first few light rains were the times I liked best.

Several times Marly came to work bundled in layers of sweat clothes. She looked cozy, a little too informal for work, but then, she was the boss. Occasionally, during spirited discussions on *Gayline*, she would get heated up and remove both her sweatshirt and a lightweight sweater underneath, so all that remained was her thin short-sleeved tee. Personally, I preferred to wear thicker turtleneck sweaters, but

I had no problem eyeing her toned biceps. It was a pleasant distraction. Knowing she would be there at work perked me up and got me going on mornings when I felt a little depressed. I also looked forward to the variety of subjects on *Gayline*. Some days we had special guests or topics of particular interest to me. For example, today's topic focused on veganism and a national group concerned with the treatment of animals. Yin-Yang called and I put them on the air, listening intently for which position they would take. As they reasoned how we humans are designed by nature to be meat eaters, I found myself examining my own views. Their comments made me question ideas I might not have considered or ones I took for granted, and their descriptive, impassioned argument prompted a visceral reaction in me.

"How many of our ancestors could have lived without the benefit of animals?" they asked. "Wolves don't agonize over running down a hare, snapping its neck, and tearing apart its warm flesh, now do they?

"Your previous caller thinks we have a responsibility to protect higher life forms, that we should revere all living creatures as sacred, and that those who don't are somehow morally repugnant. Dogma, I say. Dogma isn't truth, it's, well, dogma! What about plants? Plants respond to their environment, to music, to being touched. Do they have souls? Should we be restricted to eating fallen seeds and fruit? What if I step on a bug? How could I live with myself? By the way, I do respect all living things and I'm grateful some give their life for mine.

"That woman is entitled to her belief, but her moralizing is ill-conceived. I have a right—by design—

to be a kindly, meat-eating, fur-wearing mammal, even though I don't choose to do that, just as she has a right to be a new-age moralist with an underfed brain who avoids stepping on bugs. I'd like to know if this woman believes in the Bible. Does her God condone eating meat? Or fish?

"You know, I love animals. I do. I've owned pets—and not eaten them! I believe in humane treatment during the course of animal husbandry through their ultimate demise at the slaughterhouse, which I admit has room for improvement. Maybe that seems like a contradiction to Miss Bleeding Heart, but it makes perfect sense to me. I'm Yin-Yang and that's my opinion."

"Bravo!" Marly applauded. "Or is it brava? Bravx? Yin-Yang you're a marvel. Are you still there? Yin-Yang? They hung up. I think I'll make a bumper sticker in their honor: *Omnivores Are People Too.* Ya think? There you go folks, two completely different yet sane arguments. And me, I'll eat anything covered in chocolate."

Yin-Yang had not minced words, but then neither had our previous caller. I liked how it was impossible to tell if Yin-Yang's voice came from a man or a woman. It forced me to think of this person as a human being first, without bringing in any of my own preconceived ideas about how their gender might influence their views. Marly rarely interrupted when Yin-Yang was on a rant. These controversial subjects were perfect for inciting listeners to respond, some of whom wouldn't ordinarily call in.

Ten minutes remained until the top of the hour and part of that time was needed for commercials. Marly continued to ad-lib and joked about "nutritious nutria" when a call came in. I laughed to myself as I listened to the falsetto voice with the New York accent on the other end of the line. I figured it was one of the Queens From Queens, a drag group that put on shows for a variety of causes. Thinking we could squeeze in another quick comment, I put the new caller on hold without taking any information. I motioned to Marly.

"Time for one more caller," she said. "Hi, welcome to *Gayline*."

"Am I on the radio?" the unnatural voice asked.

"Yes, and who do we have here?"

"There's a bomb in your building." *Click.*

Chapter Fifteen

A bomb in the building? A shiver rippled my skin into hard little bumps and set my hair on end. My eyes and mouth opened wide in horrified disbelief. I clasped my hands on my headphones, ready to tear them off and dash for the exit, but first I looked to Marly for her reaction.

"Hey, a bomb threat." She laughed. "Haven't had one of those in months. The homophobes are at it again." Then in a mock-authoritative voice, she intoned, "This is a test of the emergency broadcast system. If this had been a real emergency...we would have had to break open the champagne I keep hidden in my locker. Woo-hoo! Thanks, everyone, for a great show. Talk to you tomorrow—same time, same place—and if I'm hungover, you'll know I drank that champagne all by myself."

I cut to a commercial. Men and women were bustling about the hallways. Betty, the office manager, knocked on the outer glass of Marly's booth and motioned for us to go outside. She opened our booth door and warned us to get moving. "Forget the commercials." She clapped her hands together like a schoolteacher calling her students to order. "The eighteen-pack is on. You're off the air. Come on. Out!"

Marly and I took off our cans and joined the others filing down the hall toward the exit. Betty's butt swayed in a quick rhythm as her hurried steps propelled her to the front door. Once outside, I could hear the approaching wail of a police siren. One car arrived, then two, then three. The sirens wound down while the red and amber lights swirled hypnotically. Approximately thirty employees milled about in the parking lot.

"Step away from the building," a bullhorn honked. "Move to the rear of the parking area."

I moved toward my car, hoping it was parked far enough away to avoid any damage in case of an explosion. I looked at the faces in the crowd, but no one seemed concerned in the least.

Betty lit a cigarette and puffed away beneath a tree. My mouth was dry and the faint smell of cigarette smoke irritated my nose. I swallowed hard and moved upwind to join her in the shade.

"Does this happen a lot?"

"Oh, it hasn't happened in a while. Don't worry yourself about it. We have one every now and then. It's probably nothing, no big deal, but we still have to take them seriously."

"Have the police ever caught anyone? Do they know who it is?"

"Well, hon, they always happen near the end of Marly's show. What does that tell you?" She took a long drag on her cigarette. We watched as bomb-sniffing dogs were ushered into the building. "You might as well go to lunch," she said. "It'll probably be about two hours before they let us back in. Patsy is going to miss her gardening show. Oh, well. See you later." Betty stubbed out her cigarette and fished her car keys out of her purse.

I went to my car and tuned the radio to KZSD. The eighteen-pack held eighteen CDs, mostly soft pop compilations suitable for general audiences. Paul Simon was crooning "Cecilia." I searched the crowd for Marly, but she was nowhere to be found. Lunch held no appeal for me. It was early and I felt a little queasy. I started up my station wagon, stopped briefly at the gauntlet of questioning officers, and drove home.

My apartment seemed smaller than I remembered. Concentration was impossible. I bided my time, wondering if the phone would ring, waiting until it made sense to return to work, wondering if returning to work made any sense at all. What kind of loony place was this radio station? Jennifer never mentioned bomb threats. If Marly and her show were a continual target, what did that make me?

I paced the cramped rooms of my apartment. To ease my anxiety, I wiped up a few small messes. Noticing a few crumbs sprinkled on the kitchen floor, I got out a broom and followed up with the mop. The floor was dirtier than I had realized. I got on my hands and knees, working away with a scrub brush until I noticed my clothes were not moving freely over my body. By then, I felt committed to my task and figured I'd change clothes when I finished. The kitchen cabinets caught my attention. They were poorly designed, unless one meant to collect dust. The corners were yucky. I dampened a sponge from a small bowl filled with warm water and went at it.

"This apartment is certainly cleaner than when I moved in," I muttered aloud. "I'm going to have to talk to Marly at some point. If I'm going to quit, this bomb threat would be a good reason. What am I saying? I don't want to quit. It's been weeks already. Who am I kidding? I'm not going anywhere. Marly needs me and I need her. In all the commotion, I wonder where she went? I should go back to work and see if she's okay. Look at the gunk on these cupboards."

I dumped the gray water down the drain. The phone rang. My heart raced at the sound of Marly's voice.

"Are you okay?" I asked.

"Never better. I was wondering if you're coming back in." I looked at the oven clock. It was almost two.

"There's a detective here who'd like to ask you some questions."

"I'm coming right now." I downed a cup of yogurt, changed my slacks, pulled off my top, ran a washrag across my neck and underneath my arms, and threw on a lightweight sweater. My heart pounded against the shoulder strap as I buckled my seat belt and drove back to work.

When I arrived, I noticed a police car remained parked out front. Mustering courage, I marched into the building. If I acted like this wasn't a big deal, just as Betty said, then maybe it wasn't. The regularly scheduled programming played through the front lobby speakers. I nodded to the receptionist, my tight-lipped grin little more than a contorted grimace.

A wave of relief flowed over me when I caught sight of Marly sitting comfortably in her office. Her broad grin faded as she grabbed me by the shoulders. "Are you okay, girlfriend? You don't look so good."

She stood, and on impulse I hugged her forcefully. "I was so worried," I said. "I was afraid something might have happened to you."

She returned the hug. "Hey, I'm okay. It was a bomb scare, that's all. We're used to them around here. Don't worry. There are never any bombs, just wackos who call in to get attention."

"So, you're really okay?" I loosened my grip and we fell apart.

"Forget it. It's good for the ratings. We've already been on the news and tomorrow it'll be in the paper. The detective was here; actually she's an agent for the FBI. I gave her the air check from our show. Before I forget, here's her card. She wants you to call her around four."

"The FBI? Me? Why me?"

"You took the call."

Chapter Sixteen

I put the business card Marly gave me into my back pocket. It upset me to think something bad might happen to her. I squelched an urge to comb my fingers through her tousled hair and hold her again, as if my arms could provide a secure blanket of protection. Yet I knew it was more. I could not diminish the intense attraction she aroused in me, but I felt it best to stop thinking about her.

Before I let my imagination run wild, I picked up some paperwork left over from the previous day. As I stared at the page, the words ran together and my thoughts sharpened. Marly was obviously not interested in me, and more to the point, she was my boss. To threaten the time we shared working together by suggesting a relationship would be far too risky. I was sure I was not her type. Besides, I was a poor choice—recently separated from Ted, an emotional basket case, hardly a good prospect. I considered the possibility that my attraction to her could be a typical example of rebound. After my failed relationship, she took me in. It was gratitude, plain and simple.

We were fundamentally different. Marly was very casual about her dress, her manners, her workspace. Again, I wondered what her house must look like. I still felt uncomfortable in casual work clothes, though at Marly's suggestion I was trying to loosen up. I always wore a little makeup. She probably didn't even own any. I could not bring myself to wear sweats, or yoga pants, which seemed inappropriate. Why bother getting dressed at all if you could wear pajamas twenty-four seven?

Our differences added up to more than our choices of clothing and our obvious departure on levels of neatness. She was spontaneous, zany, quick-witted, and charismatic. She could control a crowd, hold court in a roomful of listeners. I had always focused on quieter pursuits. As a volunteer at Jennifer's school library, I enjoyed interacting one-on-one with the kids. I was not a wallflower at parties, but I did not feel a need to command attention either. It was my choice to be soft-spoken, a matter of style to get my point across without making a fuss. If we paired up, Marly's personality would run over me in no time while I would be caught in analysis paralysis. I decided we would not be a good match.

I had witnessed her quieter pensive moments, sympathy, and compassion. There were times, in Balboa Park for example, when I cried on her shoulder and she offered words of comfort. I remembered what she had said about how difficult it had been for her to find a love match. Despite our differences, maybe we would click in bed. Her sexual passion would surely be a reflection of the passion she showed for life in general. If we kissed, I bet it would start soft and gentle. And I would love to get my hands on her breasts, massaging and smoothing over them with my fingertips, then moving down her waist over the round curves of her hips and onto that nice bottom. Mmmm. I would show her my passionate self, the deep, mesmerizing, soulful side of me. We could relate like that. Yeah. Then she wouldn't think I was

a boring librarian type. The smell of her hair while kissing her neck would get me so excited...I would make mad love to her, caress her, lick her until she moaned and called out my name. Yes. And I'd come just by pleasuring her. Yes, I would. Yes!
"Claire?"
"Yes!" I thrust the paperwork onto my lap, inadvertently crunching it in my curled hand. My posture stiffened.
"Claire, you've been staring at the same page for twenty minutes. You're obviously not yourself. Why don't you take off now and we'll pick up again tomorrow? I think this whole day has been a bit much for you." I looked at her with a doe-caught-in-the-headlights expression. "It's okay," she said. "Go on home."
I felt an ascending warmth flow through my body and wondered if I had turned red. My thoughts embarrassed me as surely as if I had spoken them aloud. I mumbled something and decided to leave while I had the chance. As I drove home I began to relax, knowing the station was behind me for the day.
My phone was ringing as I entered my apartment and I fished it out of my purse.
"Thank God you answered," Ted said. "I heard what happened."
"Hey, I'm fine." In brief detail, I recounted my experience, the caller with the peculiar accent, and the subsequent evacuation of the building.
"I want to see you," he said. "Have dinner with me and Jennifer tonight. We can get Chinese, my treat."
We met at the restaurant. Ted and I nodded at one another. Jennifer greeted me with a big hug. At our table, she fidgeted in her seat.

"Dad said I shouldn't talk about the bomb thing because he doesn't want me to upset you. But, Mom, you know how I feel about your job. And, geez, now this happens."

Ted took up her cause. "I think Jennifer's right. This show you've gotten yourself mixed up in could be dangerous. Think of your family. I'm sure there are other jobs out there. You seem more confident now that you've been working. It would be easy for you to find something else that would be a better fit."

I was somewhat surprised, not by Jennifer's concern, but by Ted's. It was the first time since our separation that he expressed genuine interest in my well-being. I wasn't sure if he was being selfish for the sake of the kids, or if there was more to it…something in his voice and manner, a certain tone I recognized from years of being his wife. He was worried because he still cared. Did he still love me after all that happened? Maybe it shouldn't have mattered at this point, but a part of me yearned for familial affection. I managed to pass off the subject with the promise that I would consider what they had said.

We shared several favorite dishes as we had done so many times in the past. As we picked over the last of the cashew chicken, it began to feel like old times. There was no animosity. Ted refrained from bringing up other touchy subjects. I figured he was trying to make me feel more secure. All the same, I was suspicious. As we walked out of the restaurant, he pulled me aside.

"I have something to tell you," he said. "Today made me realize how important you are to me. If there had been a real bomb…" He trailed off and surprised me with a hug. I did not have time to respond before he let go. "I've been angry and I've been getting in my digs, but I'm going to try to be better so you won't hang up on me." His nervous laugh turned into a throat-clearing sound. We said good-bye.

Later, I realized his reaction toward me regarding the situation was much like my reaction had been toward Marly.

Chapter Seventeen

At day's end I was totally exhausted. I let my clothing fall to the floor in a rumpled heap, showered, and bundled up in a cozy robe. I picked up the guitar, but my eyes kept wandering to the locked front door deadbolt, an ineffective barrier to my anxiety over everything on my mind. Even sleep did not bring peace. I tossed throughout the night.

The next morning I walked into KZSD with newly opened eyes. I noticed the receptionist's clothing, the bright color of her lipstick, and little things out of place around the lobby. As I unlocked the door to Studio B, I thought it opened too easily. Who else had a key?

I answered each phone call on *Gayline* believing at any moment I would hear the falsetto New York accent. No threats came in, though there was plenty of on-air talk. Our phone lines remained jammed throughout the show. All the local media outlets had picked up the story. I wondered if the publicity would affect the show's ratings for a long while or if this was a mere blip. It was possible there would never be a bomb, that the whole event was a calculated plan to boost listenership. Did Marly know something, or the someone who called in the threat? Whatever the source, it definitely stirred the pot. People were talking. The wall clock minute hands spun around twice and the show ended. I stopped by Marly's mailbox, which was crammed with messages. I took the slips of paper back to her office where she was firming up lunch plans over the phone. I declined an invitation to join her and the unnamed party, instead choosing to go home.

It was early to be considering lunch, though I was glad to be home. My apartment had become my refuge, now personalized by the matching curtains and throw pillows I'd sewn. To fill a little time, I sorted my laundry into lights and darks, and checked the pockets for tissues and spare change. I pulled out a business card I did not recognize and read the small print: Laurel Emerson, Agent, Federal Bureau of Investigation. My jaw clenched. Someone important obviously felt this bomb threat was not a harmless prank meant to generate gossip or boost ratings. I fingered the raised print on the card and read it several times. I had neglected to call her the previous day, and wondered when a good time would be. After laundry? After lunch? After work? I did not want to talk to Agent Laurel Emerson.

"Agent Laurel Emerson, please." I waited for what seemed like an eternity. There was no Muzak on hold. I gripped the phone tightly as I thought about what to say.

"Agent Emerson."

The smooth sound of her voice brought me back. "Hi. Agent Emerson, this is Claire Larson from KZSD—except I'm calling from home, I mean my apartment, not that it matters." I was flustered beyond comprehension. I was not guilty of anything except my association, perhaps sufficient cause. My fumbling sounded suspect to me. Would she think so, too?

"I'm glad you called." Her voice was mellow, like creamy butter that had reached its melting point. I immediately felt calmer. She suggested I meet her after work. Would a simple early dinner be okay? I could hardly say no to the FBI. Besides, I had nothing to hide.

Back at the station, I repeated Agent Emerson's admonishment to not speak of the phoned-in threat in any detail.

Marly laughed. "You're so serious—you crack me up. As if I had some kind of insider information. Get real. It was broadcast live. Yeah, details heard only by me and ten thousand of my closest friends. Oooooh!"

I felt silly and wondered if what she said was true. Did we actually have ten thousand listeners, or had she flung out a round number? To get through the day, I pretended we only had a few dozen listeners so I wouldn't be nervous. Ten thousand, hmm. Had I made any mistakes on the air that morning?

Keeping busy that afternoon was easy. Our office received an unusual amount of attention from others in the building. Patsy, who had missed her gardening show, swung by with a sarcastic comment, as did several others. No one seemed particularly bothered, plus there were so many threats these days directed at all kinds of minority groups that turned out to be nothing. Others mentioned it in jest or with the same importance as a high school fire drill. I had no reason to take it lightly, but judging by everyone else's reaction, I could see my own was one based on inexperience. By the end of the day, I was laughing off the event with feigned ease, yet I was thankful Agent Emerson didn't think it was funny any more than airport security found gun jokes amusing. I picked up my purse in readiness to leave for our meeting.

"Hey, before you head out, I have a favor to ask," Marly said. "I'm running up to L.A. for a four-day weekend over Thanksgiving and I need someone to feed my cats."

"You want me to do it?"

"They're not that tough. I think you can handle it, assuming you're going to be around. You get the time off, too, you know."

"Oh. Yeah, sure." I hadn't wanted to think about the holidays what with my family in disarray. Jonah had mentioned a ski trip to Colorado with a couple of school buddies. I had no such avoidance.

"Here's my address. Want to follow me home?"

"I'll be there later. I have to meet someone first."

Marly raised an eyebrow ever so slightly and smiled.

Chapter Eighteen

Outside the submarine sandwich shop I stood watch for Agent Emerson. Passers-by wearing sunglasses caught my attention. Would she be wearing a listening device disguised as simple earbuds? It occurred to me that Agent Emerson did not know what I looked like either. A dark-suited woman walked into the shop and my eyes followed as she paused at the order counter.

"Excuse me, ma'am," I heard a voice say. "Do you have the time?" I turned to the petite woman by my side.

"Four thirty." I scanned the interior of the sub shop for the suited woman, and then the parking lot for a likely individual. I shoved my hands deeply into my pants pockets and shifted my weight from one foot to the other.

The woman persisted. "That's the time?" she asked in a smooth tone. The voice was familiar, but I couldn't be distracted from my search. "Claire? I thought we could take our sandwiches to that park across the way."

"It's you?"

"Yes."

Soft blondish-brown curls from a grown-out perm lay softly around her heart-shaped face. Her makeup looked tired. She wore cotton slacks, a sweatshirt with a howling coyote printed on the front, and her plain white shirt poked up above the ribbed neckline. I was stunned by the sight of this diminutive, unassuming woman. She could have been a daycare worker or an invisible shopper at Walmart, but an FBI agent? As we walked to the counter, I wondered if she was an impostor. I ordered a turkey club. She declined my offer to pay for her meal, and I instantly regretted asking. We walked in silence with our bags of food to the park and sat on a bench. After a few bites, she made comments about the weather and the pretty sunset, and then broke from the small talk. She flashed her ID and asked to see mine.

"We've been following a number of cases. We think your suspect is tied to bomb threats received at other locations. The advantage we have in your situation," she said between bites, "is the tape from the radio show. We've matched it with other voice prints."

"Do you know who it is?" I asked. She shook her head. "This whole thing makes me very nervous. Everyone at the station thinks it's a joke, but you don't, do you?"

"It's my job to investigate these matters. Why do you suppose the others at the station think that?"

I felt she was pumping me for information. I didn't want to spread rumors. Speculation, that's all I had heard. Innuendo. Nothing concrete.

"I don't know anything," I said, wondering if I had unwittingly become a party to a conspiracy. For all I knew, this whole thing could be another radio station prank. I tried to appear casual as I popped a few corn chips into my mouth and chomped down. The sound was amplified, deafening. I inhaled loudly and choked, then in spasms coughed out a spray of soggy particles. She slapped me on the back rather hard given her size. I waved her off and took a swig from my water bottle. "I'm okay. I, uh, breathed in a crumb." I was afraid to look at her for what might show on my face. From the corner of my eye a guilty tear escaped. I blotted it with my napkin. I had nothing to hide, but what about Marly? Would a lawyer advise me to keep talking? I crossed my legs and stuffed my hands beneath them.

Agent Emerson sipped her drink. Her affect seemed so casual. Her size made her look younger than her actual age, early fifties I guessed. She stuffed her waxy sandwich wrap into the empty bag and gently touched my arm as if she were a caring girlfriend.

"Claire," she said, "you're not under suspicion. I met you here to get away from the radio station. It's a little chaotic there and I didn't wish to be overheard. I thought this neutral environment might make you feel more comfortable." The lilting deep tone of her voice did not match her look. "I'm not ruling anyone out, nor am I pointing a finger at anyone. I'm trying to get answers so I can solve a case. If you have something to tell me, you have my number. I appreciate your time."

She deposited the bag in a nearby trash bin. As an afterthought she waved to me, and then crossed the street to the parking lot. In the deepening light, I lost sight of her in the sea of cars.

My food felt like a hard lump in my stomach. The chips had lost their appeal, but I sat for a while sucking the salt off individual corn curls and flicking them onto the grass for the birds. If Marly knew more than she was telling, I was in the middle between her and the FBI. It was a long shot, but nonetheless it had me wondering, and given the nature of our interview, had Emerson wondering, too.

    I checked my pocket and pulled out Marly's address. I determined the best route to her house in Pacific Beach and decided to get going before the remaining light disappeared.

Chapter Nineteen

I parked in front of Marly's house, a 1950s cottage-style bungalow located on a street dotted with an eclectic assortment of old houses and new condos. Some had a second story to take advantage of the ocean view, a far prettier sight than her dying lawn. The walk up the front steps was lined with disintegrating terra-cotta pots as evidenced by the little piles of rust-colored debris encircling each one. Bedraggled geraniums cemented into the arid soil spilled over the tops as if trying to escape in search of water. I half expected to see an old stuffed chair on the porch and a tire swing hanging from a frayed rope. The front door was ajar and I heard music playing.

The screen door rattled in the frame against the rap of my knuckles. I rang the bell. "Anyone home?" The door creaked loudly as I entered. "Hello?" Two cats tore through the kitchen. The back door slammed and Marly appeared. She greeted me with a bear hug.

She invited me to sit, an all but impossible task as her furniture was covered with magazines, dirty dishes, wrinkled clothing, CDs, and anything else that might have rightly belonged in a closet, on a shelf, or in the dishwasher. She hastily gathered an armload of items off a chair and motioned for me to make myself at home. As I moved to the chair, a shaggy brown cat raced in first and nestled into a padded corner. I sat anyway, my bottom barely touching the front edge of the cushion. "MayMay! Down." The cat ignored her. "You, too. Down!" A black cat with white markings jumped from the kitchen table like a falling ten-pound domino. Marly placed her pile of stuff on the table.

"These are my cats," she said unapologetically.

"Is that the Hawaiian 'Mei-mei' for 'little sister'?" I asked as I turned to pet the matted feline purring behind my back.

"Actually, it's May, short for Mayhem. Believe it or not, she's pretty old. The black-and-white one is Maelstrom, but I just call him Mal."

"How descriptive."

"I got MayMay because Mal was so wild; I thought an older cat would be a good playmate. But instead of being a calming influence, she became more like him. Oh, well. Let me get you a beer."

Her house was as I imagined. To my relief, the door to her bathroom and bedroom were closed. She showed me where to find the cat food, kitty litter, toys, and treats. I was reluctant to lean against any of the countertops in the kitchen lest I become permanently stuck. We moseyed to the backyard and sat on a couple of old Adirondack chairs with peeling paint, where we sipped beer and talked about the show. I thought she might bring up my meeting with Agent Laurel Emerson but then I realized she did not know for certain we had met earlier. Rather than open up that can of worms, I took a swig of beer and didn't mention it.

Marly lit a tiki torch, and we rested our drinks on an old wooden wire spool that served as a table. The bohemian atmosphere reminded me of my younger days at college. She excused herself when the phone rang. I liked being at Marly's house despite its disheveled interior and rustic yard. I did not have a patio, only a tiny balcony at my apartment. I enjoyed sitting outside in the unseasonably warm weather.

    I assumed that living in my apartment was temporary, though I couldn't say where I would go next. To hear Ted tell it, he was planning his future with little regard to me. Despite his threats about hiring lawyers, I had not heard from one. I didn't know if he was waiting for me to file for divorce, or what would happen. The other night at the Chinese restaurant he had been genuinely concerned about my welfare. Was it for Jennifer's sake, or did he still care? Did he think we should reconcile? Did I? These thoughts confused me, overwhelmed me, and ultimately made me close my eyes.

    Marly came out of the house and walked up behind me. She stroked my hair and gently rubbed her fingers into my scalp. The tension that consumed my body eased away. Using a delicate circular motion, her fingers rubbed my temples and found their way to my shoulders.

    "You are so tight. That bomb threat scared you, didn't it?"

    "Mmm. I guess it did." My whole body cried out for a massage, for release.

    "This is what you need, isn't it, girlfriend?"

    "Mmm." My eyes jolted awake. That word, "girlfriend." I felt my pulse quicken. I was definitely horny. I turned toward her. It was too dark to read the expression on her face. Was she coming on to me, or was I projecting?

    "The house key," I said. "Just bring it to work next week, okay? I have to go."

"But I thought we could go out later. It's Friday night."

Using her bear hug technique, I squeezed her silent and made a hasty exit into the night.

Driving home, I tried to lose my demons by weaving in and out of the congested evening traffic. Ridiculous, I know, but when I arrived home, I pushed my apartment door shut with more strength than needed and leaned against the cool wood panels as if to protect myself from an unseen force. I locked the door and turned the handle on the dead bolt. The problem was I brought the intruder in with me. Wherever you go, there you are.

I was glad to be home. My head spun from the activities of the past two days. I felt overwhelmed. A bath, yes, a good long soak would calm me enough to sleep. Before I could turn on the tap, my cell phone rang. It was Ted.

"I wanted to check in," he said. "I'm worried about you."

"I'll be okay. I need time for things to settle down. I'm a little tense."

"You need some TLC. I could come over there and give you a back rub."

I stopped mid-breath. Was this another come-on? Marly was touching me more often as we continued to get to know one another. She was like that with her friends, but I was not used to it. It was impossible for me to separate my fantasy from the truth, whatever that was. And Ted? He hadn't been interested in me sexually for months. It was as if I had broadcast my unmet needs over the airwaves and a couple of takers had stepped forward to meet the challenge.

"Claire?"

"Oh, sorry. Um, look I was getting ready to step into the tub. I'll talk to you later."

"Wait! I called because I was hoping we could all get together for Thanksgiving dinner next week. You don't have to cook. I'll take care of everything. Come over around three, okay?"

I accepted and then got him off the phone.

The warm water flowing into the tub felt reassuring on my hand as I tested the temperature. It was almost too hot to get in, but I dipped myself down until the heat enveloped the bulk of my body and encased me in a comforting cocoon. I rested until I caught myself falling asleep. Eventually, the water cooled down to a pleasant tepidity. I reached for the smooth soap, which felt peculiar beneath my pruned-up fingertips. I let the scented bar glide down my arm and over my breasts. As I cleaned my privates, I mused over who would be the focus of my pleasure. Would it be Marly, who captivated most of my waking thoughts? Ted, whose renewed interest reminded me of the years we had cared for one another? Or, maybe an unknown person I could meet tomorrow? Fast decision—Marly. The woman who filled my fantasy life could not be dislodged by the illusory presence of others. She filled me with desire and then left me wanting.

Chapter Twenty

"Well, if it isn't Glover Hayes, my favorite nemesis wannabe. Does your radio station know you like to call *Gayline*?" Marly smirked.

"Humph. I hear you're trying to boost ratings again. Can't you come up with something more creative than a bomb threat? It's old news, baby."

"Not older than the average age of your audience, Glover. Instead of protesting water fluoridation, why not propose adding Viagra? That'll keep your listeners 'up.' And speaking of ratings, your closed-minded attitude gives my listeners renewed motivation to be involved in the community. You're always welcome on my show."

"I'll have to have you on mine someday, even though I'd risk losing a few listeners."

"Is that a challenge?"

"Call it what you like. You gays make a lot of noise, but you'll never convince me you're normal. You'll always be on the fringes of society. You act so smug on the air. I doubt that would be the case after an hour on my show."

"Folks, you heard it here first. Glover has slapped me in the face with his latex gloves. The duel is on."

Marly and I grinned and exchanged the thumbs-up sign. Her appetite had been whetted like a little girl given a dollar for the ice cream man. She pointed at my control board. I forgot what I had been doing. The phone lines lit up—one, two, three. I popped in a cart for a commercial—Carlos's store, CondomMania—and took the first line. Marly was onto something. My excitement grew as caller after caller commented on how Marly should conduct herself on Glover's show, topics that could be discussed, and suggestions ranging from the absurd to outright protests that she was playing into enemy hands. Some called her a traitor and others congratulated her courage.

That afternoon in her office, we turned on *The Glover Hayes Show*. I was amazed at how intently she listened. Her keen ability to focus on the less obvious aspects of his show impressed me. Marly explained that in order to effect a potent strategy we would need to know our opponent. I was only vaguely familiar with the program. Glover dispensed with a few local issues that must have been ongoing themes before he addressed the challenge with Marly. Interestingly enough, the comments he received from his callers were not too different from the ones we had received. Most were supportive of his long-standing negative position on gays and added to his diatribe of generalized intolerance for the supposed good of the public and family values. What I wasn't prepared for were the callers who had heard the challenge on *Gayline*. I was intrigued to hear one familiar voice in particular: Yin-Yang.

"I want you to know I fully support this exchange of ideas," they said. "There are those within the gay community who would silence bigots. As much as I wish for and work toward tolerance, I believe unwavering ideology is destructive because it's not conducive to growth. If we don't move forward, we'll inadvertently contribute to our demise. To have progress, we must foster fresh ideas. There will always be extremes, but we have to be careful if we are to label extremists as being inherently bad. Extremists must be heard. To censor them is to censor free speech. Personally, I want the freedom to say which so-called extremists are ahead of their time, and which ones—those espousing hate, for example—are cowards or who work to bring us down. Unfortunately, that's not always apparent. Ideas need time to evolve, just as people need time to accept new ideas, and your audience needs to hear our message."

Yin-Yang wrapped up the call by heartily endorsing a spirited verbal jousting match. They could have made the same speech on our show. This was a special person, one I wanted to meet, and I wondered anew why they kept their identity a secret. Most callers are not given the time to lecture on the air. It was to Glover's credit that he did not interject his own thoughts until Yin-Yang was through speaking. When it came to appealing to our respective audiences, we were more alike than different.

Marly and I spent a good deal of time over the next week brainstorming the best ways to take advantage of her time on Glover's show. As usual, Lourdes sent daily emails offering up her own suggestions, as did many of Marly's other friends and fans who proposed everything from elaborate practical jokes to formal debate. Marly's presence as a voice for the gay community in San Diego was a responsibility she embraced when the occasion demanded it. As a charismatic player in a position of power, she was entreated by her audience to maintain a staunch pro-gay stance. True to her form, she frequently laughed it off. She could not be all things to all people, and it reminded me that her show was primarily for entertainment and not a political forum. There was no single all-encompassing "correct" gay viewpoint, and to try to find it would have been as pointless as a radio show without an audience.

We laughed at the outrageous suggestions, yet I could not be sure she wouldn't glom on to one and try to make it a reality. Though I knew of others who had played practical jokes, it never would have occurred to me to come up with one of my own, and if I had, I would not have been able to carry out the plan. I was much too shy and wouldn't have liked the attention. Nor would I have enjoyed embarrassing another person, however playfully, in the name of fun. Just for the moment I allowed myself to privately entertain an exception. What if someone were to place a hint in Agent Emerson's ear about Glover? Would that be so bad? Suddenly, feeling bad felt good, until it occurred to me: What if he was already a suspect?

Chapter Twenty-one

There was no specific day set aside for Glover's radio show challenge, and I wondered if the whole thing would die a quiet death. Marly dropped the subject and spoke of her upcoming holiday travel plans. She would be leaving for L.A. on Wednesday night after the show.

Thanksgiving morning I sat curled up on my living room sofa dressed in cozy pink velour loungewear. Silent marching bands and colorful floats paraded across the muted TV screen. I sipped my coffee and tried to relax, but it bothered me that I wasn't cooking this year or contributing to the family dinner. I couldn't seem to rationalize I had somehow earned the privilege of kicking back. Seeing my family would be awkward. Holidays were often stressful no matter what one did. I took a last swallow of cold coffee and left for Marly's.

In the morning fog, Marly's vacant home took on a haunted quality. I apprehensively turned the key in the front door lock. The blinds had been drawn shut, and it was dark and cool inside. MayMay rubbed against my shin leaving a haze of brown fur on my pant leg. Maelstrom meowed noisily from the kitchen. I fed the cats, refreshed their water, and scooped out the litter. Marly had made a cursory attempt at house cleaning. A few dishes rested in the drainer and paper clutter had been stacked in piles around the living area.

One pile had already toppled. As I neatly restacked the magazines by size, I took a moment to notice the variety of publications: *Out*, *Billboard*, and on the cover of *Curve*, a teaser insinuating sexual pleasure was literally in the hands of women. I flipped through the crisp pages of *Curve* and found the article. The page was dog-eared.

Having eaten their kibble, Maelstrom chased MayMay over the coffee table. Mal's claws scraping across the wood sounded like a scratched record album, the needle ripping off the edge as he flew toward her in pursuit. The two tussled behind my chair. I hastily got up and the two scattered, leaving puffs of fur floating in their wake. Magazine in hand, I headed toward a closed door and a little privacy, smoothing out a rumpled rug on the way.

The bathroom doorknob, an old-fashioned crystal, turned with some effort. I nudged open the door with my shoulder. The room interior caught me off guard, and I gawked at the sight. It was logical to think this room would be another example of Marly's messy personal style, so I was not prepared for what I saw. Beautiful brocade material draped one side of the shower enclosure. The cloth, which screamed "Expensive!" was tied with a heavy gold cord. Behind it was a light, flowing linen with lacy eyelet cutouts in a daisy pattern. The shower itself was exquisite with eggshell-colored tiles bordered with marble accents, a look straight out of *Architectural Digest*. The flooring showcased a rougher dark mottled surface streaked with red, grays, and gold, which I guessed was slate. A fluffy oval cotton rag mat was placed before the shower. The drapery was reflected in a sculpted gold-framed mirror hung above the marble-topped washbasin that was further complemented by gold-trimmed faucets. For all its extravagance, the room was not overdone.

Mal tried to squeeze past me. I pushed him out with my foot and closed the door behind me. It was obvious neither cat was allowed inside. I felt as if I were violating Marly's space by not having asked permission to be there. In the mirror, I caught my wide-eyed stare. I reached for the towel draped over a door hook. The puffy absorbent twirls held a hint of dampness. As I brought the towel gently toward my face, I caught the familiar scent of her shampoo and paused to inhale deeply as if I could breathe her in. I sat on top of the covered toilet seat wondering what to make of this splendor—in the bathroom of all places. Eventually, I turned my attention back to the *Curve* article, but after reading the same paragraph several times I had to admit my thoughts were elsewhere. The room in which I sat was an enigma. I had to reconsider my preconceptions about Marly. In her absence, she had shaken me.

This room posed another question, one I had to answer. I tiptoed out of the bathroom and closed the door. The door to Marly's home office was open—a room full of furniture covered in a collage of papers. On the other side was a closed door, undoubtedly her bedroom. I turned the handle slowly, cautiously poked my head through the doorway, and peeked inside, being careful not to let the cats in. I paused to take in the dimly lit room without further intruding upon her private space. Silently, I pulled the door closed until the latch clicked into place.

The cats tussled beneath the sofa, and on another occasion I could hear myself saying, "Good-bye kitties," while petting their furry heads, but today I left her house without uttering a word.

The air outside was saturated with moisture. I could see the cloud bank rolling in from the ocean in thick curls. Its misty breeze cooled my face and woke me from my reverie. By the time I drove back to my apartment complex the clouds were breaking up. I was not in a hurry to return to the close quarters of my apartment and chose instead to sit on a wood bench in a nearby green area where I mentally replayed the interior of Marly's house. The sun played peek-a-boo with the marine layer until tired of the game, burned off the remaining low-lying clouds. When the white puffs all disappeared, I went inside.

It was early afternoon and I had to get ready for my family Thanksgiving dinner. Passing my hand over the clothes hanging in my closet, I paused at several selections: too summery, too casual, too tight—nothing seemed appropriate. Clothes brought back memories. I needed new clothes. I chose a pair of slacks, a silk knit sweater, and scarf. The scarf felt constricting. I retied it several times before I ripped it off and threw it back in the drawer. The sweater was too hot. I changed into a cotton pullover. Still too hot. I rolled on extra deodorant and settled on a short-sleeved sweater set, pearls, and matching earrings. I folded a jacket over my arm for later.

In the car I checked my appearance in the visor mirror. I looked like a modern-day Donna Reed, the archetypal mom. I had chosen a costume to fit a role, and yet felt strangely out of place. It must have been important for me to still feel like a mom. If I dressed the part, then perhaps I could convince Jennifer that deep down I was still the same person she had known her whole life. The problem was I didn't feel like the same person. It was too late to change clothes again. I pulled the Volvo up the driveway to my old house and set the brake.

Chapter Twenty-two

I knocked lightly on the front door and let myself in. I felt odd, as if I were an intruder in my own house. I could hear a football game on the radio in the background. Before I could announce my presence, Jennifer came running in her stocking feet to meet me.

"Mom, I'm so glad you're here. Wait'll you see what we've been doing."

She grabbed my hand and pulled me toward the backyard. Ted stood next to the outdoor grill squirting drippings from a turkey baster onto the bird. We greeted one another cordially. He closed the grill lid, turned the rotisserie back on, and wiped his hands on an old apron I recognized. Ted never was one for cooking, and I figured the barbecue had been a regular stand-in since I'd left.

"Are we having something else besides barbecued turkey?" I asked, immediately regretting the remark. Was it hostile? Witty? Sarcastic? I didn't want to start off on the wrong foot.

"Jenny's made a salad and I bought a few prepared things. I hope that doesn't bother you—that it's not all homemade."

"And Dad and I are making fruit bread. It's rising in the oven."

"That's great," I said. I had always been the cook, ever since Ted and I set up housekeeping and decided to establish our own holiday traditions. In truth I felt naked arriving without so much as a dish to pass, and though I had been told to just show up, I felt inept, inadequate. They didn't need me to make Thanksgiving dinner. My throat tightened. "Do you have something to drink?"

Jenny, who had been standing out on the patio in her socks, which were surely dirty by now, dragged me back in. I consciously shifted my focus—be positive, appreciate, don't be negative. Don't mention her socks! We sat in the living room and chatted about what was going on in her life, at school and such. Jonah called from the ski lodge in Breckenridge and we all had a chance to talk to him. I felt better having a phone conversation in the familiar surrounds of my old home, and did not wish to spoil things by dwelling on my son's decision not to come home for the holiday. This year was different, needed to be different. Change was good. I began to relax again. Jenny and I slashed the top of the fruit bread and put it in to bake. We picked out serving platters for the side dishes Ted had bought at the supermarket.

The mesquite-flavored turkey was tender and juicy, and I enjoyed it. Unfortunately, the store-bought stuffing was salty and dry, totally inedible, and Ted had forgotten about serving gravy. I passed it off as inconsequential but was secretly pleased. My parents called near the end of dinner, and later Ted's folks checked in. All evening I teetered on the brink of an invisible emotional chasm, as if any moment I would either burst into tears or let loose an inappropriate apologetic flood of maternal anxiety. The phone interruptions provided a needed break. Conversely, Ted was at his best. He seemed genuinely happy to have me around, and he playfully embellished his role as host, twirling the barbecue fork until I smiled.

Amber, Jennifer's friend, came over later in the evening. She greeted me with enthusiasm. Seeing her reminded me of the last time we met in Balboa Park on Labor Day when I tried to hide from her. I felt more at ease having her in my home—my old home, that is—until she gave me a lingering, expectant look. Before she could speak, Jenny jumped onto the landing and the girls ran upstairs. Whatever was on the young girl's mind would have to wait. She and Jenny had been friends since grade school, and of all Jenny's friends, I felt closest to Amber. I suspected Amber was uncomfortable with our uncertain familial situation. It didn't bother me that she knew about the disarray in our family life. I was glad Jenny had a confidante, a girlfriend who could offer support and help her over the rough spots. However, with the girls upstairs, I was alone with Ted.

I wasn't sure what to do next. A smattering of dirty dishes by the sink could have used a rinse before being loaded into the dishwasher, but Ted shooed me out of the kitchen. We sat down in the family room and I could sense a speech was imminent.

"That went pretty well, don't you think?" he asked.

"Yes. You did a good job on the turkey."

"Thanks. I've been cooking a little, and not just barbecuing, either. Did you notice I didn't have the TV on?"

"Yeah, just the radio."

"And the house is clean."

I looked around, but of course I had noticed.

"Jenny and I have been working at it. It takes

time, but if we break up the chores we get everything done. We could get a maid, you know."

"Well, that's your business," I said.

"I mean, if you came home." He paused, but did not wait too long for my response. "Maybe you were feeling overwhelmed. Two teenagers are a big responsibility. Now we've—I've only got Jenny here, and it's a lot of work," he acknowledged. "I could've been a bigger help. I know what you used to do because now I'm doing it myself, and Jenny. We both do all the chores and the shopping."

I didn't know what to say. Ted raced back in.

"And you can keep working if you want to. Maybe not at the radio station if they're going to blow it up. I'm sorry, that wasn't funny. Just think, though, you could do something you like, part-time, and you wouldn't have to come home to a big mess because we're going to be different. I'm going to be different," he said, pointing a thumb at himself.

"I can see how I might have been driving you away," he continued. "It's been happening so slowly over the years it kind of got away from me. What happened between us...I think, maybe we weren't thinking clearly. Actually, I'm not entirely sure what happened. Life can be stressful. It is, but we don't have to take it out on each other. Things kind of boiled to a head, and well, we both did things. I'm not proud of the way I acted. I could have handled things differently."

He gestured more than usual as he spoke, and I let him take all the personal space he needed. I was not inclined to reach out to him, or to interrupt.

"The kids are growing up. Jonah is already out of the house and Jennifer will be off in a couple more years. We should be enjoying our life together. We had so much. And what about all of our plans? I don't want to throw it all away. I know I'm partly responsible for making a mess of things. What I'm saying is, I'm ready to go to counseling—together. Please, say you'll come home."

"Home." The vibration moved over my lips and tongue and put a tickle in my throat. I was unprepared for his plea, and I certainly hadn't expected an apology when I had never offered one to him. I still wasn't sure what to say, so I said nothing. His recent change in demeanor wasn't an act, it was a prelude to this monologue. I had the sense he had rehearsed, though his words came tumbling out in an ever-increasing emotional stream, washing over me like an unexpected tide. His message was unmistakable—he wanted me home and he wanted to make our marriage work. He could not have forgotten what had transpired before our breakup, but it was possible he had lessened its importance. During our separation he could have come to terms with his anger. Loneliness, sadness, and regret remained. My affair had been a short-term event over a long-term marriage. He missed the good things about our relationship, and frankly, so did I.

I cleared my throat and bravely jumped onto the elephant in the room. "Do you want to pretend that 'it' didn't happen?" I asked.

"Claire, that's not everything. It's, well, I think we drifted apart. Or…or maybe I was neglectful and you reacted. Then I reacted. We were in a downward spiral. It's not like you were with another guy. I can forgive you. Look, I'm sure I've been a jerk. If you can forgive me, too, we can stop this stupid game and be together again. I want you home, where you belong, beside me."

"Maybe you're lonely."

"No! Well, yes, I am, because my life is supposed to be with you. We all make mistakes. I've said I'm sorry. I still love you. I need you. I'm pleading with you, for Christ's sake. Don't you want to come home?" Our marriage had provided many of the things I wanted in life. I did have wants, new things I had become more aware of since living apart. I wanted my daughter with me. Even though I had not been at KZSD very long, I was sure I wanted outside work, and maybe something that would lead to a career. My tiny apartment was pathetically austere with its squared-off rooms coated with a thick layer of glaring white semi-gloss paint. I missed my home, our home. Ted and I had made plans, lifelong plans, with goals worthy of sacrifice. My family had always come first, and yet here it was Thanksgiving and it was all we could do to pull together three of us for dinner. How can you have a turkey dinner without gravy? Some wife I turned out to be. The friends we saw as a couple remained distant. I missed my friendships, including my husband's, and, yes, the closeness, though not the intimacy. Obviously, I had made mistakes. Achieving happiness out on my own thus far had been elusive, but there was one thing I knew with certainty, something that had become clearer since being apart from Ted. I knew it whether I felt secure or lonely, capable or vulnerable, strong or a mere shadow of the perfectionist ideal I tried to achieve. It was the one overriding part of my inner being I could not deny.

"Ted, I'm gay."

Gay? The word sounded like a metal spoon hitting the bottom of a pot. I clamped my jaw shut. Ted's face twisted in bewilderment.

"Honey, I think you're confused," he said. "Men aren't the only ones to have a midlife crisis. Look, you don't have to answer me now. I'm probably putting too much pressure on you. Yes, I'm sure of it. I shouldn't have brought it up so suddenly. You obviously need time to think about this. We'll talk about it again later, okay?"

My reply, one he apparently did not want to hear, left me with mixed emotions and unanswered questions. It was tempting to revisit our old life and imagine it with improvements. Not all couples have sex. We certainly went for long periods without it. What if one of us couldn't perform because of a medical reason? Would we divorce? I had spoken my vows, "for better or for worse." I did not say, "except if I'm gay, or we can't do it anymore." My stomach churned with guilt and I began to feel queasy. It was true I had behaved badly, but I had also seen a side of Ted I did not care to see again. I chewed my lip while I considered our fate.

"Don't throw it all away," he said slowly. "Promise me you'll think about it."

Chapter Twenty-three

We were in a lovely room—a hotel suite? I knew where everything was; my personal items were as they used to be when I lived at home. There was a man in the room and I wanted him to leave. I felt aroused and I knew my real lover was hiding somewhere in the room. The man vanished. I breathed in relief and let go of a pang of guilt. A bright light in the bathroom caught my attention. It was so bright, I could not see past the radiance. Shielding my eyes with my left hand, I searched for the wall switch with my right. Then I saw her, Marly's smiling image inside the gold-framed mirror. I felt the switch. Oddly, it was in the off position. I turned it on and reached climax.

I woke up with a gasp. The pulsing between my legs faded and my breathing returned to normal. Light streamed in through the blinds I had forgotten to close, yet I was in no hurry to leave the comfort of my bed. I turned away from the brightness and reviewed mental movie scenes from the previous night: Ted pleading with me to return home, Jenny's long hug good-bye, the cold steering wheel in my car as I drove back to my apartment. I shifted my thoughts to "coming attractions"—Marly's cats.

On the way to her house, I swung through the drive-thru for a Cafe Americaine and almond croissant. When I opened the front door, MayMay and Maelstrom ran to their food dish and meowed even though a handful of kibble remained uneaten. As they crunched up the fresh meal, I breakfasted and contemplated my confused, utterly tangled, complicated life. In the welcome privacy of Marly's home, I picked up a copy of *Curve* magazine and read it cover to cover. I flipped through *Lesbian News* and *The Advocate*. She had many gay-themed magazines piled around her living room. After looking at each one, I replaced it in the stack where I had found it so nothing would be out of place when she returned.

And so it went for the next two mornings. In between articles I tried to make sense of it all. I watched Mal thoroughly lick MayMay around the ears and then bite her. My goals in life were incongruous. Nothing quite fit into place. Strong coffee was not the answer. I did, however, come up with a good idea for Marly's upcoming appearance on Glover's radio show.

Monday morning I saw Marly at the station. She gave me a bear hug and I gave her a big squeeze in return.

"Missed me, huh?" she asked as she batted her eyelashes at me.

I blushed. "Yes, but not as much as your kitties did. They ignored me."

"Typical. They ignore me, too. Thanks for taking care of them. I owe you dinner."

I asked about her weekend in Los Angeles. Part of me was hoping to hear of a rekindled long-distance relationship with a sharp-tongued beauty, a suitable companion who could be counted as a significant other, someone she could have spent a wild weekend with closing down the gay bars around West Hollywood. Judging from her reply, no such person existed and no such event took place.

I felt a little rusty returning to work after a four-day hiatus. Whatever happened in L.A. was irrelevant; we were back at work and Marly was her usual self on the air.

"Listen, puke-for-brains," she growled into her mic, "if you think computer sex with minors is harmless, maybe you'd like to do it from your prison cell, that is, when you're not being raped."

"Oooh! Now who sounds frustrated?" said the male caller. "It's harmless. I'm doing the kids a favor. They're not getting STDs. They ought to thank me for being online."

"It's arguments like yours that give respectable criminals a bad name. You're a pedophile, got it? Hiding behind a phony log-in name doesn't make you any less of a predator. You stay away from kids. Do you hear me? I've got a picture of me mooning the camera. I'll email it to you so you can kiss my ass! What a moron. Thank him for being online? *Thank him*? I want to arrest him. Claire, help me to the throne room so I can spew."

The sound effects CD. I frantically looked up the correct track and played it. Retching noises reverberated through the studio and into the halls of KZSD. The receptionist happened to be walking by our booth. She laughed and waved. I was laughing, too. How could I be so disgusted, yet at the same time have so much fun? My daughter had warned me about *Gayline*—and I liked it!

Emails had piled up over the long holiday weekend. Lourdes had sent several. Yin-Yang expressed revulsion toward the online pedophile. As usual, I sorted through the mess to delete spam, lame jokes, and other assorted drivel. As I paged down the long list of new messages, I noted one addressed to my attention from Agent Laurel Emerson and reflexively brought my hand to my throat. I glanced at Marly.

She looked up from her mail. "What?"

"I got a note from Agent Emerson, you know, the FBI lady."

"Yeah," she said. "Now that you're here, she never wants to see me anymore."

Did Marly think Agent Emerson and I were in cahoots, plotting to see if we could trip her up into admitting she was behind the bomb threats? I couldn't tell if she was kidding, but my discomfort wouldn't let me believe otherwise.

I laughed uneasily. "Oh, yes, I'm in tight with the FBI—the Female Bomb Inquiry." I hoped I hadn't sounded too stupid.

"Between us," Marly said, "I pretend it doesn't bother me, but, well, I've had a few letters and I have to turn them over to her."

"Letters?"

"Yeah, threatening messages beyond the normal 'I hate you' kind, or 'You're going to burn in Hell forever.' You'll see one eventually. It comes with the territory. I try to shrug them off, but sometimes I can't help thinking about the weirdos out there. For all the false alarms, every now and then you hear about someone actually taking a shot or setting a fire."

This was the scary part. I always felt secure with Ted. When we walked down the street together, I felt no matter what came up, he would do his best to protect me. Fortunately, we had never encountered a dangerous situation that would have put him to the test. I had never received hate mail or hate email for being straight. It never came up, a total nonissue. It was part of the old cocoon.

Chapter Twenty-four

Ah, Christmas. Tiny glitter lights sparkled in the palm trees, cheesy carol renditions wafted through the supermarket, and display ads filled the newspapers. The world around me was much the same as in years past, except I wasn't feeling especially merry. Gifts would be a problem this year, not so much because of the expense, but because I had no idea what to do. Clothes seemed a good standby gift for the kids while I considered more special items. Buying Ted a gift was complicated. I wasn't sure it would be appropriate. I assumed he would buy me something nice as part of his effort to win me back.

My life had become complex in ways I could not have imagined. The gift-giving dilemma took on minor importance when compared to my relationship problems. Before I "went gay," as Ted put it, I didn't have these concerns. Since moving out, I rarely communicated with my parents, who assumed I needed time to sort the details of my life before rejoining Ted. My relationship with Jenny had improved, though her desire for me to return to her father created an unsettled tenuousness that I hoped would hold through this uncertain phase. She had visited me a few times in my apartment where we sang along with the guitar, made fish tacos, and tried a new gingersnap recipe. Jonah might as well have been living on another planet for all the times we spoke. He was hard to reach, and when we did connect he sounded very independent as if to prove being away at college was a mere way station for his eventual launch into the world as an adult. This child was no longer a child. My sister's support and feedback were helpful, but I didn't fill her ears with every little thing during our weekend phone conversations.

I kept busy at the radio station, and in fact, it increasingly became a refuge for me. There had been no further bomb threats. Agent Emerson called once to clarify a minor detail. I had not heard from her in quite a while, and that was fine with me.

Christmas also meant volunteer work. Lourdes was managing the annual food drive for people living with HIV/AIDS, an event Marly promoted on *Gayline*. KZSD was one of the designated drop-off points. Donations piled up inside Studio B, and when our adjoining rooms became too much of an obstacle course, the packages spilled out into the hallway.

When Lourdes came by to collect the foodstuffs, I couldn't help but remember how I had called her "Piranha." I tried to let it go, to forgive myself and move on. My sister had helped me realize how my sudden surge toward being judgmental was an aberration, a typical case of turning my insecurities around and looking askance at others. I was my own worst critic, and it didn't have to do with anyone else. It wasn't too much of an effort for me to back off and get reacquainted with the "live-and-let-live" side of my personality. Working at *Gayline* helped me appreciate and feel gratitude for the many forms of diversity that took shape within our community. Of course Lourdes hadn't heard my horrible comment that day, but I feared she knew, as my efforts to engage her in conversation were unsuccessful. Her answers were monosyllabic or brief at best, though Marly assured me she was like that with everyone. Lourdes preferred to communicate by email, and it appeared it would remain that way.

I offered to drive a load of donated items to the final drop-off point for the food drive, but Marly insisted her pickup would hold more. We lugged the donations to her truck until our studio floor became visible once again. Marly drove to a central distribution center where, with the help of other volunteers, we unloaded everything into a room already overflowing with stacked cardboard boxes and heaps of paper bags filled with canned goods and other staples. When the work was done, Marly and Lourdes hugged. I extended my hand to Lourdes. She ignored it and hugged me instead. Her arms encircled me low around my waist and I wrapped my arms around her in return, feeling the long braid that tumbled down her back in a thick cord. She smiled at me ever so slightly without exposing her underbite. Relief swept through me. I grinned back and thanked her for the opportunity to help out.

"Let's get something to eat," Marly said to me. "I owe you dinner, remember?"

I hesitated, as I could see there was more work to be done straightening up, but Marly swung her arm beneath mine and escorted me away. I felt a little sweaty from our work and hoped she would choose a casual restaurant. On the way, she stopped for gas. I waited in the pickup and listened as Marly addressed a woman on the other side of the gas pump.

"Here, girlfriend," Marly said as she handed the woman a business card. "Have you heard of my show?"

The woman, thirtyish and unassuming, examined the card. "What makes you think I would be interested in this? I'm not gay."

"Yes, you are," Marly said. "You just don't know it yet."

The woman harrumphed and turned her back. I felt embarrassed. Marly finished filling her tank and hopped into the cab.

"Why did you do that?" I asked.

"Because she is. Did you notice she didn't throw the card away, she stuck it in her back pocket?"

It was a detail that had not registered with me, but it was true. "Marly, do you have that 'gaydar' thing, that ability to tell if someone is gay or not?"

"I can tell most of the time. She was gay, trust me."

Unfortunately, I did. I squirmed in my seat. There was no use pretending. If Marly already knew about me, I couldn't hide from the invisible gaydar power. But she did say "most," not "all" of the time. I wanted her to know about me, and more, to make a move toward me. It would be far too humiliating for me to approach her only to find out she wasn't interested. That would make going to work unbearable. Yet, it was equally unbearable to sit idle when we could make better use of our time. Betty had given me an employee handbook that stated office dating was acceptable if both parties agreed, but after one "no" response it was considered harassment to broach the subject again. By now, it would have seemed likely to hear of family, old lovers, casual dates. I was reluctant to pry into her private life, but it was time to know.

Chapter Twenty-five

"What's this? Are we going to your house?" I asked as we drove west through Pacific Beach past Ingraham Street.

"Surprise! I'm making you dinner."

When we arrived, I was delighted to see her house was cleaner than when I had cat-sit. The stacks of papers and magazines were mostly gone. MayMay brushed against my legs and I patted her furry head. I went to the cupboard for the kibble. Maelstrom meowed nonstop at full volume until I set the food bowl on the floor. The floor was clean. The countertops were clean. Four kitchen chairs were arranged neatly around the table. Centered on top of an old placemat was a straw basket filled with pinecones.

"Been reading *San Diego Home and Garden*?" I queried.

"And I thought you'd approve," Marly replied, feigning hurt.

"Oh, I do, I do." My coming over was not as impromptu as it first appeared. I smiled, acknowledging my presence merited the effort to clean house.

She ripped open a bag of mesclun greens and lightly fluffed them in a salad bowl. I offered to help with the pasta, but she insisted it be her effort. I set the table, and then relaxed in the living room where I teased the cats with their favorite toy, a long plastic rod much like a fishing pole with a dancing feather lure.

The fresh mushroom-stuffed ravioli was excellent. It was a modest portion, just right for two. The remaining garlic bread stayed toasty warm wrapped in aluminum foil. I took one last piece, in part because I was nervous about dinner coming to an end. A pair of candlesticks remained on the kitchen counter. Had she planned on using them and changed her mind? Was she coming on to me? I swallowed hard and washed down the dry bread crumbs with my wine.

"Everything was delicious," I said. "Thanks."

We cleared off the table. She washed, I dried. A patter of small talk filled the space. I wanted to ask her important questions but couldn't find an opening. As a friend, I didn't understand why it was so hard for me to bring up these subjects: family, friends, lovers. We moved to the living room and I decided to ease into the topic.

"If you didn't have a home office," I said, "you could have a roommate. I mean, if you wanted one."

"Actually, I did once. She stayed a couple of years."

Silence. Rats! This was frustrating.

"Do you like living alone?" I tried again.

"It's okay. How about you?"

We were playing hot potato. "I guess what I'm trying to say is, I'm curious about your past and your private life—if it's not too personal. You never say anything about your family. Do you have any brothers or sisters?"

She didn't reply, but got up and returned with an album she retrieved from her office, then motioned me to join her on the sofa. The oversized book creaked as she opened the green vinyl cover. Inside, a few black-and-white photographs from another era had been inserted underneath plastic-covered pages. Newspaper articles and awards lay loose stuffed between pages. She lifted a faded ribbon.

"This one was for winning the spelling bee at school when I was in sixth grade. See? Here's the clipping." The yellowed newspaper looked as if it would crumble from age. A smiling girl held the very same ribbon. She was a younger version of the woman who sat by my side, front teeth protruding slightly in a cocky grin. I read the caption beneath the photograph.

"Your last name is Mesterhazy? Turn on a light. I want to see this."

Marly slapped her hand over the old article and flipped the page. She turned toward me, tilted her head, and smiled. "Now you know why I use all those funny names: Mostacolli, Mastroanni, Michelangelo, Mistletoe, anything but Mesterhazy."

Now we were getting somewhere. I pushed onward. "I bet your folks are proud of you."

"My dad left when I was little, and Winnie and I don't talk anymore. Besides, she lives up in Hesperia."

"So? My mom lives in Minnesota, but we still talk, sort of. Right now our relationship is, well, it's not strained exactly, but she doesn't understand why I'm separated so we haven't been talking as much as we usually do. You call your mom Winnie?"

"That's her name, Winifred. I used to call her Mom until we had a falling out. She was disappointed in me and let me know it. I was her only child and she apparently had expectations—like a husband and grandchildren. She's never forgiven me for being gay."

"Ugh. Why do parents take these things like a personal insult?" I shuddered to think what my own mother would think, or do, or say, if or when she found out about me.

Marly gazed at me through her dark lashes. Her raven hair framed her face becomingly. I looked into her eyes, their blueness deep in the soft faded light.

"I like you just the way you are," I said.

"Thanks. I know you do, and that's one of the things I appreciate about you."

She draped her left arm over my shoulder and pulled in slightly. I could feel her fingers glide behind my head as she threaded them through my hair in a loose grasp. She drew me near. Our foreheads touched, our noses brushed together. Hair strands tickled around my eyelashes, and I could feel her breath, warm, garlicky, inviting. My eyes were closed, but I knew my lips could not have been any closer to hers without touching. Then, it happened. My top lip brushed against hers with a feather's touch. We paused in space; her breath trembled. In unhurried anticipation, I parted my lips slightly. Her bottom lip touched mine. Maybe it was me who leaned in a little more to feel the softness of her mouth. The pressure between us increased as our lips fit together. She pursed a little. We released enough to create a tiny pop. Our lips drew together once again. I slid my hand up her arm, gently following each recognizable contour until I felt the soft down of her face. She moved her right arm around my back, drawing me in closer. The hardness of the album cover was an unwelcome intrusion. Our lips parted. Marly slid the scrapbook onto the coffee table and turned her full attention to me.

We embraced again and kissed, slowly, slowly, then deeply. It was my fantasy—a kind of deliberate madness. We were opposite magnets drawn into place. My lips followed hers in a passionate rhythm. Moisture passed over my lips, onto her, onto me. I heard a barely audible sound—mine—as she pressed her tongue into my mouth. She licked my lips and kissed my check, my chin. As her lips passed over my neck, she made an animal-like growl and breathed into my ear. My fingers luxuriated in her thick mop of hair. Her body. I wanted to touch her body, and impetuously grabbed for her breasts. They were voluptuous, round, warm, and sensual in my hands. I was in heaven. I thought fleetingly about the last time I had felt someone else, Crystal, whose sole desire was sexual. Was Marly's? What about work the next day? My God! What was I doing? In a panic, I pushed away. I held her by the shoulders at arm's length. Her breasts heaved with the rise and fall of her breath.

I felt guilty, afraid to speak. What about Ted? Did I have unfinished business to take care of before I could move forward with him, or Marly, or my own life in general? And the way I grabbed for her breasts with no subtlety, like an uncouth teenager. I felt out of control, and as usual, embarrassed.

"This is what you wanted," she said haltingly. "Isn't it?"

I waited a long time to answer as I thought of the repercussions of work and family. "I, I don't know. I mean, yes, but now I'm not sure." My thoughts raced ahead. Until now, I had only given consideration to my own selfish fantasies and nothing to reality.

As we sat in the growing silence, her bewitching face and compelling closeness dared me to kiss her again. In the dim light, I saw a woman, felt a woman in my hands, felt urgency deep within myself. A part of me wanted to try again, but I was terrified. My heart raced. Was it too soon? The risk was great, the reward both uncertain and unbelievably tempting. My frustration mounted. When I sensed her patience—or mine—could be tried no further, I whispered, "I can't. I think I have to go. I'm sorry." I tried to gather my wits about me, but I couldn't put my thoughts into words. I found my purse and reached inside for my keys.

"I drove you here," she said in a soft, regretful voice.

I felt slightly tipsy as we got into her pickup. I crossed my arms in the chill air and kept them there even when the cab warmed up. We drove in silence. I wanted to ask what she was thinking but could not bring myself to speak. I wasn't sure what to do when she pulled up next to my station wagon at KZSD. She sat facing forward, both hands on the steering wheel. There would be no bear hug. I touched the back of her hand. The tension of her grip did not soften, and I pulled my hand away.

I said, "I'm not sure about a few things. I need to think this through."

"Of course. That's what you do."

"And...um, I'm not sure what's in it for you."

Marly took her hands off the wheel. "Me?" Finally, she turned her head. It was impossible to see what she might be feeling with her face in dark shadow. I was more afraid she might say something sarcastic, words that might make me feel sorry we ever kissed when I wanted to cherish the moment, the memory, forever. I clutched the door handle and let myself out before we could make things worse.

"I'm sorry," I said.

The cab door shut with a harsh metallic clank that disturbed the night air. I got into my car and firmly closed the door, accentuating the divide between us, so much greater than I dared imagine. The seats of the Volvo felt stiff with cold, an unwelcoming plank beneath my backside. She waited until I started up before driving off into the night. Augh! Was I making the biggest mistake of my life? I found my way home feeling more lost than ever.

Chapter Twenty-six

I wanted to slide my head beneath the water in the bathtub. No, I wanted to drive to Marly's house and seduce her. Perhaps it would be better to take a job at another company. Or go home to Ted and Jennifer. Make biscuits. Buy a dog. Wake up like Sleeping Beauty. Unfortunately, it was time for work.

It was chilly beyond the cozy warmth of my bed covers. Procrastination is not my long suit when there is work to be done, but I waited, thought, dozed a moment, and berated myself for being a coward. When I had pushed my tardiness to its limit, I got out of bed and put on a pair of slacks. Too wrinkled. I put on a cotton skirt and sweater set. Not warm enough. I threw on a pair of old but serviceable jeans from my closet, found a clean turtleneck and pullover, walking shoes, and a scarf. I picked up coffee and blueberry scones for two on the way to the radio station and arrived decidedly late.

As I approached Studio B, I could see Marly poring over the daily log. I had to bang my elbow on the glass to get her attention. She opened the door and we grunted our "Heys." She cleared a space for me to put down the cardboard coffee tray. I set out the coffee and scone I bought for her next to her own double-cupped grande and half-eaten scone.

"Yours is in your booth," she said.

"My what?" I peered through the dividing glass

that separated our small rooms and saw another grande on the counter. I went in and picked up the blueberry scone she had laid on a napkin. "I like blueberry. I brought you blueberry."

Marly picked up her two blueberry scones, one in each hand. "This is kind of funny, don't ya think?"

Both scones were identical in appearance.

"Yah." For some reason I answered with my Minnesota accent.

"Claire, do you think we're that different?"

"Noooo," I continued in singsong affectation. "Maybe not."

Marly rolled her eyes. I sniffed my scones. A little crumb tickled my nose and I laughed. Marly threw her half-eaten scone at me. It hit the glass between us. Startled, I fell backward off my stool, tipping it over. Marly tromped in and reached for my hand. I pulled her down.

"Here! Eat this!" I pushed a scone toward her face.

She resisted and the breakfast treat broke in pieces.

"I don't see you eating any, girlfriend."

She grabbed a large hunk in her fist and tried to push it past my teeth. Some got through, but my laughter spit it out. It landed in her hair. With exaggerated disgust, she extricated the moist crumb and then sprang into action, smearing the gooey particles into my hair and onto my face. We tussled on the floor shrieking hysterically until our slaps lost strength and our laughter broke down into punctuated exhalations. We lay beside one another on the studio floor, our legs entwined below the knee. Our faces rested close enough to feel our breath pass between us.

"Did you always know about me?" I asked. "That I'm that way…like you."

"At first I wasn't sure, then later, yeah, I could tell."

"I don't understand how gaydar works. This whole gay thing, it's new for me…and it's scary. I don't know what I'm doing. I feel out of control."

Our lips were dangerously close. I was too near to focus, though I had no urge to move away.

"I thought about what you said," Marly began, "about what's in it for me. I'm not doing this to satisfy your curiosity. I'm not your first."

"How do you know?"

"Hey! What's going on in there you two? You're on in three minutes."

We looked up to see Betty, her large frame, fists on hips, looming through the plate glass. Marly leaped to her feet and locked the door to Studio B. She unfurled the blinds, which dropped with a tinny, metallic clatter, and then hopped on her stool.

"Girlfriend, get busy. It's showtime!"

Chapter Twenty-seven

The days between Thanksgiving and Christmas were filled with indecision. Usually I'm prepared and get my shopping done early. This year was different. Making up my mind about gifts was as tricky as making up my mind about the rest of my life. Where would I live? Would we share custody of Jennifer? Could I be happy with Marly? Should I go back to Ted? One minute decision "A" seemed like the right thing to do. The next I had cast it aside in favor of decision "B," which lost ground to decision "C." In spare moments I roamed the mall, ruminating on my future with no satisfactory answers.

Curiously, the best part of my life was my job at KZSD, and I had accidentally tripped into that spot headfirst. If the best I could do was the result of unpremeditated thought, what did that say for the choices ahead? I did manage to finish my Christmas shopping, except for Marly's gift.

The station held a party and gift swap in the employee lunchroom. Earlier, I had pulled Zach's name. He liked the leather bow tie I got him and he wore it often. I received a scented candle from a fellow in advertising, and Marly donated her fruitcake to the food bank. I was hoping to get a few gift ideas for Marly but came away with nothing.

I wanted to get her something special that would let her know how important our friendship was to me, but unless the item was solely practical it seemed to carry unwanted romantic overtones. I didn't want to send off another mixed message after I had been open about my inner conflict. To start a romantic relationship before I was ready to proceed would have been emotionally irresponsible. My sexual fantasies had kindled into a private inferno, sparked by the fire of our kiss. Fear was the cold sleety wind that tamed the flames of my passion. Aside from regular bear hugs, Marly and I kept a friendly distance. We never agreed to exchange gifts anyway.

Jonah arrived from university the day before Christmas. I picked him up at the airport and drove him to our old house where he would stay for a week. In the car, he chattered on, animatedly embellishing stories I had only heard snips of over the phone. He looked older. His jaw had grown square and he had adopted a trim goatee and mustache popular with the young men.

Ted had turned on the icicle lights outside the house. They looked welcoming and festive even in daylight. Jonah and his dad slapped each other on the back in man-to-man style. He and Ted looked more alike than ever, both the same height, though Ted was broader around the shoulders and had filled out around his midsection. I knew Jonah's thinner frame would one day mirror his father's. Jennifer had on a pretty outfit I did not recognize. These new gaps in our lives made me feel left out. To get past self-conscious feelings, I focused on our interactions instead. It was Christmas Eve and we were all together.

We opened gifts, ate spiral-cut honey-baked ham and sweet potatoes, and talked to relatives on the phone. I was not expecting friends to drop by, but several neighbors made an appearance and stayed for wine and cheese. In polite company, no one asked about the separation, and I purposely left my job out of the conversation, all the easier since I had taken the day off. I had a pleasant time, a pertinent reminder of the benefits to being part of a married couple.

When the evening wound down and the children were upstairs on the computer, Ted and I sat by the Christmas tree. The tree lights made the merlot in my glass glow like a cabochon garnet. I touched several ornaments, remembering their history. They looked fuzzy around the edges, and then began to blur. I had lost track of how many glasses of wine I had consumed, obviously more than intended. I tried to count: four? Five? Eyes closed, I sank back into my chair. Feeling my head spin, I forced my eyes open. Ted noticed I was fading fast and picked up a small package hidden beneath the tree blanket.

"I know we said we weren't going to exchange gifts," he said, "but I couldn't resist. It's to let you know, well, that days like today are important to me and they always will be...forever."

I finished off my wine and set down the glass so I could use both hands to remove the beautiful gold damask wrapping paper. I held the small square box, examining it from various angles as if doing so would reveal its contents. I opened it. Inside was a black velvet jewelry case. Ted got on his knees to peer at the gift. He swayed in and out of double vision. I refocused on the box and lifted the hinged top.

The multicolored Christmas tree lights scattered a rainbow of dazzling rays within the diamond. It was a princess cut, likely a full carat placed in a beautifully crafted white gold setting. In a word, it was exquisite.

I never had a diamond ring. Ted and I had married young, and I always wore a plain gold band, that is, until recently. My throat closed up and my ears began to hurt. As the colors merged into a kaleidoscopic abstraction, I heard his words: "Will you marry me, again?"

Chapter Twenty-eight

I awoke to the sensation of his hand tracing the lines of my back. The sheets were familiar. They smelled fresh, a striking contrast to my breath, which delivered stale, earthy undertones from the red wine. Saliva surrounded my thick tongue and coated my teeth like kindergarten paste. The diamond ring felt heavy on my finger.

"Good morning," Ted cooed.

I rolled over, feeling the smooth sheets across my naked body. Even with the blinds drawn, the morning light caused me to squint. I kept one eye shut. "Oh, Lord, did we..."

"We could."

"We could've last night...or, we could now?"

"Would you like to?"

"Uh, can't think yet. I should get moving. What timezit?"

"Ten thirty."

"*Ten thirty?* Shit! I missed the whole show and I told Marly I'd be there."

I sat up, but Ted took my hand before I could get out of bed. "Hold on. I called the radio station and told them you needed a personal day."

"You did what?"

"It's Christmas. What could be more important than being with your family?"

My eyes were wide-awake, but the rest of me

felt woozy as if the drink had not worn off. My head hit the pillow. The room spun and I could feel my body spin with it. Suddenly, my temples pounded and queasiness gripped my innards. Maybe I did need a sick day. I pushed the pillow aside and rolled onto my stomach. Ted resumed his light caress. His fingers flowed in a delicate dance over the curves of my shoulders and slowly my malaise melted away into the softness of the bed.

"What happened last night?"

"I helped you upstairs and put you in bed. Nothing happened. You passed out."

I couldn't remember. I doubted him and touched myself to be sure. Reassured of the truth, I rested more easily.

His caress relaxed me. His fingers curled through my hair and gently eased the tension from my scalp. I was feeling much better, though peeved he had called in sick for me. To say anything negative would have ruined the moment and I was not eager to let this guilty pleasure end before it had to. I let him run his hand up and down my back. He had not touched me in a long time. The sensation of flesh against flesh was water to my dehydrated body and I drank it in. I had a vague recollection of the last time we made love—a perfunctory, passionless exercise. I had not come. There had been times over the years when he loved my body, genuinely, thoroughly, and with great care. I knew this was an attempt to seduce me, and I did not resist because I was in need of soothing. To relax beneath a caring hand was a dream worth staying awake in half slumber, until he ran his hands over my bare bottom and between my legs. I flung the sheets back and went into the bathroom where I locked the door and ran the shower. I placed the ring next to the sink.

"Will you marry me, again?" he had asked. Again? It wasn't over. We were still married.

I replayed the conversation in my head. It stayed there as I drove to work. Along the way, I nibbled on Christmas cookies to help settle my stomach. The crumbs fell carelessly into my lap.

"Well, look what the cat drug in." Marly eyed me suspiciously as I entered her office. It was one o'clock. "Didn't think I was going to see you today."

"Sorry," I mumbled. "My evening took an unexpected turn."

"Is that a good thing, or a bad thing?"

"I said I was sorry. Just give me something to do."

I didn't want to rehash the last twenty-four hours and was positive Marly would not have wanted to hear the details involving Ted. She gave up her seat at the computer so I could get online. It didn't take long to become absorbed in work. I saved a number of funny emails, some showing pictures of Santa and his reindeer in un-Christmas-like situations. I chuckled to myself and hoped the messages would give her a laugh.

Marly handed me a separate package. "Here," she said. "Agent Emerson dropped this off. It's a caller ID thingy that will work with our old studio phone. Not exactly a Christmas present, is it?"

I opened the package and examined its contents. "Hmm, I've seen ones like these. I'll figure it out." The device looked innocuous enough, but it was irksome to think this matter was too pressing to wait until after the holiday season.

A party atmosphere lingered at the station between Christmas and New Year's even though we were busier than I anticipated. People off from work took the opportunity to call in during the show or sent emails. We received many packages, most of them food items we gave away. After New Year's Day passed, I figured we would all get serious about our jobs.

Jonah went back to university, and Jennifer to high school. Without the distraction of my kids around, I refocused on the work ahead. Marly and I had a backlog of projects. The challenge to appear on Glover's radio show had not been forgotten, and I could not wait to tell Marly about my idea.

Chapter Twenty-nine

Attention *Gayline* fans. Your choice is clear. The year-end numbers are in and, *ta-da!* We've now got a two-point-six share, up from two point one. That's huge! I'm so happy I could just *plotz*. The word is out. That's why I shout. We're hot, we're hot, we're hot!" Marly tapped her hands on the countertop to the beat of her impromptu rap. She grabbed her cans before they slid off her head. "Hey, Claire, my lady fair. Are you having fun over there?"

I broke into a smile and nodded.

"I can't *hear* you. Talk to me."

Just as quickly, the smile dropped from my face. I pointed at myself. Did she really want me to say something—out loud—over the air?

"Claire's shy, folks, but get her alone and, mmm, hubba hubba! If you'd like to hear from Claire, and I know I would, give us a call here at KZSD AM 780. Lines are open. In the meantime, let me tell you which popular show host saw a marked drop in his share."

Marly kept talking. In seconds, all the phone lines flashed. This time they weren't calling for her, they were calling for me. To pick a line, to touch the button would be Russian roulette. Which caller would ask me to go on the air? Which one to remain the silent call screener? A cold chill ran up my spine. Why was Marly doing this to me? I closed my eyes and made a random pick.

Line two: "I'm interested in what you have to say."

Line one: "You should speak up."

Line three: "Go ahead, take the plunge."

Line one: "Are you free for coffee and private conversation?"

I let the open lines continue to blink and motioned for Marly to break. I crammed in a commercial cart with enough force to knock the equipment backward.

"Are you nuts?" I squeaked through our open intercom. "They want me to talk. I can't do that."

"Why not? Do you think I let anybody on the air? That's why I have you."

What was this about? Was she playing a game with me? *Gayline* was her show, not mine, and now she wanted me to join her on the air? Stretching, stretching, always stretching, until…I contorted into an unrecognizable pretzel. Everything had been going well lately and I didn't want to ruin our forward progress. According to Marly, her program had become more interesting since my arrival, and the production value had improved over time. We sounded like a real show, the kind one could hear on a major station. I felt a flush of pride as I switched carts and ran Condom-Mania's latest commercial featuring the Queens From Queens. Marly tore off a piece of duct tape and used it to wrap the connecting wire adjustment between her headphones. It was a sad commentary, one our listeners couldn't see. Marly certainly deserved better. We needed to be in Studio B with its dual rooms, but our equipment was shameful, and the station manager refused to upgrade only for her. I signaled for Marly's return.

"Marly Maxipad here in your ear. We're back

with more yak. Okay, Claire, I know you took some calls. What's the verdict?"

I switched on my mic and swallowed hard. "Hi. I'm here."

"Well, I'll be hog-tied with a silk scarf. I got myself a sidekick. What say you, pard?"

"Um, just don't kick me in the side."

"Nosiree! We'll be as easy as a cowgirl in a haystack. I can tell that's enough talk for now—ha ha, just a little foreplay. Don't want to wear you out. I won't put you on the spot—at least until tomorrow."

I sighed with relief. I was off the hook. I was also still on the air.

"There she goes again, folks—breathing heavy into the mic. I told you she was hot!"

I slapped down my slider and turned off my mic. The cold chill I felt earlier had turned clammy, a sensation that now extended from the base of my spine to the top of my head. My fingers were freezing and my armpits were dripping. I felt a hot flash coming on. In seconds, my face and neck radiated enough heat to warm the room. Water filled my eyes, my throat choked, and my chest felt as if squeezed tight by a boa constrictor. Why was Marly doing this to me?

In her office after the show, we fast-forwarded the air check cassette to replay our interchange. Marly, of course, came across strong and daring. My utterance could only be described as timid. She switched off the tape and coached me. To begin, she suggested, our interactions would be brief and natural, like when we spoke to one another alone. Listeners would not want to hear long dissertations. That was Yin-Yang's realm. Nor would they expect to hear comedy. That was Marly's genre. I should be myself. Oh, yes, that again. It was hard to know who I was, and I wondered if and when my life would calm down so I could figure it out. Adding to everything, I now had an audience.

"Claire?"

I turned around. Betty crowded the doorway.

"Claire." She enunciated my name with a sharp smugness. "You are in violation of federal airway laws. If you're going to be on the air, you have to have a license. Agent Emerson is here to see you."

Three words and...busted! As Betty waddled off and Agent Emerson came into view, I felt ashamed and embarrassed.

"I'm so sorry! I didn't know. You aren't going to arrest me, are you?"

Agent Emerson looked at Marly and then at me. They both burst out laughing.

"No, Claire. I'm here on another matter."

"Don't worry," Marly interjected. "You don't need a license."

I was speechless. I felt like an idiot. *Dumb, dumb, dumb.* I looked at my shoes.

"So, um, what brings you by?" I asked Agent Emerson.

"I want to make sure the caller ID system I dropped off around Christmas is working properly. Your case is active. I can't reveal any details about our investigation. As you know, the display shows the phone number from the incoming caller and it also has a memory system. In case you get any more bomb threats, whether from the original caller or from the copycat we think is out there, we'll have a record of the call.

"Unfortunately, we don't have the manpower to commit to a wiretapping operation given that the threats are spaced so far apart. If that changes, we can revise our tactics. In the meantime, this will suffice. Most calls of this nature aren't made from a home-based landline; a cell phone is a more likely scenario. The phone number will be revealed and we can zero in on a general area by the cell towers it pings."

Dressed in a business suit, her words carried more of an official air than they had during our first dinner meeting when her casual affect and gentle probing made me feel suspect. Today, her mannerisms were more formal, adding weight to the serious nature of the investigation. I looked at Marly for any telltale hints. If she knew who was behind the calls, would they stop? Marly did not look concerned in the least.

The three of us walked to the studio. Agent Emerson called the studio line on her cell phone to be sure everything worked okay. Since hooking up the square black device with the digital readout, I had not paid it much attention and had become used to seeing it on the counter. The small box grew to ominous proportions.

"Maybe he'll never call again," I said.

"Perhaps not," said Emerson. "Or, maybe he will."

Chapter Thirty

Though I had promised to go on the air with Marly, I wheedled an extra few days of waiting on the premise I was listening and learning how best to contribute to the show. I'm not sure she bought it, but the end result was the same—a delay. In spare moments, I started playing little conversations in my head, asides that wouldn't overshadow or misdirect her patter.

"Tomorrow's Monday," I said to Deena during our weekend conversation. "I don't know if I can do it."

"Of course you can. You underestimate yourself."

"Please. You're always saying that."

"Because it's true. Claire, you're on the right path."

"How can I be sure? My life is so different, nothing is familiar anymore."

"Great! You're not walking in circles."

"Very funny. You should go on the air."

"How about I visit instead? You and I need face time."

I agreed. It would be good to see her. Some things were best shared in the same room, not over the phone.

The prospect of her visit was much more pleasant than the mental exercises I put myself through wondering why Marly wanted me to go live. Speaking on the air seemed contrary to my whole purpose on *Gayline*. Marly needed a board operator so she didn't have to do what she was asking of me. It didn't make sense. What did she think I might add by throwing out a word or two?

"I have a major case of the jitters," I said to Marly as we readied for Monday's show. She made notations on the daily log and I wasn't sure she heard. "I'm really nervous about going on the air. I need more time to get used to the idea."

"No sweat. I won't bug you."

I twined my ankles and feet around the legs of my stool until I was tightly entangled. Marly began her show with a list of community events. Topics changed with the few callers who rang in to voice opinions. It was a slow day. Nothing much was being said, and I didn't have anything to add.

In the second hour, she nattered on about a ski trip gone awry. Her story didn't have much punch and I was getting restless. I listened impatiently as I leaned off to one side of the counter. My feet dangled next to my stool and I fidgeted with a pen.

"We couldn't get our rental equipment fixed and we were freezing our butts off. It was so cold. Really, really cold."

I brought my mic in toward my mouth and opened up the line. "How cold was it?" I droned. I was afraid I sounded bored.

Marly's eyebrows lifted in astonishment.

"How cold, you ask?" She looked straight at me, her blue eyes wide.

I swallowed the stone in my throat and came back at her. "Yeah, how cold was it?" My sound level matched Marly's.

"It was so cold…it was so cold, the Saint Bernard drank his own brandy."

"Do tell."

"It was so cold, the mountain packed up and went to Florida."

"That's cold."

"It was *so* cold, our words froze as we spoke and we had to look in the snow to read what they said. It was so cold, Ivy O'Neal's venom froze!"

"Ow! That's cold."

A phone line flashed, then another. Marly was revitalized and listeners were responding. I patched through an unexpected caller.

"Glover Hayes," Marly gushed. "How flattering. I must be on your speed dial. What's troubling your little mind?"

"You know damn well. I can't have you trashing Ivy without speaking up. Do you think all your listeners are anti-family?" Glover didn't wait for an answer. "Ivy has my respect and gratitude for her good works. The woman has values—family values. She's a loving, giving person, and the world would be a better place if there were more folks like her in it. She stands up to evil. Personally, I find her an inspiration."

"And personally, Glover, you speak in such glowing terms, if I didn't know better I'd say you two were having an affair. Do you meet after hours behind the abortion clinic?"

"Marly, how on the one hand can you decry gay bashing, and on the other advocate murdering children? You perverts deserve what you get."

"Strange logic there. Your mind's like a smelly diaper—in need of changing. But I won't hold my breath. Or, maybe I should—*peeuw!* Time to go, Glover. Your ice floe is double-parked."

I cut off the call and checked the time. We needed to fill four minutes before the bottom-of-the-hour break. Glover's words ricocheted through my brain. I could feel anger well up inside me as I took the next call. "*Gayline.*" How dare he! "What's on your mind?" *I don't understand how Marly stays so calm. Her barbs were cutting, but I know her words were meant for entertainment and to get a rise out of her audience. It sure got a rise out of Glover. His personal attack was genuinely hostile, the creep. Family values? Yeah, right. This makes me want to...* "Sorry, hold on a second..." *Oh! I know how to get back at him. When Marly goes on his show...* "What's that, sir? Abominable? I'll say. Hold on while I patch you through." I focused and repeated the word in my head as the caller broadcast over the air: *Abomindabuilding?*

I threw the receiver at the phone base, recoiled, and charged out of my booth. Marly looked at me as if I were crazy. I seized her wrist, and as I yanked her out into the hall, her cans flipped over her face and onto the floor.

"Claire, what are you doing?"

I struggled to pull her down the hallway.

"He said, 'A bomb in the building!'"

"We've got three minutes to fill. Take him off the air and get the guy's number."

I stopped tugging and whipped around. "Do you think this is a joke? This is the real thing. I can tell." Before we took another step, I had to know. "Tell me the truth." I panted as I held Marly by the arms. "Is it because this bomb threat is another one of your gags? Because if it is, I don't think it's funny."

"It's not a gag. I don't know who's behind it, I swear!"

"Let's get out of here." We sprinted down the hall, passing others on their way out. The warning flew from my lips in unbridled terror. "*Bomb threat!*"

Chapter Thirty-one

"It's all a blur," I told Agent Emerson as we sat in our office later that afternoon. I glanced furtively at Marly. "I shouldn't have picked up the phone because I was preoccupied. I don't remember the sound of his voice, just him saying something like, 'Hey, lady, I hid a bomb in the building.'"

Agent Emerson recorded our remarks using a handheld device smaller than a pack of cards. "Do you remember taking out your air check cassette?" she asked.

"I didn't take it. I grabbed Marly and dragged her out with me."

"Are you sure you had one in?"

"Yes. I don't know what happened to it."

Marly sighed.

The agent continued. "Did you notice anything unusual today?"

"Not before the show. Afterward, the police dogs were sniffing a long time around certain cars, but it was nothing. We were all agitated. I guess my screaming set everyone on edge. And Betty, she couldn't wait to get in her car and leave. I got the sense she was biding her time, annoyed almost, because they wouldn't let her drive off right away."

"Oh, she was annoyed all right," Marly chimed in. "How long did we have dead air? I don't need her yelling at me about how *she* had to run into Studio A again to put on the eighteen-pack."

"I'm sorry it didn't occur to me to start up a CD. Geez!"

Agent Emerson clicked off her recorder. "Let's not start blaming. It would have been great if we could have gotten a tape recording of this guy. Let's be glad we have the phone number. It's more than we had before."

The formal part of our interview was over. I regretted there was nothing new I could add, no clues that would help the investigation. I wondered about the phone number retrieved from the little black caller ID box but knew better than to ask. San Diego was heavily populated, and you'd have to be pretty stupid to commit a crime like this without a throwaway phone. I didn't understand how it would help. We bid our good-byes and I headed toward the studio. As I reached for the door, I had a flash.

"Wait! Don't touch anything." I blew past Marly and ran toward the front entrance. "Wait!"

My hands flew with excitement as I told the agent my thoughts. She nodded and creased her brow. Skimming through the contacts on her cell phone, in no time she contacted the San Diego police detective who had been here earlier. We went inside and waited while guarding the entrance to Studio B.

The detective returned and without comment went to work. He opened his case and applied dusting powder to the doorknobs. Inside the studio, I directed him to the cassette player where I was certain I had installed our air check tape.

Every morning I put in a fresh cassette, and I was sure today was no exception. After the evacuation when we had been given the "all clear" to reenter the building, I immediately went for the tape knowing that Agent Emerson would want it. I pressed the "Eject" button, and as the front face slowly dropped, I was stunned to see it empty.

    The detective examined the cassette recorder. As was my habit, I kept the equipment neat at all times. Now, I could see a wide fingerprint on the plastic cover, and I knew it wasn't my own. I always closed the cassette cover near the top center with the tip of my index finger. My thoughts ran wild as I imagined who could have come in to remove the cassette. Could a company employee be a saboteur? The detective lifted off a perfect print. "It's a beauty," he said. "Thumb." He dusted the surrounding area.

    "I need to see Betty," Emerson stated.

    "Not Betty!"

    She looked exasperated with me. "I need personnel records of all current and past employees going twelve months back. You're all getting fingerprinted."

    I was relieved Agent Emerson did not chastise me in front of Marly, whose stifled smirk showed her amusement at my outburst. I wondered again why Marly wanted me to join her on her show, and I hoped she was not laughing at me or using me as a foil.

    A few days later, the police department brought in a young, attractive brunette to do the fingerprinting. One by one, we were called to the main office where she had set up at a desk. I was instructed to give a slight roll of each finger onto a clear substance. Then, she helped me roll each of my fingers onto a pre-printed form designed with separate boxes to accommodate each finger and both thumbs. The special paper reacted to create a dark print. We finished with both palm prints. Cleanup was easy as there was no messy ink. She handed me a pre-moistened towelette, but I felt better after washing up in the ladies' room.

As expected, there was much talk on *Gayline* about the bomb threat including speculation about who the criminal could be, whether it was a disgruntled employee disguising his voice, and his possible motives. The subject was beginning to wear me down. I declined to go back on the air. Let Marly run the show, *her* show. To rid myself of the workday, I found my thoughts turning to my upcoming visit with Jennifer. At midafternoon, I asked to leave and went home.

The early morning fingerprinting left me with a lingering sense of uncleanliness. A leisurely hot shower did the trick to rinse away the vestiges of the day. I felt tired, though it was barely five o'clock. I arrived at my old house shortly thereafter.

I had agreed ahead of time to make dinner for Ted and Jennifer. At her request, I put together my special meatloaf sliders. All the ingredients were in the refrigerator. Fifteen minutes before it was ready, I placed a pan of dinner rolls on the oven shelf. Jennifer made the salad. Ted pulled up right on cue and we all sat down together at the dinner table. It felt good to eat home cooking. I had little inclination to make anything special for myself, but cooking for family felt worthwhile. I decided to start treating myself better.

Jennifer showed me her school science project for the upcoming fair. The poster board backdrop was pasted over with computer-printed lettering. The subject matter was a far cry from middle school rock collections. A thick paper explaining the sensitive environment of Agua Hedionda Lagoon was neatly encased in a dark jacket. Pictures of algae, native plants, birds, and wildlife adorned the backdrop. It was a well-researched project.

"Sweetie, I'm so proud of you. You've definitely earned an 'A.' When's the fair?"

"Wednesday morning in the gym. Can you come, please, Mom?"

Jennifer's hopeful expression faded in the lingering silence.

"Well, you know, um, I have to work. Maybe I could swing by in the afternoon."

"No, we have to clean up during first lunch."

"I'm sorry."

"Me, too." She slumped on her bed with her head down. I could feel a mother/daughter talk coming on. She started.

"What happened after Christmas? I thought you and Dad... And now he's acting weird again, especially after that second bomb threat. He's trying really hard, Mom. Why can't you?"

Her words pierced my heart, her disappointment a crushing blow. She couldn't understand the separation wasn't about her, yet from her point of view it was. Every day when she came home from school, I was not there. I missed out watching her create the science project. I wasn't there to provide guidance on her homework or listen to the day-to-day interactions at high school. How could we cuddle together on the sofa and watch a DVD if I wasn't there? There was no substitute for the hole I'd left behind. I felt selfish and guilty for not feeling the romantic love Ted and I once shared.

I pinched the bridge of my nose and sighed. "I'll try harder, honey. I promise. I know Daddy's trying, but this isn't like a high school romance where we can say we're sorry and start up again. We have some serious personal problems to overcome. Please understand this isn't about you. It's going to take a little more time for me to sort everything out. Hey, I've got a great idea. Let's go find Daddy." I tousled her hair and gave her a hug. I decided to jump in.

The three of us settled in together on the sofa with a bowl of popcorn and laughed at an old Robin Williams movie. Two rounds of Yahtzee followed by herb tea filled out the evening. Jennifer went to bed, tired and happier. I sat with Ted until the tea was cold. It was my move. We went upstairs.

Chapter Thirty-two

As I hurried toward Studio B, the sound of my shuffling feet reminded me of saddle shoes on old linoleum in junior high hallways after the second bell. I hated being tardy. Marly was on her side of the booth sorting through new CDs. I hung up my bag out of the way.

"Hey, sorry I'm late. I got stuck on the freeway."

"Yeah, whatever. Look who's got a new CD out. We'll play it later. Here." She handed me the jewel case. "Since when do you take the freeway?"

Caught without an umbrella! "Oh, um, I spent the night at my old house. I told Jennifer I would try harder." Marly looked at my day-old clothes. "It's an experiment," I added.

Marly went about her business, and as usual I couldn't tell if my words made any sort of impression on her. My first thought was to explain myself, my situation, but it would have been inappropriate to tell her of my intimacies with Ted—not that there was anything to tell. I tried to convince myself that after our long break, sex would be exciting and I would feel uplifted. It seemed like cuddling would be a good place to start, but after a while, my tension increased. I didn't want him touching me, and my body broadcast that sentiment loud and clear. His body felt wrong next to mine—his fuzzy hair, his size, the smell of his skin. Where was the fragrance from Marly's shampoo? Thoughts of touching her soft curves kept popping into my head. Being with Ted was not working. I wanted my own space and rolled away. Ted sighed, then rolled over, too. He had made a romantic effort and I couldn't follow through merely to alleviate his subsequent disappointment. We slept on separate sides of the bed. Though tempted, I could not share that part with her without telling her more. And what of the romantic moment Marly and I had shared at her house? I didn't want to diminish our brief interlude or make her think I was using her. Rather, I remembered the words of the Bard: "The lady doth protest too much, methinks." I kept my mouth shut.

I turned my focus to the CD, a "Best of" collection from Nina Mills, a popular local artist. I read the liner notes and queued up a few tracks to refresh my memory of her soft pop hits. I had seen her perform at a coffeehouse and was favorably impressed. Because I was familiar with her music and knew a little about her—although it never occurred to me she might be gay—I felt more confident making comments over the air. I would give it another go. When the time came, I played the first musical number indicated on my log. Marly made a comment and then asked her listeners for their feedback. Before the phone lines could ring, I took an opportunity and switched on my mic.

"The first time I heard Nina's music was a year or two ago."

Marly's face lit up. "She speaks! Yes, go on."

"Nina can really swing, but I prefer her soft hits."

"Soft tits?" Marly asked as she ran the words together. "Can we say that? How soft are they? And more to the point, my dear Claire, do you speak from personal experience? Oooh, baby, talk to me!"

I switched off my mic and drew my hands to my mouth in horror. I couldn't believe she said that, but then, it was what *I* had said. I laughed through my fingers until I couldn't hide any longer. Marly asked for the next "soft hit," enunciating with exaggerated clarity. This time, I did not feel she was laughing at me, though plainly the joke was at my expense. It was funny! Instead of feeling embarrassment, I felt invigorated and wondered if our ten thousand listeners were laughing, too.

The show was lively and passed in a wink. We joked about the interchange again in her office. I loved to see Marly's face when she laughed. It lit up with an incandescence that brightened the dull room; even the scuffed walls seemed to sparkle. Her resplendent energy swirled around me, permeating my soul. Her dark-rimmed blue eyes drew me in, rendering me utterly hopeless, a lovesick teenager fawning over a matinee idol.

"Claire, I didn't think 'soft tits' were your thing." She gave me a knowing look.

"It's better than crap, I mean, *rap* music." I remembered Marly's breasts, so firm and shapely. I secretly admonished myself for behaving crudely the evening I grabbed her body. It was likely Marly was also remembering our time together. I was grateful she did not speak of it further.

Then, it dawned on me—I had a vague intuitive sense of what Marly saw in me. She was able to look beyond my insecurities and appreciate my foibles. I had experienced so many embarrassing moments around her, yet I was the one making myself uncomfortable. I had always been quick to admonish myself. In a way, it was the easy thing to do—admit blame for the sake of others. Why I had cast myself in a fool's light, I did not know. I knew I could be different. Others might laugh at me and I would not crumble. More importantly, I could now laugh at myself. I could be self-assured without being perfect. In fact, I could give myself permission to be imperfect, be flawed, the same as I would allow that in others. I could relax and be myself, and others would like me. It was a relief.

Marly had fostered that empowerment. I wanted to give her a big bear hug, the kind we had shared often, until recently. I appreciated what she had done to bring out the best in me, yet I knew if I did hug her, I would not want to stop there. Better to close the door of her windowless office and bring her close to me for a nice, slow, tender embrace—a light kiss. At least it could start that way, as most of my fantasies with her seem to do, and—

"Hey! Anybody home?" Marly waved her hand in front of my face.

I snapped out of my reverie and hoped she had not noticed I was blankly staring at her. To cover my tracks, I decided to tell her something I had been waiting to say. "I had a thought about Glover Hayes. We need help from the Queens From Queens to carry it off. Here's my idea…"

Chapter Thirty-three

"I'll tell you," I said to Jennifer and Ted after we settled in at our usual table at the Chinese restaurant. "It's as if I broke through a wall at work. I can do the board op, answer the phones, make comments, and follow the thread of conversation. I've got this multitasking thing down. My transitions have smoothed out. Everything flows."

"That's great, honey." Ted smiled.

"Ted, can you listen in at work? Once?"

"Mom, Amber said she heard you talking on the radio."

"What?" Ted looked confused.

"That's what I'm telling you. Marly and I talk back and forth on the show. I make comments and don't lose track of the board op."

Ted gasped. "I thought you talked to Marly on the side. You mean people can hear your voice over the radio?"

I nodded.

"And do they know it's you?"

Again, I nodded. Ted's smile faded. Tension deepened the lines in his face. He loudly crunched a handful of fried noodles. Lately, he seemed to be getting used to the idea of me working with Marly. Now, I wasn't so sure. Jennifer clammed up and pretended to play with her chopsticks.

"You spend a lot of time with her, that Marly,

don't you?"

Shit. I could see the glare in his eyes, his lids narrowing as he zeroed in on me.

"It's my job. I enjoy it."

"This isn't like you. A few weeks ago you told me you were petrified to say anything on the radio. You've never called in to a radio show in your entire life and now you talk on one? What else does she have you doing?"

"You talk like she has some kind of power over me. Being on the air is a thrill. It gets my adrenaline going—in a good way. And yes, I have been going through some changes, changes for the better."

Ted fingered the noodles and crunched a few more. He didn't want to say anything that might break our truce, but he didn't have to; his sour expression told me everything I needed to know. He gazed at a nearby goldfish tank and my eyes followed. The orange-and-white fins of the small, fat specimens undulated like gossamer on a breeze, a sharp contrast to the stiffness of the moment. No one spoke for what seemed like an eternity.

Finally, Ted turned to me. "After you move back in," he said authoritatively, "we can re-evaluate your work situation. I'm sure your new job skills would transfer to something even better, like a volunteer post." He forced a weak smile.

I debated whether to voice my objection to his attempt to control me. The food came, a welcome distraction. Rather than say anything in front of Jennifer, I decided to hold off. I stuffed my mouth with shrimp lo mein, then picked at vegetables on the other silver platters, eating more than I should have. My fortune read: You will make life an adventure.

Back at the house, it took a long time for my food to go down. Ted and I made small talk to fill the empty space. He tried to involve me in a domestic decision regarding the kitchen cabinets. Resurface? Remodel? It didn't matter. I was in the kitchen, but I felt like an outsider. The house was no longer my home. It was any other house. I excused myself, took a magazine into Jonah's room, and paged through without reading. Rain began to fall. Usually, the hypnotic dripping sound would lull me to sleep. I lay in bed thinking for a long time about the matters in my life I had not fully accepted. I could not make myself feel passion on the inside by putting on an outward act. Nor could I deny the inner passion I felt by outwardly behaving coolly.

At work the next day, I declined to make any comments over the air and I had little to say to Marly when we were off. She respected my pensive mood and did not press for an explanation. My silence was not in any way an acquiescence to Ted's implied request, and I hoped he did not pick today to listen to *Gayline* lest he think it was so.

I did have one cheering thought: Deena had made good on her promise to visit by buying a ticket online. At her request, I didn't tell anyone she was coming. Our time together would be short, Saturday and Sunday, and we had a lot of ground to cover. I was looking forward to her visit, but mostly I felt mildly depressed.

To lift my spirits, I decided to get to work on my idea for Marly's appearance on Glover's show. I called Carlos from CondomMania and asked him how I could reach the members of the Queens From Queens. He gave me several numbers. As drag performers, the stage names of the "ladies" were apt: Miss Swan, Lucinda Street, and Cocoa Barr. Carlos thought his husband, Trevor, aka Cocoa Barr, would be the best person for my plan. I called Trevor and he agreed. The plan was a good one in rough form, but he wanted to speak to the other girls to see if either of them had any better ideas. The thought that my devious machinations might work brought a smug curl to my lip. I was a changed woman, indeed.

Chapter Thirty-four

Low, dark clouds threatened rain the evening I picked up Deena at the airport. We took a chance with the weather and ate at an outdoor Mexican restaurant in Old Town. The chilly air was warmed by gas-fired heat lamps placed strategically around the patio. The plane ride had tired her out. In my eyes, she looked great. Our waitress mistook us for twins, a common occurrence over the years, even though she is older and weighs more than I do. As we talked over dinner, I once again tried to understand how gay women found one another. Despite our resemblance to one another, Deena confirmed no woman had ever propositioned her.

The next morning I came out of my bedroom to find Deena folding the sheets and putting the sofa back together. A fine rain had drenched everything overnight. She insisted it didn't matter if we passed on our planned day at the beach.

"I came to see *you*," she said. "This is still better than Minnesota."

In the cozy confines of my apartment, it felt safe to open up to her, to tell her in depth about the challenges I had faced since moving out. It didn't take long for us to get into the heart of the matter. We sat at the kitchen table and rehashed the events of the past year.

"Since my affair, I've seen sides to Ted I didn't know existed," I said. "He never used to be hostile.

And I don't remember him being so controlling."

"I don't think he was," Deena replied. "I'm sure he feels out of control now. Look at it from his point of view. He wants you back, and he's willing to make some concessions, just not a repeat of what happened before. He's afraid."

"Well, I'd like some improvements, too, but getting a housekeeper isn't going to change our underlying problems. I feel guilty because this is mostly my fault. Don't give me that look. If I wasn't gay, we wouldn't be going through all this."

"How do you know if you're really gay? Couldn't this be some kind of phase? You used to be attracted to him. Maybe you need a break. Did you ever think the reason you went off with Crystal was because you needed a change, something completely different?"

"When Crystal came into my life, I was more than ready to be with a woman. I couldn't imagine how it would ever happen, and suddenly there she was, wanting to be with me. Oh, Deena, it was so erotic! It felt so right—the sex, I mean. Ted and I did have something when we were younger, but it's not only Ted. I'm not interested in any man. It's true, for a time I did like men, but at some point I stopped fantasizing about them. I've been in denial for years about my shift to desiring only women. This isn't easy for me, you know."

"I know."

I fixed us chai tea and we moved to the sofa.

"I've been struggling with this for a long time. A lot of couples don't have sex, or so I've read."

"So?"

"And what if it were for a medical reason? Anyway, it's not only the lack of sex. I don't have the old feelings, that 'in love' feeling. I've been trying to do the right thing by Jenny, giving the relationship another shot. I can't force it."

"What about counseling?"

"Counseling could provide the affirmation that I'm not a horrible person. I admit I behaved badly. So did Ted. He probably thinks if we start doing it again, he can turn my head around, like I'd stop being gay. Jenny feels like I've abandoned her. I should've waited until she was out of high school."

"Well, it didn't happen that way. Don't worry, she doesn't hate you. She loves you very much and she misses you. From our phone conversations she understands more than you give her credit for, trust me."

"Well, it doesn't matter how long I try, I can't be who I was before. Letting go is so hard. Here I am, starting over in the middle of life, but it's not all bad."

"Then tell me about the good things. You like your job, right?"

"Yes. It's such a stretch for me. Marly doesn't push me to be on the air every day. I've got the board op down, so when I do feel like saying something, I don't lose track of everything. She's been great. I couldn't have done all this without her. And she's so much fun. We laugh and I help her plan the show. She's also very interesting, very intense, and challenging me every step of the way. You know how some high-energy people can be draining? Not her. I've never met anyone like her. Somehow she intuits the parts of my personality that need to come out and she's there tugging away. She makes me feel I have so much hidden potential. I know, you'll probably say it's fate that I got this job."

"Oh, were you telling me about your job, or

about Marly?"

"Deena, you know Marly and I are just good friends. It's hard to admit I didn't know myself as well as I thought. Or maybe I've changed because I do see myself differently. Marly is a complex person, and Ted is, well, more predictable—and I'm not saying that because I've known him longer. I have to resolve more of my old life before I can take on anything else."

"Of course you do."

I was glad Deena had come. It was good for me to air my feelings knowing she would be a good listener. Deena had always been there for me. I couldn't have asked for a better sister or friend. When we were teens, she used to tell me to be patient with life. She assured me I would find my way even if I didn't try so hard. We frequently disagreed on this. It was my nature to try hard at everything. I felt the more effort I put into something and the more I knew about it, the more control I had over it. Because this one trait served me well over the years, I could not imagine being able to loosen up enough to be able to "go with the flow" like Deena suggested.

I admired Marly for being her own person and found inspiration in the way she set and tackled her life goals. She had a talent for mixing together ambitious plans with spur-of-the-moment fun. It was easy for me to get caught up in her charismatic style, the way she grabbed life without reservation. That verve, added to her striking beauty, made it all too easy for me to fall deeper into my infatuation. But I did have control of myself, and I was not going to launch into an affair designed to temporarily curb my loneliness or sexual frustration. I hadn't changed my core, a methodical planner able to rein in my urges until I knew myself and the situation better. Discovering her intentions regarding the two of us was still important because until I knew she was honorably sincere, I would not plunge into those mysterious, uncharted waters.

"I guess I've always played it safe," I said. "For the most part, I like to be fairly sure about the outcome before I'll act. At my job, that doesn't cut it. I have to be spontaneous. I guess I have changed."

Deena nodded.

Chapter Thirty-five

As the week progressed, the heaviness slowly lifted from my body. Instead of shuffling with leaden feet down the hall at KZSD, by midweek I walked with a spring in my step. The change was apparent and Marly commented on it.

"Yes," I told her. "Since Deena's visit, I feel I've turned the corner."

"Does this mean you'll get back on the air?" She raised an eyebrow. "The reason I'm asking is I've got this fun idea for us, and I was hoping you'd brainstorm with me."

"Sure. Why not?"

She opened her laptop and went over the notes she had taken. We tossed ideas back and forth in a spirited exchange. By the time we finished I couldn't wait to get back on the air. We practiced trading lines until we polished our work and I felt comfortable saying my part.

Early in the first hour of the next day's show, Marly sat next to me on my side of the booth so I could see her cell phone. She set up the skit.

"Listen up my friends, Claire and I are about to get interactive with you on social media. Pull down your pants, better yet, pull up your Twitter feeds and get ready to play Marly's Movie Match-up. Use hashtag MarlyKZSD and be sure to follow me. This is where we test you to match up our questions with some of the most popular movies of all time. Not a movie buff? Find someone who is because we have awesome prizes today."

"That's right, Marly. Movie passes to the LGBT Film Fest will go to the person who comes up with the first correct answer."

"We're watching the Twitter feed to see your answers in real time. We'll give you a question, and you tweet the movie that answers the question. So if I ask, 'What movie do you watch while sipping a blended whiskey drink with bitters and vermouth?' You'd say..."

"*Manhattan.*"

"Got it? Here's a hint: today's theme is about what's happened in the world. Let's get started. What did residents of Nevada watch after the last ice sheet melted?"

"Get those thumbs working. I'm not taking calls. Give me a movie title. Marly, look here. Someone got it. *On the Waterfront.*"

"Fabulous! PonyassGirl we'll DM you—and all our winners—for your info."

"Wow, look at all the answers coming in. Too late. Time for the next question. What movie do you see after you smoke recreational marijuana?"

"*Into the Wild*? Not quite. *It's a Wonderful Life. Weeds*, that was a TV show."

"Here it is: *La La Land.*" I wasn't used to Twitter, but was catching on fast.

"Ooh-la-la! We have another winner. Next question: What do ranchers watch when it's too hot during the day to do their jobs? Yin-Yang tweeted *Brokeback Mountain*. Good answer, but not the one we were looking for. *Texas Chainsaw Massacre*? What? You're nuts. Think, people."

The tweets came in so fast, I could hardly keep up. "Ah, here we go. *Midnight Cowboy*. But look at all these other good answers. I like *Silence of the Lambs*. That's just as good. Marly, don't you think she should get a prize for that?"

"Obviously, some of you out there are smarter than we are. Okay, Josie23whatever, we're going to send you some tickets, too."

"Next question: What movie do you feel like seeing after the latest round of health care cuts?"

"Oh, man, look at all the replies. *Day of the Dead. Night of the Living Dead. This is Spinal Tap*? Cute, but no. And the winner is: *No Country for Old Men*."

"No country for women, either."

"Or immigrants, or poor people, or people of color. If we had elected Hillary Clinton instead of *Slumdog Millionaire*, we would have watched *Sense and Sensibility* instead of *A Nightmare on Pennsylvania Avenue*."

"Or *One Flew Over the Cuckoo's Nest*."

"Or *Psycho*. You know what Hillary wanted to do when she found out about Monica?"

"What?"

"*Kill Bill*. Ugh! Politics. Makes me want to scream 'Help!' Hey, that's an old movie, too, remember? With the Beatles?"

We had gone off script and Marly filled the airwaves with spontaneous remarks that I played off of until we took a commercial break. The phone lines never stopped blinking. We were clicking, big-time! Our callers loved the skit and couldn't wait to tell us their favorite movie match-ups. Some continued to play on Twitter after our game was over. Time flew faster than a weekend in Las Vegas. When the clock hit eleven, I thought it must be wrong. We had just gotten started.

We stayed in the studio and played our air check. My words sounded clear and my levels were the same as Marly's. The sound of my voice, though peculiar to my ear, fascinated me. The calls we received on-air and off were positively inspired. I was concerned someone might complain, but no one said anything negative. They liked the biting political humor.

"We'll have to do that again soon," Marly said. "I think we make a good team."

"That was so much fun. We got through most of the skit, but you carried the show. It amazes me how you can go off on a tear. It's okay to say all that stuff, isn't it? It felt kind of dangerous."

I could see Betty coming our way, a sure sign our fun was about to end. I gestured to Marly, who pushed open the door with her foot.

Betty did not enter the studio. "The GM wants to see you, *both* of you. He's in his office waiting." She smirked with a haughty air. As she turned and walked away, on impulse I stuck out my tongue and made a face. Marly laughed.

"I've never met the GM," I said. "I hope we're not in trouble."

"Our General Mangler? Ah, Fred's all right. Come on. Let's get this over with. Oh, and take a hint, don't say anything while he's talking."

Fred was chatting with an earpiece clipped in place when we walked into his office. We sat and waited. I don't know what I was expecting, but Fred didn't look like a man with a position of authority. I realized I had seen him before walking through the halls. It never occurred to me he might be the station manager. He paced with a sharp edge as he conversed. Faded blue jeans shredded at the heels exposed flip-flops, and a tweed jacket fuzzy with age fit snugly over his Hawaiian shirt. His thick head of silver hair contrasted with his boyish face, making it difficult to guess his age. His call ended abruptly, and he did not introduce himself to me before he spoke.

"I got a lot of calls on you girls today. Lately, your show has been attracting attention. It's got me thinking about the direction we need to take."

I swallowed hard in anticipation for the bomb to drop. He couldn't make us change our format now. Though Marly sat expressionless, I could imagine what she was feeling. Fred was still on his feet, pacing within the narrow confines of his office.

"You might think *Gayline* is about you or the gay demographic you appeal to," he continued, "and in a way it is. I give you free rein, which we can do here at a small station. You get to program your own show as long as you follow the log and play the commercials. But from my point of view, it's about the advertisers. I don't mean to sound trite, but I'm driven by the bottom line. I'm a numbers man. The long and short of it is this: I've got advertisers who want to buy airtime and I want to give it to them. They're complaining about the scheduling of their ads and that won't do. That's why I've called you in here."

The dust of the Mojave had settled in my throat. I couldn't have spoken even if I'd wanted to, but at this point I was trying to hold back tears. I clutched the arm of my chair and hoped he wouldn't cancel the show altogether. The thought of having to get another job made me clench my teeth.

"I think the best thing for the station is to rearrange programming to better accommodate the advertisers, shuffle the deck so to speak. And the best way to do that is to change your show—from two hours to three."

"Three?" Marly blurted out. "We're getting three hours. They like us! They like us! Woo-hoo!" She turned to give me the high five, but I was unprepared and shrank back. I didn't know what to make of this news.

"Yes, well control your enthusiasm," Fred deadpanned. "This is conditional. Personally, I don't care what you say on your show as long as you produce numbers and don't get obscene. We can't afford a fine, and I don't want the Indecency Police crawling up my ass. As you know, we would have dropped *Gayline* last fall if it hadn't been for your few loyal advertisers holding you up. Since then, your share has increased steadily and significantly with the addition of your new call screener. The two of you seem to have some kind of chemistry, and I want you talking back and forth every day throughout your time slot.

"Now, Claire, I realize you have limited experience and you haven't said much, but so far I like—or I should say the advertisers like what they hear. If CondomMania still wants to advertise, that's fine, but we've got mainstream businesses that want to be heard on *Gayline* and they're willing to pay to get it. Of course I'd like to give it to them. It's a commitment, one I hope you're ready to take on. You two have a synergy when you get going. That's a rare commodity, and I want to capitalize on it.

"Furthermore, you'll both get a raise, but I want you to act like it. Keep coming up with fresh material like you did today. Demographics show you're pulling listeners from the competition. Your new schedule starts Monday after next, nine to noon for a three-month trial, maybe longer. I'll have your new pay plans to Betty later this afternoon. If you're not happy, let me know. Here's forty bucks. Lunch is on me. You're excused."

Chapter Thirty-six

Marly and I went for Thai food in Hillcrest. All the things Fred had suggested—no, told us—about how to handle the show spun around my mind like a skipping record album on a turntable.

"He didn't exactly wait for an answer," I said as I reached for the pad thai. "He assumed we'd go along with whatever he said. I want to be sensitive to your needs because *Gayline* is your show, and well, he kind of insisted I get involved."

"Fine by me. You're part of why we're getting extra advertising revenue," she said.

"I don't want you to be resentful."

"It's not like we're trading places, but you do need to participate more. I told you, I think we make a great team. The numbers back it up."

"I caught what he said about you almost losing your show last fall."

"But I didn't, did I? Believe me, I'm getting what I want out of this," she said. "We get three hours. I'm not sure you know what that means to me. Plus, we both get a raise."

"How much?"

"Who cares?" She laughed. "And if all goes well after the trial period, I'll insist on a laptop for the studio, since he won't let me use mine, the freakin' weirdo. And anything else we need to play MP3s and wav files. And a six-pack CD player. That cart machine has to go, not to mention everything else."

"Like a new stool so I don't have to sit on duct tape. Well, first things first."

Her eyes twinkled at me from across the table and my hunger shifted toward something other than food. I squirmed in my seat.

Over the next few weeks, I focused almost exclusively on the show. My family problems seemed less burdensome and I finally began to feel excited about my future. Under Marly's tutelage, I learned how to effectively brainstorm, a stimulating mind exercise where we blurted out ideas in rapid-fire bursts. One of us would write them all down, regardless of their initial merit, then we would cull the losers and work on the ideas with potential. During my drive home I thought of other ideas we missed, and over dinner I would fine-tune conversations we could have on the air. I kept a notepad handy just in case.

In a way, it reminded me of my college days when I had to come up with themes for composition class. I hated to admit it, but what it pointed out was how boring my life had become over the years. What I had done while raising my family had been of prime importance at the time and I did not regret my life, but with Jonah already out of the house and Jennifer not far behind, it felt satisfying to spend time on myself for a change.

I feared the extra hour and increased participation on *Gayline* might worsen my relationship with Jenny. Instead, I found my enthusiasm was contagious; I even shared some of our scripts with her. She laughed at the notion that her staid old mom exchanged racy and satirical repartee on the air.

As for my relationship with Ted, well, frankly,

I lost interest in trying to make things better. He experimented with various approaches and long looks: puppy dog loyalty, the you're-the-most-fascinating-person-in-the-room look, outright leering, "I've got to have you, you're so sexy!" eyes, and more often a sad resoluteness that what he wanted would not come to pass. He stopped trying to lure me into contrived remodeling projects designed to bring me home. After sleeping a few times in Jonah's room, I didn't return and nothing was said of it. We moved on to conversation that involved non-emotional topics, and in our civility we became almost too polite.

Chapter Thirty-seven

The extra hour of *Gayline* meant more than an extra hour of time needed to produce the show. We had to prepare in the afternoon and into the evening because our mornings were filled with scheduled airtime. Listening to an entire air check was out of the question. We fast-forwarded our cassettes to the important moments to hear how our scripts went over, and rather than lament the lost "could have" or "should have" saids, we wrote down the funny lines for use at a later date.

From a practical standpoint, we couldn't script more than a short part of the whole show. The rest was impromptu banter fed by the subject at hand. The quality of our callers improved. I patched through many first-time callers who offered refreshing ideas, and our audience was much more likely to add to the merriment by tossing out a comedic throwaway line. Our show progressed by giant steps, and I struggled to keep pace. Fortunately, Marly was supportive. The extra workload had not weighed her down. In fact, her mood had been light and easy, much like her on-air persona.

More and more, late afternoons at the station progressed into carry-out meals at Marly's place or soup and sandwiches at mine where we worked into the evening. In the past few weeks, I noticed her house had become less cluttered. Magazine piles disappeared.

"Look at this," she said as she plopped down next to me on her sofa one evening with an accordion file. "I've been clipping articles, you know, the kind of things we can make fun of on our show. They're filed alphabetically by subject matter."

Even without the expectant look on her face, it was obvious she was trying to impress me. I smiled and riffled through a few sections. The letter "A" contained information on astrology, animal behavior, and adult situations. "B" was stuffed with book reviews. In "C" was a handwritten note that read: "Hey, kids, no time to take driver's ed? Take our crash course."

I smiled. "That's cute. You can develop this."

"You mean, we."

I moved my fingers to the back of the file. "Z" had the most paper in it.

"Those are ones I haven't filed yet."

"Marly, this is wonderful! What a great surprise." I pulled out an article at random. "'Doctors on Drugs.' Ew. That's scary."

"I don't trust doctors," Marly said. "You won't catch me going to one."

"Can we get a second opinion on that?"

"If you're into drugs, you want to go to a doctor. They've got the best drugs."

"I remember in Minnesota there was a pharmacy with a big sign outside that said: 'See Don for Drugs!' It was as if the pharmacist was a drug dealer. Hey, where's the pencil? We should be writing this down."

Our work took form; we ripped it apart, added to it, crumpled it up, smoothed it out, threw it away, and rescued it from the trash. To remain focused on one skit at a time was a challenge. The surge in popularity that resulted from our expanded format further distracted us from our task. Our regular listeners were excited and they let us know it; they called during *Gayline* in greater numbers. Marly's friends took to calling and texting her more often after hours. To get anything done, she turned it to silent mode and set it aside.

Visitors to her house were another matter. Work stopped and party time began when several of her friends showed up unannounced. On the plus side, it gave me a chance to meet new people and get to know her friends better. Carlos from CondomMania stopped by with his husband, Trevor. It was delightful to finally meet them both and match faces to the voices I'd heard on the phone. Trevor showed me pictures of himself as Cocoa Barr in a performance with the other Queens From Queens, and I could see how in that role Cocoa would be the best person to carry out a needed assignment for our plan with Glover. One of the other Queens, Lucinda Street, offered help with video technology, something that would come into play later, and I felt relieved to mark off more obstacles from our to-do list.

Eventually, I became weary of the parade of admirers surfing the wave of our success. Marly had more energy for it, but I could tell she was also becoming annoyed by the interruptions. We decided to spend more evenings at my apartment where visitors, announced or otherwise, were rare.

Chapter Thirty-eight

Jenny and I walked along the beach in Del Mar. Locating a parking spot had been a challenge during Spring Break, but our toes called out for the gritty feel of sand beneath our feet. The air was a little cool for sunbathing, but that didn't stop the tourists and locals who staked out a square of beach trying to get the first tan of the season. Their pasty white bodies lay in uneven rows on patterned towels of myriad colors. As gulls cried overhead, we wound our way through the crowds and waded a few inches into the chilly water of the Pacific. The calm surf echoed hypnotically between the water's edge and the sand cliffs. Waves rolled up and flattened out as they spilled onto the shore. Sandpipers poked their beaks into the wet sand and then hastily retreated on their spindly legs to escape the next incoming wave.

"You don't seem upset these days like you were when I moved out."

"A lot's happened, Mom. I guess I understand now why you and Dad split up."

"I wanted it to work out. It couldn't, you know. It wasn't about how hard we tried."

"Yeah, I know. I've been having regular sessions with my school counselor. She's been helping me understand what it must be like for you."

I turned to her. "Oh, I didn't know that."

"And...she's been helping me—with me." She laughed uneasily. "Because you used to like boys, and I like boys, and well, what if it happens to me, too? I was pretty freaked about it for a while. I didn't say anything to you, 'cause...I don't know." She shrugged. "Amber and I have talked about, um, your change, too. I hope you don't mind that I told her."

Jenny's hair sparkled with red highlights as it gently blew across her face. She turned toward the ocean and her hair billowed behind her back. I pulled a strand away from her eye.

"No, I don't mind."

"Dad's doing better these days, too. He doesn't say things like, 'When Mom comes home we'll all do this or that.' It's not like he avoids the subject. We've talked about it. It's just...he knows you're not coming home. And you're so involved with work these days, we hardly ever see you."

"I hope you don't feel like I'm abandoning you, honey. I love you so much. One of the hardest things about all of this is I'm not with you more."

"I can take my driver's test soon. When I get my license, Dad says I can borrow the car to see you. Then we could visit more often."

I shook my head and sighed. "You're turning into a wonderful adult, and I'm afraid I'm missing these important moments in our lives. Pretty soon you'll be like Jonah, off and running at college somewhere."

"I'm thinking about going to Cal State if I

can't get in to UC. Maybe you'll have your own house by then and we could be roommates."

I laughed with her. We embraced and I kissed her salty forehead.

"I love you, sweetheart."

She hugged me and murmured in my ear, "I love you, too, Mom."

I took her hand as we strolled down the beach. Everything in time. I wanted to hear more about the boys she liked. I wanted to blindly assure her that she wouldn't wake up one morning and feel gay. The signs had been there for me, and I would have recognized them long ago had I known what to look for. Less than a year ago I felt my world crashing down around me as if, like Chicken Little, I could look up and see another world ready to fall on my head. Now, I could envision some attractive possibilities.

I wanted Jennifer to know that I might have another relationship one day, a woman friend. I daydreamed of Marly, with her impish smile waiting to greet me in the morning. Marly, with her quick wit and penchant for the absurd. Marly, with her one-of-a-kind train of thought leading anywhere. Marly, with her mercurial personality—sensitive one minute, outrageous the next. Marly, the sexy, inviting temptress. Except for an occasional bear hug, she had been keeping a respectful distance for quite some time—since the night we kissed. She and I spoke cursorily of family life and such. I had told her about visits with Jenny and Ted at the house. She listened, but rarely asked for details.

Her friends became a welcome substitute for the ones Ted and I left behind when we stopped seeing other couples. I missed some more than others, and since we'd lost touch, wondered how strong our bonds had been. Perhaps we had friendships of convenience, a couple to accompany another couple so we wouldn't have to be alone with our spouses. For now, splitting the workload with Marly was all I needed.

In addition to feeling comfortable with Marly's friends, I was more relaxed in other ways. I toned down my wardrobe without compromising my basic ideas of how one should dress for work. Neat blue jeans and less fussing with my hair and makeup no longer made me feel self-conscious. Conversely, Marly took more care with her appearance. She purchased a few nice things for herself, trading worn garments for trendy sweaters and new jeans. In the warming weather she donned lighter-weight wrinkle-free tops instead of sweatshirts meant for the rag pile. I didn't know if she dressed better and kept after her house clutter as a concession to me or if some of my neatnik habits were rubbing off on her.

On the air, her animated spirit and outlandish commentary inspired me to break out of my shell and toss in my own zany ideas. Not all of our skits were winners. When they didn't go well, I counted on her to be silly, to change the subject, or to make fun of the bit and ourselves. She had an amazing ability to come up with the right words without additional preparation. In many ways I was her opposite: more conventional, slow to act, easily embarrassed—character traits that provided the kind of contrast that provoked conversation or led to humor. I didn't want those parts of my personality to dampen her wild energy, for without it, *Gayline* would go flat. Fred was right. We had a synergy that fed on itself to create a better show, a mix of straight lines, zingers, and one-upmanship without competitive hostility.

My adapting to being on the air reminded me of what happened with her cats, one wild, the other calm—but not for long. I laughed to myself thinking about how those two master shedders had shown no compunction in covering my slacks with their fur. Heaven knows when Marly found time to clean house. Then, there was that bathroom. And her bedroom! What was that all about? Marly, ever the enigma.

Chapter Thirty-nine

Though not first on my list, squeezing in time to follow up with Cocoa Barr regarding Marly's visit on *The Glover Hayes Show* had to be done. We would be foolish not to capitalize on the event, especially now that *Gayline* was receiving more attention. I did not feel our new on-air repartee should change our plan with Glover. It had always been Marly versus Glover; their ongoing rivalry started long before I came on the scene. Of course, Glover was not aware of the plan we had concocted, and the best news was we got a lucky break—an intern working at Glover's radio station agreed to act as our mole and provide invaluable extra help.

We needed to pick a date and stick with it, or else this showdown with Glover would be forgotten. Marly and I figured the best way to pin him down was to start talking about it on *Gayline,* something we did at every opportunity. Start the publicity and the rest would fall into place. Bait the trap. Cook the bacon over the campfire and the bear will come around. It was almost too easy.

"Good morning, everyone. Your host Marly Meshuga here. This portion of *Gayline* is brought to you by S. Cort Massage Service where the customer always comes first. And, speaking of being first, we've already got our first caller—a real April fool. It's Clover Days, I mean, Glover Hayes!"

"Clever Ways, you mean."

"Touché, Glover. Let the sparring begin. Confirm a date already, will ya?"

"How about May Day? Easy to remember and it'll be here before you know it."

"Not to mention a distress signal. Not surprising. Your show is calling for help."

"And your show is beyond help, along with your antiquated station. That's why we'll use our studios here at KQEW."

"Okay, but then we're using my time slot."

The deal was struck and sealed with sarcasm. The one-month cushion was needed in case something didn't go well with Cocoa Barr completing her part of the plan. Then it occurred to me—if we were planning something for Glover, would he be planning something in return? Would we be prepared for a practical joke or a vicious attack? What if he got the upper hand and made us look stupid? The key would be to stay in control of time, to plan the minutes and not leave anything to chance.

Word about the showdown date circulated quickly. By the middle of the second hour, the phone lines were buzzing with the news. Putting regulars on the show would wait for another day. Our caller list was expanding rapidly, and while I would not forget the loyalty of past supporters, new ones were now equally important. At the top of the third hour, Marly and I decided to skip our written bit and stay with callers who were providing an endless stream of lively conversation.

As an active participant on the show, rather than screening calls, it was easier to pick a phone line and let the person talk. If he or she strayed from the subject, Marly or I cut them off and I would patch through another caller.

As I patched Yin-Yang through, I realized that except for frequent emails, we had not heard from them in weeks.

"May Day's a Saturday," they said. "Switch it to April thirtieth. This is an important moment. I know I'll be ready with my ear to the radio. Got my popcorn and soda. I can't wait to hear what's going to happen. I'll see if I can help you get publicity—as if you need it."

"Thanks Yin-Yang," Marly said. "Claire, who's next?"

"*Gayline*, you're on the air."

"You can't make Glover look like a fool," the voice said. "I swear I'll blow up your building. I'll do it today! I can do it and I will."

Wide-eyed, I looked at Marly. My jaw dropped. I was about to head to the door, but Marly beat me to it. To my amazement, she locked the door with us inside.

"I'll blow you sky-high in a New York minute," he chortled in his undefined accent with its fake falsetto that tended to break as he spoke.

"Don't cut him off!" Marly yelled.

The hallways of KZSD began to fill with employees. Zach knocked on our window and motioned for us to leave.

Marly yanked the window blind cords, which fell in a clatter, visually sealing us away from outside interference. I could hear others knocking on the glass.

"You dykes oughta get out now while you got a chance. Your building is wired. I've been waiting for the right moment to get rid of your kind."

The black box! I grabbed it and wrote down the phone number, just in case. The dull thuds of a fist pounded on the studio window and resonated inside the booth. Marly plugged her cans in my studio and set up the extra mic. I was glad she was in there with me. Adrenaline surged through my body. I didn't want to believe there was a bomb in the building, but I was scared. My whole body prickled. I glanced at our air check tape to be sure it was recording.

"I've got a whole stockpile of goodies," he said. "Take your pick. Should I set off the whole building, or just Studio B?"

"Oh, my God," I cried. "He knows where we broadcast!"

Marly commandeered the mic. "*Duh.* Everybody knows we're in Studio B. You're an impotent nobody who's trying to get some attention. Destruction is the coward's way. Why don't you do something constructive for a change? Oh, but that would take more guts and brain cells, something you're short on."

The pounding amplified on the double-paned glass. I wanted to peek through the blinds, but Marly put a hand on me as if to say, "Don't look." I could hear muffled yelling. They wanted us out. Marly would not be dissuaded.

"I bet you're in with those religious loonies out in East County. Well, you can tell Ivy and the pastor out there that if anyone is abnormal, it's people who go around committing violent acts. Anarchy to the anarchists! I hate bigots. You're sick!"

"You're sick," he countered. "Your life is an abomination!"

His New York accent was faint, as if he had left the city many years ago. I was sure this was our original caller. Listening to him, I was both spellbound and repulsed by the consequences of his dangerous intrigue.

Marly lobbed the next volley. "You're so scared of people who are different than yourself. Take a look in the mirror, mister, and you'll see something really scary. I know I'll never change your mind, you pea-brained miscreant. It's you and your beliefs that are a threat to society. You belong in prison. The God I know is tolerant."

The doorknob rattled as if being forced. A key clicked in place and the door swung open.

"I hope in your next life you're gay!" Marly shouted as Fred grabbed her arm. I popped out the air check tape from the cassette player and shoved it in my back pocket.

Chapter Forty

Squad car lights pulsed in slow rhythm and crowds milled nearby as the police herded employees away from the building. Fred took us aside in the parking lot.

"What kind of a stunt was that?" he asked. Marly and I knew better than to reply. "You know the company rules, and some rules are made to be kept. This offense is grounds for discipline. You don't have carte blanche, you know. That third hour doesn't entitle you to special privileges. Employee safety comes first. I'm sure Agent Emerson will have a few things to say. I can hardly wait. You bullheaded creative types are going to be the death of me!"

He raised his arms and splayed his fingers in frustration as if he could strangle the air. I swallowed hard and chewed on my lip. His speech over, he strode off in the direction of the police. The dogs had arrived. Two German shepherds strained at their leads and barked menacingly at the entryway to KZSD. Our bravado at staying inside Studio B fell away. I felt vulnerable and shaky, my knees nearly giving out as I tumbled onto the grass.

"You okay?" Marly asked as she sat next to me.

"Yeah. I wish I knew if we were doing the right thing. You don't look so hot yourself."

"Must've been the cold pizza I had for breakfast."

My stomach churned. Knowing I'd have to see

Agent Emerson didn't provide relief. I hadn't heard her name mentioned in quite a while. In fact, the new format had kept my mind occupied with more pleasant thoughts, and except for a few reminders like the caller ID box, I had done a pretty good job of putting those old worries behind me. Despite Emerson's concern, I had begun to believe it was all talk. Today's show changed my view. We had a nutcase out there who could very well target our building, or us. My head began to swim, and I lay down on the cool, wet grass. I could feel the rectangular bulge of the cassette tape in my back pocket. Whoever he was, his voice recorded on tape was too near for my personal comfort. I had to see Emerson, the sooner the better.

When the police gave us the all clear to leave the parking lot, Marly and I went to a local eatery where we both pushed food around our plates. Every few minutes, she checked the cell phone that vibrated next to her. Finally, she answered it. It was Agent Emerson. We headed back to KZSD to meet with her.

For once, Marly and I had little to say. In her office, we each picked up reading material, and I noticed she flipped through her mail without looking. Agent Emerson arrived. I was expecting her to grill us, or at least give us a dressing down as Fred had. She glanced at us without making eye contact.

"You can't put yourself in danger and expect us to rescue you," she said.

"Here," I said as I handed her the cassette tape. "You'll want this." I looked at Emerson expectantly, but she remained silent, no questions, no further admonishments for our behavior, no explanations about anything.

"I need to go," she said. "I have a lot of work to

do. At least we know it's not Stephanie or one of her friends." With that, she walked out.

I bit my lip. Marly doodled on a magazine cover, and eventually looked up at me. Her dark-rimmed blue eyes conveyed a sadness I was reluctant to fully interpret. Her hair stuck out in funny directions and lines creased her brow. It had been a wild day.

"Okay, I give," I said. "Who's Stephanie?"

"Someone I used to know." Marly drummed her fingers on the desktop. "We were always trying to make our relationship work. It was frustrating. It didn't work out, obviously. She was too crazy, kind of the obsessive type. At first I liked all the attention, and maybe that's why we got together, but then she was like gum on my shoe. We lived together at my place. What a mistake. I had to take drastic measures to get her to leave. After she moved out, she harassed me by phone—just a lot of calls, no bomb threats or anything. It took a temporary restraining order to get her to stop."

"Why didn't you tell me before?"

"What for? Stephanie's got a screw loose, big deal. Given our history, of course they had to check into it. Agent Emerson's ruled her out as being the mad bomber type. Besides, why do you care about my ex when you're still having a relationship with yours?"

"I am not! Did you think we were getting back together?"

"Hello! You've been sleeping at your old house."

"Well, yes, for a while I was, but I slept in my son's old room." I paused, looking for the right words. "I can't even do that anymore."

Marly looked confused. "You still didn't say why you cared."

I wasn't sure what to say. Of course I cared, cared because I wanted to know more about her private life and about the past relationships she had guarded rather closely until now. How long would it have been before Marly told me about Stephanie? In these past few months if she had been thinking I was sleeping with Ted, it was no wonder she held back, assuming she was still interested in me.

"I do care," I said cautiously. Her eyes had a silent beseeching quality that allowed me to go out on a limb. "I cared enough not to go headfirst into something until I was sure it was the right thing."

Marly touched her finger to my arm. "And now? Is this the right thing?"

She was giving me the go-ahead to explain my feelings. "I didn't want this to be some meaningless fling for you."

"No way. I've had plenty of opportunity and I'm done with that. It's not what I want."

"I work for you."

"We had to meet somehow."

"I'm older than you."

"So?"

"And you said you weren't interested in a relationship because you wanted to focus on work."

"That's true. And look how you've helped me make *Gayline* so much more than it was. The show is going great. Claire, it hasn't been easy waiting for you to come around, but you're worth it." She smiled a little and put her hand on my leg, her touch warm through my pants.

"We're so different."

"Are we? I thought we'd gotten past that. You have to stop confusing who I am on the air with who

I am off the air. Think about how we get along when we work together. It's true, I'm kinda out there and you're kinda quiet, but underneath it all, we connect on a very personal level. You can't deny there's an attraction. I don't feel like I should be trying to convince you. You have to believe it from your own experience."

I took her hand. "Then I'm ready to try again. Okay?"

She nodded. My heart quickened as I passed my hands up her arms. She closed the door with her foot, and in the privacy of her office we embraced in a prolonged hug. I sighed as I took in the fresh scent of her hair, the gentle herbal essence returned as if in a long-forgotten dream. I breathed deeply to experience the musky smell of her neck and felt desire stir within me. My lips felt their way along her neck as they brushed lightly over the fine hairs. The softness of our breasts where they met beneath our clothing felt incredibly erotic, and I found myself moving rhythmically in a slow dance against her body.

She whispered into my ear. "Claire, I really like you. You're good for me, and it's been hard for me to think about losing you to someone else. I know you have strong ties to your family. I've been trying to show you how I feel by getting you more involved on the show and in my life. I hope you're truly ready, because I want you."

She threaded her fingers into my hair and with her fingertips she lovingly massaged away the tension. It reminded me of the unforgettable evening we kissed. I let my forehead rest on top of her shoulder as she made careful rotations on my scalp, taking time to reach and undo all the tightness of the day.

My arms fell loosely to the narrow of her waist. She curled one of her fingers around a strand of my hair and with her free hand stroked my back. Her caress was intoxicating. The office environment vanished as I focused on her touch, savoring each moment to the fullest in case she should pull away and our time would be over. I had waited so long to feel her body close to mine, and though I could imagine myself falling asleep in her arms, I did not want to miss one second of her presence. I felt transported.

In recent weeks I had tried to keep my fantasies in check to protect myself from falling even more deeply than I already had. I wanted her more than ever and contemplated what to do. Declaring my feelings had been a bold step, and I had been rewarded. Marly's arms felt receptive and as soothing as a warm, natural, spring-fed pool. I felt surrounded by her comfort. To be true to myself, I would not plunge in over my head; I would take time to get used to the water.

Chapter Forty-one

After work I wanted to go with Marly to her house, back to her sofa to pick up where we had left off months ago; our unfinished embrace with its raw edges yearned to be smoothed. I didn't have the excuse that we needed time together to brainstorm a new sketch because the one planned for today's show had gone unused. What I needed was private time to reflect on the day. I flicked on the radio as I drove home and listened to the news report of our latest bomb threat. Agent Emerson was being interviewed.

"We have voice recognition," she said. "We believe this is the work of a locally based individual."

"Do you anticipate an arrest in the immediate future?" asked the reporter.

"No comment."

At home I chose to ignore my phone messages. Instead, I sat on my sofa and gazed absentmindedly out the window until my stomach growled. I hadn't eaten much at lunch. Comfort food called: macaroni and cheese, steamed broccoli, mint tea. After dinner I lazed on the sofa, letting small bites of dark chocolate melt completely on my tongue followed by sips of red wine before consuming the next morsel. My thoughts were scattered in faraway places, dotting the landscape of my mind like silos across miles of rolling farmland. I recognized the ringtone I'd set up for Ted and answered. "Hi."

"Honey, it's me. Didn't you get my message? Sweetheart, you're in way over your head at this radio station. Think about what you're doing, about the kids, and me. We're worried sick about you. It's insanity over there. What are you waiting for?"

"Hey, slow down. You're in a panic."

"Of course I'm in a panic!"

"They're just threats, that all."

"How do you know? That's the way these things start. Why take a chance? You're risking your life, and for what? It's insane! Stop doing this to yourself—and to us."

"Ted, I really don't think anything is going to happen. It's—"

"Claire, stop it! Listen to yourself. You're deluding yourself. What do I have to do to make you come to your senses?"

I held the phone away from my ear. Ted's desperation tugged at my heartstrings. "What has Jenny said?" I asked.

"She wants you to quit. She wants you safe at home. Don't you think this charade has gone on long enough? I've said it before, I'll say it again, you and I need to go to counseling. You can take a break from your job. I'll continue to support you while you get your head together if you're not ready to move back home now, but you have to stop this nonsense. Now! Before it's too late."

"I'll get back to you. Give Jenny a hug for me."

"Claire, wait!" The volume of his protest faded as I moved the phone away from my ear and ended the call.

I'm not sure of everything that passed through my mind that evening as I lounged on the sofa. There were so many things: Marly, the caller's slightly nasal New York accent recorded on tape, the restraining order against Stephanie, holding Marly, how to handle events for Glover and Marly's showdown, Marly's bedroom, her funny cats, her everything.

I called Jennifer the next morning before she left for school to assure her I was okay. Mornings were not her time. She sounded calm, which may not have been a true representation of her feelings. She said nothing about my returning home or quitting my job. I was concerned Ted might be embellishing the drama of the situation and somehow making me out to be a crazy woman. I had to rely on my relationship with Jenny to believe she could decide for herself if I had lost my mind. I was glad she had ongoing sessions with her school counselor. There was a part of me that felt I was too close to the situation at work to see it clearly. Maybe Ted correctly perceived I was in denial as I had completely wound down from the day's events. As an outsider, he would have a different perspective. I was not afraid to go to work. This in itself could have been cause for alarm, yet for some reason the next day I found strength in confidently walking through the front door at KZSD and past a newly installed armed guard.

I met Marly in Studio B. We exchanged quiet smiles and embraced in a long, close hug. The morning had a dreamlike quality. I felt as if I were floating slightly outside myself. I brought in a cup of coffee, my second of the day, to pep up for the show.

"You're listening to *Gayline*. Marly Marvelette here with Claire Coconuts taking your calls. Talk to me."

Engaging with callers got the neurons firing in

my brain. Before long, the first hour passed. In the second hour, I became more animated, and by the third, I was tired from laughing. Our listeners encouraged us not to fall victim to a faceless entity. Stand proud, produce the show, do not be deterred; that was the message we heard again and again. Unseen forces of negativity would always be present. To give in would mean "they" had won. Going off the air was not an option. Toning down the show was not an option. Not being gay was not an option.

Betty approached our booth as we signed off the air. She clicked the glass with her decorated nails, which we could not hear through the soundproofing. Marly opened the door. Betty's body language and demanding presence, usually so solid and uppity, had gone through a sea change. Her shoulders slumped and her face was drawn with the heaviness of age.

"Thought you'd like to be the *second* to know, I gave my notice today. I'll be leaving at the end of the month," she said in a monotone. "Oh, and Fred wants to see you." With an uncharacteristic sigh, she slowly shuffled off as if she had suffered a personal defeat.

Marly and I looked at each other and contained our mirth beneath silent smirks. That battle had been won. She would not be bothering us anymore. We walked into Fred's office and sat down.

"Claire," he barked. "You're a call screener first, air talent second. Do your job."

I grimaced, but kept quiet.

"Marly, don't you turn into our next security issue. I've got my hands full as it is. Hmmm…consequences, consequences. I've been mulling it over. First, pull another stunt like the one you did yesterday and you're off the air. Maybe for a day. Maybe for a week. Maybe off for good. Do us all a favor and don't put me in the position of having to decide.

"Actually, something's come up and the synchronicity is killing me. Betty gave her notice today. She's been a good employee, been here a lot longer than you two. But I also know there's no love lost between you—Marly anyway, I don't know about you, Claire. Consequences...for your misbehavior. You two are assigned to put together Betty's going-away party. Make it look like she's been your best friend or there'll be hell to pay. Got it? Now, get out of my office!"

Chapter Forty-two

Time unfolded strangely over the weekend and into the next few days of work, one moment a crawl, the next a blur. Marly and I maintained continuity with the show despite numerous interruptions. Phone calls from various media flooded the office as did email communications. We worked until midnight for several nights at the station until we caught up with the demands of outsiders. A TV crew filmed a few minutes of our show. I did not want to be on camera and turned away. Marly was interviewed afterward. Her spirited repartee with the reporter was much like her on-air persona. The evening news ran the segment, which was repeated in the morning. The media seemed to be feeding on itself with repeating links on all the popular social media sites. Eventually the monster was sated and our story fell to the back pages.

I was exhausted. The weekend came, yet Marly and I had to keep the creative juices flowing. I went to her house Saturday morning to work on sketches for the coming week. With my eyes closed, I reached into her accordion file and pulled out an article to get us going.

"Let's see…'Valentine Surprises: Practical, Romantic, and Sexy Solutions for a Memorable Holiday.' Eh, too late."

"No, don't put it back. Let's work with it."

Marly's eyes sparkled. "Forget Valentine's Day. We could have practical, romantic, sexy gift solutions for any special day. Some gifts could be all three."

"Like a satin nightgown," I said.

"Or a pre-heated dildo."

I slapped her playfully on the arm. "Quit! You're bad."

"What? I'm serious. Are you telling me you like a cold one?"

"I do not use a dildo," I stated emphatically as laughter burst through my puritanical facade.

"You don't even own one, do you? Here, you can borrow mine." Marly got up and headed toward the bedroom, but I grabbed her belt loop and pulled her back. Not to be deterred, she tugged forward. I fell sideways off the sofa startling MayMay, who scampered into the kitchen. Marly helped me back onto the seat cushion and we sat together.

Our laughter subsided. Slowly our smiles faded and we moved closer. She lifted my face with her hand and drew near. I parted my lips to meet hers as she pulled me toward her. My heart raced as we touched, and I could feel tears welling in my eyes. My throat felt tight as we exchanged a few brief kisses. Her lips were as moist and inviting as a ripe plum, her breath sweet. My hunger grew with the sensation of her tongue across mine.

She positioned herself over my lap so she faced me, her bent knees pinned snugly against my thighs. I wrapped my arms around her back as she caressed my face. With eyes closed, I savored the small kisses she planted around my forehead and cheek. Again our lips met, gently massaging, and we explored one another's mouths with our tongues. I wanted her closer and squeezed my arms around her with a passion I had hidden for months. We broke our kiss and embraced tightly, her face next to mine, her hair in my hair, our breasts pressed together yet fitting so well I could have spent an eternity in this heaven.

I had a sudden urge to feel her body but stopped myself, remembering with a hint of embarrassment how I had lunged at her breasts the first time we kissed. This time I delicately ran my right hand along her side to feel the curve I had often admired. She accepted my touch eagerly and sensing my desire leaned back so I could comfortably bring my hand to the front of her body. She placed her hands on my shoulders, silently affirming it was okay to touch. In slow motion my hands caressed the sensuous curves of her femininity.

Her face glowed as she arched her back and sighed. My fingertips traced circles around her beautiful roundness, and I could feel the distinct hardness of her nipples beneath her rayon knit top. Finally, she leaned in again and we kissed at length. She had not touched me as I had touched her, and I wondered if she would. As if reading my mind, she whispered in my ear, "Soon, Claire. Very soon."

Chapter Forty-three

April calendar pages were flipping by in my daily planner and I had a multitude of tasks before me. Marly and I had done nothing for Betty's going-away party scheduled to take place after our appearance on *The Glover Hayes Show.* Arranging a meeting with the Queens From Queens to check on their progress had become a challenge. I made time for Jenny, which I managed in small snips—coffee near her school with her friend Amber, dinners at my apartment, and a constant stream of text messages. Every day Marly and I had to produce three hours of *Gayline* and plan some kind of on-air routine for the next show. On top of everything, Agent Emerson seemed to be keeping tabs on us, calling almost daily to check in but never revealing anything new.

Time management moved up on my to-do list. The saying, "If you want something done, ask a busy person," applied to me twenty-four seven. I could not remember how I used to spend my time as a housewife. Had laundry, housecleaning, shopping, and lunch with casual friends taken a full day? Having plodded along day after day, I undoubtedly suppressed the ennui that had turned into restlessness. While the mundane tasks of my existence were important for the smooth operation of my household, they were not any less boring. It had been a long time since I had felt useful outside of my family obligations.

In little windows of time, thoughts of Marly crept into my mind: our kisses so new and exciting, the emotions that emerged when I touched her, dreams of touching her again and enjoying her sensual caress on my skin. I believed her feelings to be genuine, to run deeply through her psyche. Our romantic longings made my heart flutter. When I wished to replay the warm connection of our embrace, I remembered the feeling as if it were a special present wrapped inside a lacy gift box, the beauty inside—love.

For years I had loved Ted, and for that reason I was scared. Our commitment, once emotional and solid, had turned into a legal matter. Our romantic love had turned into the love for a friend. One of us had to file papers. I wanted to focus, to follow through with the inevitable, only I couldn't imagine when that would happen with everything going on. I was always on the verge of being overwhelmed. Next month when the mayhem would end, the timing would be better.

Now more than ever, I felt it would be appropriate to show Marly how important she had become, and if possible, to express my appreciation for the opportunity she had given me. She took a gamble hiring me for *Gayline* and we both won. I decided to buy her something special.

When it arrived, I brought the gift into the studio and laid the package next to her op board. I had wrapped the box with the Sunday comics section and tied a red bow on top. It looked a little silly, but I thought she would find it appealing.

"Hey, what's this?" she asked as she walked into Studio B. "Our gift to Betty? Wait. Let me guess." She held out her hand to stop me from speaking. I chuckled to myself as she pretended to cogitate deeply. "Hmmm. I'm picking up a vibe. A vibrator?" She shook the box. "It's a cold salami! No? A one-way ticket to Brazil? It's too big for a subscription to *Matrons R Us*. How about—"

"How about opening it up?" I said. "It's for you. From me."

Marly's countenance softened. "For me?" I could tell she was touched. She hugged me. "You're so sweet. I love it! I always wanted a box like this."

"Just open it already."

She untied the bow. Setting the ribbon aside, she pulled away the paper and opened the unmarked cardboard box, carefully removing the bubble wrap to behold her gift—a new set of headphones.

"Oh, Claire, they're wonderful! I can't believe you did this. It's not even my birthday."

"Think of it as a belated Christmas present. You deserve them. Now you can get rid of those old taped-up ones. Yuck. The equipment around here is disgraceful. Go ahead, try them on."

Marly adjusted the padded earpieces to perfectly cup her ears. The lightweight design was much less cumbersome than the old pair and let her move more freely. Volume adjustments on each earpiece were state of the art, and the overall professional styling would keep her hair from becoming entangled.

"They look great on you," I said.

"WHAT?"

We laughed and she gave me a hug.

The show proceeded apace. Every time I looked at her and saw the new headphones, I smiled. I had great respect for her talent and professionalism. If the station wouldn't get her what she needed, well, I could help a little. I popped in some CDs, something we hadn't done in a long time, and played new tunes by local artists Lisa Sanders and Celeste Barbier to elicit conversation unrelated to the bomb threats. I thought I did a good job of letting the right callers on the air. It was a relief to think about other subjects for a change.

Right before the show ended, Marly and I saw Agent Emerson lugging a heavy briefcase through the hallway. After we signed off, we met her at Marly's office. She closed the door and we all sat down. Judging by the look on Emerson's face, we were in for a sobering lecture. She removed a large folder from her case and laid it on the desk in front of us.

"I'm going to show you pictures," she said. "Tell me if any of these faces look familiar to you." She sat at an angle where she could watch our reaction.

Marly opened the black leatherette cover. We slowly perused the photos protected behind clear acetate. Some were mug shots. Others were photos taken in a variety of settings: a park, an office, at a restaurant, and in a parking lot. All were men. By the last page, I had not recognized any of the faces. In general, strangers don't stand out for me, and I hoped I had not disappointed by being inattentive to my surroundings. Marly shrugged—nothing for her.

Agent Emerson put the folder back in her case and pulled out a second. "Notice," she said, "that the first book showed only one man per photo. This next set has group shots in it. Now, take your time."

We flipped over a few pages before we both recognized a familiar face—Ivy O'Neal. She stood in front of an abortion clinic, her mouth frozen in mid-yell as if leading a chant with the group of protesters who filled out the picture. Except for the pastor at Ivy's church who carried a protest sign, Marly did not recognize anyone else in the photo. Marly and I looked at each other.

"Don't jump to conclusions," Agent Emerson advised. "Please, focus on the pictures."

After a dozen more photos, Marly pointed at a crowd scene. "Hey, here's a picture of us in Balboa Park for that Labor Day thing."

I took a closer look. "I remember some of those people," I said. "I walked through the crowd trying to get people to go on the air."

"Some of my friends are in this batch," Marly said. "And this big guy, his back is turned, but it looks like Glover Hayes. Hard to miss that physique. But I don't remember seeing him that day."

I turned the page. "Who's this tall, skinny guy? He's in a lot of these pictures." Emerson didn't answer. No one else looked familiar. On the last page was another picture of the tall, thin man we had seen earlier. He was standing with our office manager.

"Is that Betty's husband?" I asked. "Why are you showing us these pictures? Who took these?" I moved my chair back as far as I could in the cramped confines of the office.

Agent Emerson looked unfazed. "Oh, he's just a friend of Betty's."

If her comment was meant to assure me of something, I didn't know what it could be. I felt vulnerable, like a young teenager home alone who hears a floorboard creak. Someone was out there, and I felt I was being watched.

"If you don't recognize any of these people, it's okay. You need to be honest," she said. Marly and I concurred; we couldn't be of much help.

We tried to pump Emerson for information, but it was useless. Nothing could pry a word about the investigation from her lips. Her petite stature and unassuming looks seemed incongruent compared to the cumbersome albums of potential suspects she dropped back into her briefcase.

I watched her disappear out the door and turned to Marly. "I don't know about you," I murmured, "but I've got a strong case of the creeps."

Chapter Forty-four

There was a certain mystery to Agent Emerson's appearance at our office. In an indirect way, she had called our attention to several unfamiliar males who could be behind the bomb threats. What I didn't understand was if she had already zeroed in on one or two individuals, why was she parading them past our eyes? And why did she show us a picture of Betty and her friend? Every time I thought about it, the creepy feeling returned. Marly and I talked about the photos, but she was not especially interested in prying into the minutiae. That, she said, was the FBI's job.

Sleep did not come easy. I was tired the next day and felt the show dragged. I couldn't wait until five o'clock, and then I didn't want to go home alone. I invited Marly to my apartment on the pretext we needed to plan Betty's going-away party. If we procrastinated any further, the day would be upon us and we would be unprepared.

At my apartment I got out a yellow pad and the two of us sat together on the sofa. The event would have to take place in the employee lounge. In addition to the employees, there were a number of vendors added to the list. Our simulcast with *The Glover Hayes Show* would start at eleven and end at noon, which would allow us time to pick up food and decorate the room if we were quick about it. From the budget

Fred had given us, we allocated set amounts for food, decorations, and flowers. In addition, we decided an engraved plaque would make a nice presentation. Earlier in the day I had run these ideas past Fred, who agreed and added to our allowance. A personal gift would also be in order, assuming we could think of something appropriate—not the circumcised cucumber Marly suggested.

We divvied up the jobs. Marly agreed to arrange for food trays to be picked up the day of the event, which we planned to delegate to a co-worker. I offered to shop and to make discreet inquiries among the staff about a suitable gift for a send-off. Menu planning stirred our appetites; I ordered a pizza to be delivered to my apartment. I made two revised to-do lists and gave one to Marly. At my suggestion, we reviewed the event once more to be sure we hadn't overlooked anything important.

The work done, I took out my guitar. "You need a theme song for *Gayline*," I said. "Listen to these intros I wrote." I played a couple for her and she nodded along. "I saved the best one for last." I grabbed a pick and strummed a few bars with a quick build to a crescendo. "*GAYLINE!*" Three sweeps, down—up—down, and I was done.

"Ooh, I like it. Got any more hidden talents?" she asked while peeking down the front of my sweater. I set the guitar in its case. We tussled and kissed and laughed as sofa cushions ended up on the floor. The doorbell rang.

"Mmmm, food!" I sprang to my feet and opened the door. "Ted! What are you doing here?" My face stiffened and my eyes widened.

"Hi, Claire. You don't look too happy to see me.

I probably should have called. May I come in?"

I didn't know what to say, and although I stalled a second, I let him pass.

He looked at Marly, who stood by the sofa. Her disheveled hair and the cushions in disarray told a story. I hastily ran my fingers through my hair, not knowing how I looked.

Marly wiped her hands on her jeans as if she had been cleaning. "So, you're Ted." She extended her hand and walked toward him. "I'm Marly. I've heard a lot about you."

Ted shook her hand. "Yes, I've heard about you, too."

The silence in the room became thick and heavy, making it hard for us to move or speak. I didn't know why Ted had come, and he was not giving me any clues.

I had to break the awkward silence. "We're having pizza." I laughed unnaturally. "What brings you by?"

"Pizza?" He looked around the room. "Right. I thought we should talk, but I can see you're busy. I don't want to break up your pizza party."

I did not feel compelled to explain myself further. "Next time," I said, "you should call first."

"Next time," he said as he raised his voice. "I won't come!" He walked toward the door.

"I'm entitled to have a life, you know!" I yelled at his back.

He turned at the doorway. "What about *our* life? Did you think you could throw it away? Huh? And what about Jenny?" He pounded his fist into his other hand. "She's your daughter. Some kind of mom you turned out to be."

"And she'll always be my daughter. But you won't always be my husband."

With a grunt and a dirty look aimed at Marly, Ted stormed out of the apartment and collided with the pizza delivery man outside the front door. Ted marched on, indifferent to the pizza-warming box that had flipped into the air. The young man was unable to catch it. He snatched it from the ground where it had landed upside down. He apologized.

"That's okay," I said. "It's not your fault." I gave him a five-dollar tip.

Chapter Forty-five

At work the next day I made several stupid errors. Playing the wrong ad wasn't as bad as the twelve seconds of dead air we had until I realized the feed from the number two cart was switched off. My headache could have been from slapping myself in the forehead for all the mistakes I made. Ugh! Stress! By the third hour, I had regained control. Marly knew I wasn't myself and naturally carried the show.

I answered the phone off the air and ran carts while focusing on Marly's banter. Listening steadily boosted my confidence. I screened several calls to find an enlightened viewpoint on the subject at hand: gay student clubs in high school.

"*Gayline*, what's the nature of your call?" I asked.

"Mrs. Larson? Is that you?"

I paused. It was a girl's voice. No one called me Mrs. Larson at the station.

"Hello, Mrs. Larson? It's me, Amber, Jennifer's friend."

"Amber! What a surprise. Is everything okay? You're not calling about Jenny, are you?"

"No, she's fine. I was wondering if you would let me say something on the radio."

Jenny had mentioned that Amber listened to the show. I looked at the clock, almost half past eleven. It must have been her lunch break from school. I agreed to patch her through.

"Marly, we have Amber on the line."

"Hey, Amber, welcome to *Gayline*."

"Hi! Wow, thanks for taking my call. I'm sixteen and I go to high school. We don't have, um, a gay club at school or a gay alliance or anything, and we don't have a religious club either. They won't let us do anything controversial anymore. But I wish we had a club because we need one. There's a bunch of gay kids at my school and they get picked on a lot. It's hard to be gay, and I think they need support from the other kids who are gay, and understanding from the ones who aren't. Some of the guys are depressed and other ones put on this phony act. I know there are kids who are afraid and hide who they are, but I don't want to hide. I told my parents this morning."

I listened intently to Jenny's friend whom I had known for years. I could see her in my mind's eye as she looked a few years ago with beribboned braids, and then as I had seen her recently looking more mature. I was stunned by her admission and felt badly about the times I had put her off. Surely this was what she had wanted to tell me on several occasions, yet even if I had realized it on a subconscious level, it was too difficult for me to deal with her face-to-face. I hoped her parents had taken it well, and I wondered how I would ever get up the nerve to tell my own.

"You are very brave," Marly told Amber. "I know it isn't easy to say these things, especially on the radio. Your courage is commendable."

"Well, um, the other reason I called was to thank you, Marly, but mostly Mrs. Larson. She's the one who gave me the courage to say something. She has more courage than I do."

I was too choked up to reply. Maybe I hadn't

failed her after all. I had unwittingly led by example. So often, I wanted to believe that callers didn't know if I was gay, although I knew many assumed I was. Marly's comments about my sexuality had to be taken with a grain of salt, but I never refuted her audacious claims of my supposed behavior, and at times played up to it.

I cleared my throat and turned on my mic. "Thank you, Amber. I'm sorry we couldn't talk about it before today. How did your parents respond when you told them?"

"They were okay. My dad rolled his eyes, but my mom hugged me and said she wasn't surprised, that she wasn't sure what was bothering me. I know things are going to be a lot better now."

"Yes, I'm sure of it. I'm giving you a hug over the phone, dear."

Marly appeared touched by the call. Again, she praised Amber's courage for publicly coming out. I ran the bottom-of-the-hour ID and four commercials, one on a cart and three on CD, a tricky maneuver considering our CD player only held one CD at a time. Advertisers were paying more money to be heard on our show, and judging by the improvement in production value, they were paying more to produce their ads. Marly read a PSA for the San Diego Blood Bank and segued into the community calendar.

I put off a few callers who wanted to continue with the previous topic. Because Amber was a family friend, her revelation, though broadcast to thousands of listeners, seemed personal to me and I was reluctant to discuss her "private" matter with strangers who might happen to call in. While Marly read a list of upcoming events, it gave me a chance to think about

Amber's recent behavior.

Other than the fact she had tried to speak to me in confidence, I had not detected anything different about her. To me, she seemed to be a typical teenaged girl. Over coffee the other day with Jennifer we had talked about school, the environment, and driver's permits. It made me feel closer to her. I felt compassion and empathy, but most of all I wished her an easier time. At least the kids were talking about homosexuality, understanding it better. Times had changed since I was her age. I could only wonder how my life would have been different if I had known then what I knew now.

Marly was concluding her announcements, so I snapped out of my reverie to take another call.

"*Gayline*. What's on your mind?"

"Get out before it explodes!"

My adrenaline shot up. The voice was unfamiliar—a copycat!

"Hey! Wake up! This is a bomb threat!"

The man spoke in a squeaky falsetto similar to what you might hear on an animated TV show. There was an attempt at an accent, but it sounded totally fake, too. We had about fifteen minutes left in the show and I wasn't sure what to do. We couldn't draw the blinds like we had done before. Fred would want us to leave the building, copycat or not. I thought about keeping him on the line, for what, I wasn't sure, and I certainly wasn't going to put him on the air. I remembered Agent Emerson's book of photos. How could I know who was the real bomber and who was a copycat? I grimaced and decided to play it safe. Before I loaded in a music CD, I looked at the incoming phone number on the black box.

"*Ted!* What the hell do you think you're doing?" I broke into a sweat as he remained silent. "Ted, I know it's you. This is *not* funny." I turned away from Marly, furious. "Ted, stop playing games. Say something!"

"How did you know it was me?" The phony voice was gone, but he did not sound like himself.

"We've got caller ID. I recognized your number. You idiot. This is so not okay—and illegal. What is the matter with you? Have you lost your mind?" I paused, and when he said nothing, I continued. "Ted, if I hadn't figured out it was you, you could've gotten arrested. Why are you doing this?" More silence. I could hear his breath coming over the wire in short huffy snorts. I waited for what seemed like a long time.

"I couldn't take it anymore." His voice cracked as he spoke. "I was listening and I heard Amber. What's happening? Is everyone gay? Are she and Jenny... What about our son? I can't take it." He was sobbing. "Everything's upside down. Why does it have to be this way?"

Now I was the silent one.

Chapter Forty-six

After another silent pause, I said good-bye and quietly replaced the phone receiver in its cradle. Marly shot me a wild questioning look and pointed at her watch. I had no idea what was happening with our show. Should I take a caller? Was it time to run an ad? I turned up the sound on my cans. Marly could sense I was lost. Never one to let dead air take over, she picked up a flyer and mentioned an upcoming poetry slam while I gathered my wits about me. I scanned the log, found the few remaining commercial carts, and loaded them in order with the top-of-the-hour ID in last. Marly signed off and I hit the "Play" button. The show was over, and I made sure our mics were off.

She opened the door between us. "Hello. Anybody in there?"

"I'm sorry. I hope I didn't mess up too badly."

"Who was on the phone?"

I couldn't look her in the eye. The second ad ended and I started up the next. Marly shifted her weight onto one foot and stood with her arms crossed, waiting for the station ID to finish. Another jock in Studio C read a teaser for the upcoming newsbreak as I turned off our equipment and the aircheck tape.

"Well?"

"It was a copycat."

"Oh! He wasn't on the air so we don't have his

voice on tape."

"No."

"That's okay, we have the phone number."

"No!" I contorted my face. "It was nothing, um, nobody. It was Ted. Please don't say anything. It was a mistake. He won't do it again, I promise."

"Ted? Oh, great. Personally, Claire, I never make promises when it comes to other people's behavior. I'll see you after lunch." She gathered a few items and left the studio.

I dawdled for a few moments and left. Outside, the fresh moist air felt good in my lungs. I headed down the road to my apartment, but on impulse stopped at a taco stand. Crunching my way through a plate of nachos released tension, but I didn't taste much except for the jalapeños. Afterward, I felt tired. My lips stung. As I watched cars go by, I thought about what had happened. If the copycat had been someone other than Ted, I'm not sure what I would have done. But it was he. I felt sorry for the anguish he felt. I had been through my own inner conflict, now it was his turn. I could not release him from it. He would have to work it out on his own.

I put in a quick call to Deena and told her what happened.

"I'm sorry it's come to this," she said. "I'm not used to putting the words 'Ted' and 'freaking out' in the same sentence. I think of him as being so even, but…I guess when you push someone hard enough, they're going to react."

"It was sad. He sounded so torn, so confused. I feel badly and now I have to face Marly."

"Hey, you're not the one who called in a bomb threat."

"Sometimes it feels like it."

Deena was quiet. "Hmmm. Like you blew up your family? You have to stop feeling guilty. I thought you had gotten over that."

"I still have shreds."

"I think you're doing remarkably well. Give yourself some credit. You've made huge progress. I love you."

"Thanks. Love you, too. I have to get back to work."

Whatever relief I felt talking to Deena disappeared when I met Marly back at her office. She seemed distant and I wasn't sure she wanted to close the gap. As we each tended to our workstations, I could feel her drifting away. With each passing moment of silence, the space between us grew wider until I felt she had all but vanished from the room. The chasm expanded to the depths of the Grand Canyon until I feared my loudest screams would disappear into the void. The separateness of my own body felt confining as if my skin had shrunk tight. I felt itchy and scratched my arm to break the barrier. I had to break free of myself. *Out! Let me out!* I was ready to explode like a bomb.

"Will you stop scratching? You're driving me nuts."

Her voice shattered the taut invisible wall around me. We looked at one another, each of us startled by her outburst. I was back in the room aware of my surroundings. Angry red marks lined my arms in discernible rows.

"Claire, do you think we can get some work done now? Glover's intern called while you were out. He says Glover has a quiz planned for us. Don't ask me what that's about. Anyway, we've allotted enough time to do his thing and ours. We can still fit everything in one hour, but we need to tidy up our loose ends so we'll be ready. Our timing is important. It's coming up fast, you know. You know?"

"Yes." I felt silly. She'd been waiting for me to speak and I for her. Somehow her words cut the bonds constricting my body. In its place I felt an expansive floating sensation that made my skin tingle. I rubbed out the redness on my arm.

I wanted to take her in, envelop her, be a part of her. I wanted to hold her and hold her and hold her. The change in my physical body was almost overwhelming. Marly's face had a clarity I had not noticed before. I wanted my hands in her hair. Last-minute computer work made time fly, but my thoughts kept drifting back to Marly, whose presence filled me. "Let's work at your house," I said. "I can't get anything more done here today."

We packed up a few needed items and drove to Pacific Beach. It was late afternoon. MayMay and Maelstrom greeted us with conversational meows. Marly and I cleared off the kitchen table while the kitties noisily devoured their food. I had organized everything on a yellow pad. Marly rolled her eyes and got her laptop from her home office. We role-played how we thought it would go on *The Glover Hayes Show* and tightened up our timeline. Our ideas flew back and forth as the cats chased one another around the house. With only two days left before our simulcast, there were still too many unknowns for my taste. Others were involved, Glover's intern, Cocoa Barr, and a woman I had never met, but I had to have faith it would all fall into place.

Refreshments in hand, Marly and I retired to the

sofa. Curled together on a side chair in the living area, MayMay licked Maelstrom's head. I reached over and stroked MayMay under the chin and lightly scratched behind her ears. As she purred, I realized I was not focusing my attention where I wanted it to go. I turned to Marly and kissed her squarely on the mouth. She responded in kind. Kissing her was wonderful. I couldn't get enough of the incredible feeling of her lips on mine, her face touching my face, her fingers intertwined with mine. I wanted to surround her with my energy.

I broke from our kiss and drank in her loveliness. Her dark shaggy hair was pleasingly unkempt. A hint of moisture glistened on her lower lip. Her mouth felt even more luscious than it looked, and as much as I was consumed with desire to kiss her again, I felt it would not be enough. My hands clenched her hair, and I realized the depth of the passion building inside me. I pulled her toward me and squeezed her tightly, as if I could somehow move through her. She kneaded the skin on my back in a way that told me we were thinking the same thoughts. I had to know.

I whispered lightly in her ear. "I love you, and… and I want you."

"Oh, Claire," she murmured. "I've waited so long for you to say those words, waited because I love you, too." She took my hand and led me to her bedroom.

Chapter Forty-seven

Marly and I walked hand in hand toward her bedroom, and as always, the door was closed. I thought back to the time when I had been cat-sitting. It wouldn't have been out of the question for me to take a peek, which of course I did, and maybe she assumed I nosed around her house as a matter of general curiosity, but we never talked about it. I felt a moment's hesitation and Marly sensed it.

"Are you sure you're okay with this?" she asked.

I nodded and smiled. I was ready.

She opened the door. Everything was exactly as I had remembered. On many occasions I had replayed the vision of this room in my head—unforgettable. It was getting dark and the deepening shadows in the room hid its true nature. I wasn't sure what to do, nor could I admit to feeling slightly intimidated. Marly went to the window and allowed the drape to fall in front of the sheers. She lit a candle. In the soft glow, the room began to reform into familiar shapes and muted color. The dark wood furniture seemed almost black in the dim light and I could barely make out the fine detail at the top of the armoire.

She came to me and kissed my hand. We slowly embraced in a warmer version of the many hugs we had shared. She brushed her lips across my neck and chest and leisurely unbuttoned my shirt. My breathing became shallow and I was almost afraid to move my body. She ran her fingertips along the lace outlining the top of my bra and on my matching underpants where they poked above my jeans. I unbuttoned her shirt, a lightweight sleeveless denim with a pointed collar. There was nothing between her and her shirt. I could feel a change in my body, a stirring between my legs as the candlelight illuminated her beautiful round curves teasing me beneath her top. I eased my hands underneath to touch her soft breasts as I had imagined doing so many times. Her nipples hardened as I passed over them. As we kissed again, I slipped her top over her shoulders and let it fall silently to the floor. With an experienced twitch, she unhooked my bra. I breathed in deeply, paused an expectant moment, and exhaled slowly while she removed my shirt and bra and draped them over a padded wooden chair by the antique dressing table.

 I did not feel shy about our nakedness even when I caught a glimpse of our reflection in the wall mirror. Despite our slight difference in height, our nipples met together. She put her hands on my waist and began an erotic dance with her upper body. Our breasts moved together, each massaging the other with tender passion. I followed her moves. We kissed again. The sensation of skin on skin set my heart racing. I combed my fingers through her thick hair as she kissed my face and inched down my neck to the slight depression at the bottom of my throat. She gently cupped my breasts and suckled one, pressing her tongue around my areola. It was intense, divine! In a fit of passion, I clenched her hair as she thrilled me with each sweep of her tongue. A warm sensation traveled up my spine and I began to lose myself in her touch. My grip eased, and I stroked her dark shaggy locks into a lion's mane and back smooth again.

Again, Marly took my hand and escorted me the few steps to her bed. A filmy gauze drape suspended from a carved wooden frame above the bed enclosed the bedchamber. The material was divided into four parts, each covering a corner of the bed. She reached in and wrapped the gossamer material first around one section, then the other of the two posts at the foot of the bed.

The platform itself was a little higher off the floor than most. I had gotten used to the light and could see more detail with the bed curtain parted. A gracefully carved headboard was partially obscured by pillows. We kicked off our shoes as she guided me onto the bed over the sumptuous burgundy-and-gold flowered print spread and pulled back the cover to reveal gold-colored sheets with matching floral print trim. The threads felt satiny smooth underneath my skin. I felt pampered by merely being on the bed. We pushed a few cylindrical toss pillows aside to allow more room for ourselves. I could not imagine anyone not wanting to share her bed.

She propped me near the headboard and made sure the remaining pillows supported my back. I let her take the lead because I sensed that was her preference. Also, I felt more comfortable receiving her experienced hands and less sure about the art of loving her. She reclined next to me and let her fingers glide lightly up and down my bare skin. Her delicate touch was unlike anything I had ever felt. It astonished me, as I had always thought of Marly as bold, certain, definitive in her actions. Gently caressing, she showered my whole body with her nurturing touch, exhibiting an unexpected softness of spirit. I felt cared for, as if every square inch of my being was of great concern to her.

I could lie back only so long. I needed to touch her in return and soon we were locked in a passionate, undulating embrace. She reached between us and unfastened the button to my jeans. I heard the zipper slide. Her movements were deft, yet her attentiveness made me feel as if she had been practicing for me. I helped her slide off my jeans. Then she removed hers and dropped them onto the floor.

Her hand snaked along my leg and up my body. I luxuriated in her touch as I closed my eyes and felt her loving caress. The scent of the candle, jasmine with a light vanilla undertone, wafted lazily in the air. Its delicious aroma mixed well with Marly's natural scent, which I inhaled deeply. Mimicking her delicate touch, I floated my hands along her voluptuous curves. Desire surged within me as I discovered the sexy thong running between her legs. She slipped her hand beneath my panties and slid them off. Tenderly, she let her lips drift along the length of my body, kissing me from head to toe, exciting me to move rhythmically in a sensuous dance. She licked my neck and breasts until I moaned with pleasure. My breath quickened as I allowed myself to take in these long-sought moments that had finally arrived.

With thumb and forefinger, she teased me by twisting the curls of hair between my legs. My muscles tensed in anticipation. Slowly her fingertips moved into my private crease, the slick moisture facilitating her movements. A small sound escaped from my throat, a truncated note signaling a tiny portion of the incredible sensations unfolding inside me. I shifted my leg aside, opening myself to her. She relaxed me into a dream—a wonderful dream. And when I thought the dream could not possibly become more exquisite, she bathed me with her tongue. My legs tightened, my toes curled under, and I alternately grabbed and let go her thick mop of hair, her silken strokes unbinding human bonds until my goddess within released with a prolonged panting cry of delight.

A little later when I had recovered somewhat, I did my best to return the favor, taking my time as she had with me. My past fantasies were nothing compared to the reality of her soft skin beneath my hands. My senses remained heightened as I explored the sensuous sweep of her back where it curved into her behind. When I turned her over, her breasts, round and pert, flattened slightly in circular perfection. My thirst for her could not be slaked until I sipped her nectarous flower that was now ours to share. She tensed and squirmed, quieted and rocked herself, her moans a sweet melody, her breathing a syncopated rhythm, her cries an exultant refrain of joyous celebration. We lay together in satisfied exhaustion wrapped in each other's arms. Light sleep gave us momentary rest. When we were inclined to speak, our words were brief—of love, delight, and fantastic pleasure. Our desire opened like a rose, and we were moved to act upon it again and again until the candle grew tired and died.

Chapter Forty-eight

I awoke on Thursday morning to her feather touch along my breast. In half sleep I savored the sensation as I drifted in and out until the light peeking from an open sliver in the curtains caused me to turn my eyes away. I rolled onto my side toward her. A guttural purr vibrated through my throat as my hand rolled over her womanly curves. We held one another and slept again, though I was conscious of her body warming my skin where we touched. In the back of my mind, I was concerned about the time.

Maelstrom and MayMay meowed impatiently outside the bedroom, prompting Marly to sigh. She got up. On her way out, she pushed the curtain aside a few inches to let in the natural light. I recognized sounds as she knocked around the kitchen: the light tinkling of the kibble as it hit the food bowl, running water, steam escaping from the coffeemaker. She returned with a tray carrying two mugs, a carafe of coffee, and a hunk of coffee cake.

"I hope you don't mind," she said. "It's a little stale."

"No."

"And I'm out of milk."

I smiled. We breakfasted in bed, sharing contented glances between sips of the strong brew.

"Delicious." I winked at her.

"You can't mean the coffee cake."

"No."

We set the dishes aside on the tray and, propped by pillows, lounged in bed gazing at one another. To an outsider, we would have appeared like two lovesick puppies. It did not feel silly to me. I had held back for months waiting to see if our love was real, if it would be substantiated by our whole personalities and not simply by lust.

"I love you," I whispered.

"And I love you."

We fell together in an embrace. Love fueled our passions. It was incredible to me that I could feel so satisfied yet want her again. Our play had not turned serious when her cell phone alarm trilled like an old-fashioned alarm clock. She reached over and shut off the unwelcome nuisance.

"Aargh!" I did not want the little time we had to end.

"We ate already, so we have a few minutes," she murmured in my ear.

Seeing her pale skin so close to mine sent a warm tingle between my legs. For the first time since I started at KZSD I regretted we had a job that could not wait. We could not call in sick or say we were running late. We massaged and caressed one another until we could not postpone getting out of bed one second longer. She threw me a silk robe from the armoire. It was beautiful, fuchsia with black trim. The room was beautiful; I felt beautiful. My tears welled as we shuffled toward the bathroom.

Marly adjusted the water temperature in the shower before we stepped in. I circled the rosemary-scented glycerin soap along her body letting it foam playfully across her nipples, and moved in close. It was wonderfully erotic to feel her slippery body next to mine.

The inner shower curtain momentarily clung to my ankle and I pushed it against the side of the tub with my toe. "Why is it," I murmured in her ear, "that your bathroom and bedroom are so gorgeous? Well, you know, it's not like the rest of your house."

"I'm glad you approve of my decorating," she said as she lightly scrubbed my back with her short nails. "I'm not exactly Suzy Homemaker, but I like nice stuff as much as the next person. For now, they're the only two rooms I can stay after. Maybe when the cats are gone I'll do my office."

She ran her soapy hands up and down my legs and then carefully in between, followed by a thorough rinse with the handheld showerhead. If it weren't for the coffee kicking in and the fact we had to be at the station, I am sure I could have reveled all day in the drug-like stupor of our love. Work could not be ignored. Stopping our lovemaking was a momentary break, as I knew our journey had only begun.

Once we were at KZSD, it took a concerted effort on my part to focus on the daily log sheet in Studio B, and as I watched Marly, I could see she was moving much slower than usual. A creature of habit, I relied on my routine to get me through the show. I located and lined up my ad carts and CDs, and set aside music we could play in case we were at a loss for words. As we listened to the end of Zach's show, I looked at Marly through the glass partition and mouthed the three words that flowed through my mind like an endless river. She repeated the silent refrain, "I love you."

Fortunately, we had finished planning for *The Glover Hayes Show* because neither of us could concentrate very well. We managed to get through the first hour of *Gayline* without any major errors. Callers baited us in an effort to leak our plans for Friday's simulcast, but we did not give away our secret. The element of surprise was a necessary ingredient if Glover was to stew in his own juice. I had to believe everything would go as planned, even though we would be on his turf at KQEW. I felt giddy yet relaxed, and wondered if my strength would be sufficiently renewed by tomorrow. Thinking how Marly and I had sated each other in bed left me feeling dreamy. Many times I glanced her way only to find her already looking at me, sharing a smile of contentment. She did perk up, but her characteristic edginess was softened. She launched a few rejoinders and I came up with a couple myself. In the third hour we lost momentum. We had peaked early. The CDs came in handy; the music gave us a break.

After the show, I went home to change clothes and eat. As I removed my shirt, I caught a whiff of her scented soap on my skin. A slow smile spread across my face. I broke from preparing lunch to answer a familiar ringtone.

"Hello."

"Hi. It's me," he said. "Ted."

"Yes, I know."

"You probably don't want me calling you at work anymore, and I don't blame you. I called to say I'm sorry."

"You should be." I don't believe my voice carried the animosity it could have given his behavior. My response was matter-of-fact and I no longer felt guilty.

"What I did was wrong. I want you to understand

what drove me to do it. I've calmed down since then." He sounded repentant, but I was skeptical. It was possible he had a hidden agenda. "I tried to call you last night, but you weren't answering your phone."

I was inclined to hang up rather than risk a return to a former argument. "I'm listening."

"I know you have a life," he said. "It's so hard for me to accept that it's not with me. But it's not, and it's not going to be." His voice sounded strained, like he was on the verge of tears. "I want you to know, I've never talked to an attorney about us. If you want to file for divorce, I won't fight you. I know you loved me once, and I know this isn't about if you still love me or not. You've changed and we can't be together. I still love you and I want you to be happy. I guess it doesn't matter what I want because you need to be with someone else. There, I said it."

As a long silence passed between us, I could feel my throat tighten. His words were unexpected and also utterly believable.

"I know this isn't an easy call for you," I said. "The past nine months..." I did not want to sound patronizing, and considered my words. "I guess I should find a lawyer, or maybe a mediator. We don't have to make this nasty."

"It's never going to get any easier so we might as well get it over with," he said. "And I don't want Jennifer dragged through any more arguments. It's been hard on her, too."

"Yes, I know."

"Speaking of Jennifer, I'm asking this one last thing. Please don't tell her about my call to your show...what I said. Please? Will you do that for me?"

"Yes."

Chapter Forty-nine

Marly and I met in her office after lunch, working in silence in separate chairs, unified. Though she had satisfied me completely, I could feel a new energy beginning to stir and could not be sure if it was in anticipation of our appearance the next day on *The Glover Hayes Show* at KQEW, or if it was the thought of our next encounter in her wonderful bedchamber with the gossamer curtains billowing lightly from the ocean breeze. While most of our plans were in place, we had to tie up various loose ends. Marly had to run a few errands before meeting me at Glover's studio tomorrow, and I wanted to make sure the *Gayline* website had been updated properly.

Before leaving, she closed the office door with us inside, and in our moment of privacy we shared a lingering embrace peppered with passionate kisses. I held her until the scent of her hair and skin became ingrained upon my memory. It was time to part. We each had work that could not wait, and in order to be prepared and alert the next morning, we reluctantly decided to sleep apart.

When my lists were all written and I finished my calls, I grabbed dinner, drove to my old home, and picked up Jenny. It was a little chilly outside, but we decided to go for ice cream. I tried her Macadamia Nut Fudge and she tasted a spoonful of my Coffee Mocha.

"Did Dad tell you we talked?" I asked.

"Sort of. He said you were going to call a lawyer."

"Yes." I confirmed with a nod. "I'll be making inquiries. It's time."

"Yeah, I figured." She sounded dejected. "I knew you weren't coming home. Did you decide if you're going to stay at that apartment? What's going to happen to our house? Are you and Dad gonna have to sell it?"

"I don't know, honey. We haven't discussed it."

"How can I live with you if you only have one bedroom?"

I set my cup down on the bench where we sat, reached around Jenny, and gave her a hug.

"These are all important questions, and I wish I had the answers for you. Are you unhappy with Dad?"

"No, but I miss you."

"I miss you, too. I guess I'm surprised you'd want to live with me. When this all started, you were so angry and unhappy. It broke my heart. I never wanted to hurt you."

"I'm still not happy about it, but I get it. Amber told me she called you on *Gayline*. I'm proud of you, Mom. She's been talking about being gay for a long time, before anything happened with you. At first, I'm thinking like, whoa! My best friend and my mom? How random is that? Anyway, it doesn't seem so odd anymore, and in a way it makes a lot of sense. Hey, maybe I could trade off with you and Dad, you know, like have a room in each of your houses."

"That's a possibility."

Later that evening after I dropped off Jennifer, I focused on all the important relationships jockeying for my attention. Despite the rocky road ahead, I knew Jenny was going to be all right. It made it easier for me to think about the future, no matter what Ted and I decided. And because Jonah was away at school, he was largely unaffected. He could concentrate on his studies without being dragged through the day-to-day emotional roller coaster that would surely begin with legal proceedings. His room at home was waiting for him when spring semester ended, giving him a quick snapshot of family time before going off again for summer sessions. It seemed to me our son had the easiest time of it. He understood from the beginning this was our lot and he did not fight it. I wished I could have learned from him, but I had to work through my conflict to make my own peace.

Ted had made strides to cross the gap bridging the broken pieces of our marriage. I saw how hard it was for him, experienced it with him. He had made important progress that would undoubtedly help us get through the next step—our divorce. I envisioned myself going through the motions required to begin proceedings, something I had not been able to do in the past.

Even if Marly had not been in the picture, I was sure Ted and I would have chosen to divorce. I had not expected to find a relationship because I hadn't been looking. I needed a woman in my life, and thankfully Marly was there. Her presence clarified more quickly the direction my life would inevitably take. Knowing she was there would help me move my divorce plans forward. I was grateful for the time Marly and I had already spent together, and I looked forward to the time ahead, whether a month, a year, or a lifetime. Poised on the brink of unknowing, my marriage apart, unsure of my daughter's custody, and with a big day ahead—which I prayed would not be lambs to the slaughter—I drifted off into deep slumber.

Chapter Fifty

A TV van blocked the front entrance to KQEW AM 1410. Crew members milled about, clipboards tucked under their arms. I should have guessed. After all, Glover's station was tied in with Channel 67. Somehow I had convinced myself that even though the event had been well publicized, all the action would take place within the relative privacy of Glover's studio. I was wrong. I recognized the white KZSD van parked near a side entrance with its antenna perched high overhead, yet our presence seemed secondary. The additional media exposure got my adrenaline going, and I felt a moment of panic. However, I was determined not to be overwhelmed as I would have become in the not too distant past. Fear was the enemy, but I had tools to protect myself.

"Claire Larson?"

I turned. A man broke away from a crowd of bystanders. My armor snapped into place and a wave of paranoia took my breath away until I realized that given the scene, it was likely reporters would be looking for me. Thank goodness I had worn something decent. The man hailed a burly woman who balanced a mini-cam on her shoulder. It looked heavy, yet she deftly focused the lens while the camera remained stable. The reporter, whose hair was expertly sprayed in place, made sure his tie was straight and without first asking my permission, gave the cue to roll. Here was someone who was used to getting what he wanted, probably a lot like Glover. I was tempted to bolt, but the exposure for *Gayline* was too valuable and I had come prepared for whatever might happen. It was better to play along, even though I wasn't sure what game we were playing.

"Hi, I'm here with Claire Larson, better known as Marly's vocal call screener on *Gayline*. Tell me, what do you hope to accomplish today?"

I had no idea if we were being taped for later or if we were live. If the reporter had told me his name, I had forgotten it. I did not know if he was biased and wondered if this was a total setup. I felt a warmth rush through my body, and my forehead immediately broke into a sweat. He had already shoved the mic under my nose. I could not fall to an early ambush and yet my thoughts strayed to the camerawoman, who I sensed was gay. There was no time to congratulate myself for having my gaydar kick in, or wonder if I was having what might be the first of many stress-induced hot flashes. To avoid coming across as a dimwit, I swallowed, blinked hard, and gave it my best shot.

"We're here to have fun, that's all," I said, forcing a smile.

"There's talk that this so-called showdown is too lopsided. Glover's in the big leagues. As newcomers, do you think you'll have a chance to shine?"

"I think listeners will make up their own minds when they hear the show. I have to go in now. Thanks for your interest. Bye!"

I turned quickly and made a break for the building.

"Wait! Well, I guess she was in a hurry..."

His words trailed off as I strode into the crowded

lobby of KQEW. I scanned the group for Marly, but she was nowhere in sight. I quietly introduced myself to the receptionist, who asked me to take a seat—a laughable prospect. I had no idea who all the people were or why they were there. I feared they also had something to do with our showdown. When a seat became available, I darted toward it like a kid playing musical chairs. Though the game was just beginning, I wanted the whole thing to be over with as soon as possible. I waited for Marly, and waited, and waited.

My presence in the lobby was fairly inconspicuous. Most of those standing could not see me. I tried to calm myself down, first by breathing slowly, then by counting each long second. I wished I could call it off and go home. I was terrified we were in way over our heads.

"Mrs. Larson?"

A portly man with a kind expression stood before me. His image, plastered on buses, billboards, and in newspaper ads, made him instantly recognizable.

"Mr. Hayes."

"None other! Come with me. I'll escort you out of this mob scene."

He offered his hand like a gentleman and helped me up. He ignored others in the lobby trying to get his attention. Someone buzzed us in through a locked doorway and we maneuvered through a maze of cubicles. It was much like any other office, and a world away from KZSD. The furnishings were modern and tastefully done, the walls a pretty eggshell. The din in the room was muted by ceiling tiles and a beige Berber twist carpet. The cubicles also had a smattering of color that picked up the colored flecks in the carpet. In comparison, I realized how small our building was—not to mention old, dingy, and lacking in aesthetic appeal. We reached a short hallway and turned a corner. Several studios came into view. Glover stopped at a glassed-in corner office, his name emblazoned in gold on the door. He opened it and allowed me to enter first. The door closed behind us and the nondescript mumble of office sounds disappeared into a vacuum of silence.

"Shall I have my girl get you some coffee?" he asked as he fell into a large brown leather chair. He held up a KQEW coffee mug imprinted with his likeness.

Said the spider to the fly. "Water, thanks."

I took a deep breath and sat down in one of the two available chairs. Woven fabric over thin foam covered the seat, and I had the sneaking suspicion these chairs had replaced more comfortable ones before my arrival. I wrapped my ankles around the metal legs. There was a long folding table set up between us. On top, two sets of headphones lay on their sides, ready for use. I handled one. It was of fine quality, generously padded and surprisingly lightweight. He swung open a wooden cabinet door. Inside was a small refrigerator stocked with soda and water. He handed me a bottled water along with another mug. I set the mug aside and sipped from the plastic bottle. As an afterthought, he took out a second bottle—for Marly?

"Nice office." Where *was* Marly?

"Thanks. I spend a lot of time here so I had this built especially to meet my needs. I also have a small bar beside the mini-fridge. I keep my papers handy over here," he said as he gestured to a neat filing system. "The computer's hooked up with Jimmy's. He's my assistant producer, kind of like you, except he's an intern. He helps me stay organized, screens calls and such, researches on the Internet, that kind of thing. See these two clocks?" he said, pointing above the doorway. "The one on the left is a twenty-four-hour clock that digitally counts down to my show. The other's real time, although we have a seven-second tape delay."

I nodded and looked around the room. Built-in wooden shelves were crammed with books, magazines, and a few awards. Framed certificates and pictures showing him with local politicians crowded the available wall space. His office seemed an odd place to do the show. Confused, I wondered if we were going to take our headphones to another location. Then I noticed his microphone positioned off to the side.

"Where's your board?" I asked.

"Ha! Glad you asked. Look at this."

He moved his keyboard and flipped a switch. A motorized whir commenced as the front half of his desktop dropped down and then slid backward, where it disappeared into a rear compartment. An operations board popped up in its place. I was stunned, yet managed to flash a phony smile. I could not let Glover get the upper hand before we started. He was showing off, and though I was intrigued by his setup, I did not want him to know it. If we were going to get through this, I would need to put on a powerful front, no matter what I felt inside. I would not let him or his fancy equipment make me feel inadequate.

"Of course, I rarely use it." Glover waved his hand dismissively. "Jimmy takes care of everything." He flipped the switch back. The operations board disappeared and he repositioned his computer keyboard over his desk.

I crossed my leg at the knee and my foot started to swing. I was hesitant to engage in small talk. Anything could be used against me. And when all was said and done, would we be the laughing stock of San Diego, or would we be able to casually joke about this episode as merely another radio prank?

Glover broke the silence. "You seem like a nice lady. How did you end up on *Gayline*?"

I didn't like the inference and I felt my smile harden. It was a cool reminder that Glover was my adversary. This was not the time to be nice for the sake of being a lady. I saw Marly come down the hall with a decided bounce to her step. A wave of relief took the edge off my grimace. Her escort opened the door and she jauntily made an entrance. In a strong short hug, all of her wonderful energy surged into me, and I felt emboldened by her presence. Marly plopped down in the available chair as Glover rose to shake her hand. She casually tossed a white bakery box on the table in front of us and she shook his hand as if it were an afterthought.

"Man! I thought I'd never get out of there," she said.

"Where?" I asked.

"Ivy's outside with her entourage. Can you believe it? Guess she wasn't going to waste the opportunity to show off those posters of hers. What a zoo! So, Glover, did you set that up?"

Marly was armed and ready to go. "Here." She untied the thin, white string and opened the box to reveal a few pastries. "Almond croissant for me and Claire." She laid the treats on a napkin. "And Glover, take your pick: chocolate donut with nuts, or jelly filled with sprinkles, or take them both."

"Had me figured for a donut man, eh? Well, you're right. I'll take chocolate."

He looked like he'd had his share over the years. "You have the build of a donut man," I muttered and flushed red.

"True enough." Glover did not seem offended as he took a big bite and washed it down with coffee.

I was not very hungry, but ate out of nervousness. It wouldn't hurt to have a few extra carbohydrates, which is probably why Marly brought them in. If I was going to throw barbs, I had to be fortified.

A well-groomed young man opened the door. "You're on in ten," he said.

"This is my intern, Jimmy. He's my assistant producer. He works over there." Glover pointed to another glassed-in office across the hall. "This is Marly and Claire." We shook hands and he winked.

Marly hit the record feature on her phone. "Hey, Glover," Marly asked with a casual air, "you don't mind if I take a little video or some photos while we're here, do you? I want something to post on my sites."

"No, go ahead."

She handed Jimmy her cell phone and he took a few photos.

"We need to do the sound check. Excuse me." Jimmy went across the hall and put on his cans.

Glover stuffed his mouth with food. His donut disappeared and he started on the second. In a few bites it was gone, too. We plugged in our headphones and took a couple of minutes to get our mics adjusted during the sound check. I felt strange sitting behind a table in someone else's office with no sliders in front of me. Conversely, I could concentrate on what was being said and not have to worry about running the board.

Glover put on his headset and adjusted his computer screen, which I could not read. It seemed an unfair advantage. Everything appeared to be to his advantage. It was his office. He was the bigger opponent in terms of ratings. Why he felt compelled to bother with us was still a bit of a mystery to me, unless his huge ego needed reinforcement. On the other hand, judging by the additional media exposure, this event was turning out to be more important for him than I first realized. He must have wanted the boost in ratings. In any case, his equipment and setup were state of the art, and Jimmy had control over which listeners would be patched through during the show. We knew nothing of the quiz Glover had planned, but undoubtedly he would try to get the better of us at every turn. On impulse I grabbed Marly's hand and gave it a squeeze. She grinned broadly at me as if to convey she had enough confidence for us both.

We had a few things going in our favor. Cocoa Barr and Marly's friend, Kim, would be arriving shortly—the sooner the better. If they were late or got caught in the media circus outside, then we were in big trouble. However, no one knew who they were so they wouldn't be stopped for interviews. I had to believe everything would be okay.

Also in our favor, Marly and I made a great team. We had performed well in Studio B, and I had every reason to believe we would hold our own. The digital clock on the wall marked down the seconds—four, three, two, one. As the red on-air light illuminated in a brilliant flash, an energy jolt rocketed up my spine.

Chapter Fifty-one

The top-of-the-hour ID sounded clear and crisp through my headphones, which were far superior to the expensive ones I had given Marly. A mixed chorus sang out the call letters, "KQEW AM 1410, the Big Q! Your twenty-four-hour station for news, talk, sports, and more." A teaser for the news was followed by several ads. I looked around to the other studios but did not see anyone actually reading the news. Across the hall, I could see Jimmy running the board. His head was down and his arms moved as if he were conducting an orchestra.

My notepad was in my purse and I scrambled to get it out. I gave a pen to Marly and kept one for myself. Marly laughed. Jimmy cued Glover with a hand signal. Theme music played ten seconds before Glover began speaking.

"Good morning, San Diego," he boomed. "Today we have a special radio simulcast here at KQEW AM 1410 and KZSD AM 780. I, Glover Hayes, have special guests on my show, the hosts of *Gayline*, or should I say hostesses? Marly—"

"Hey, there!" she interjected.

I realized our mics were on. It was confusing not being in control of the board. I was hesitant to breathe in fear the sound would come across too loud.

"And her faithful sidekick-slash-call screener, Claire."

"Hi." My voice cracked.

If he thought we were special, it remained to be seen. Glover and Marly immediately launched into preliminary niceties about the function of *Gayline* as a community forum. They compared the way their respective shows provided a similar service to listeners, the main difference being the *Gayline* audience was predominantly gay and left leaning as opposed to the primarily right-leaning listeners of *The Glover Hayes Show*. Both featured guest speakers, political commentary, community events, and news of interest as well as an opportunity for San Diegans to speak their minds on a myriad of topics. In competition for airtime, Marly and Glover each interrupted and stepped on each other's words in an effort to control the conversation. There was not one opening in their rapid-fire exchange for me to add a word. Glover primed his audience for the next segment coming up after the commercials.

Jimmy switched off our mics during the break. As Glover typed something on his keyboard, Marly turned to me and cupped her hand near her mouth. I removed my headphones.

"Don't wait for an invitation, girlfriend. You have to jump in if you're going to say anything. The more airtime we get, the less dominant he'll seem. We've got more debate coming up." I pressed my lips and nodded. She leaned in closer and whispered in my ear. "Pretend he's not in the room, like if he called our show and we were joking around on the air. Whatever you do, don't get defensive. Don't be afraid to hit hard, because you can be sure he will." I nodded again and adjusted my cans.

I sipped water to keep my throat moist. We

came back on.

Glover took the lead. "You're never going to get much higher in the ratings. There are only so many gay people out there."

Marly answered. "We draw from a larger demographic. Our new data shows that well over half of our listeners are not gay. We hope to increase our listenership by appealing to folks who like what we have to say, who like the music we play, and who may or may not be gay."

"Olé!" I shouted. I didn't know what I was doing. Marly grinned.

"How many gays listen to your show," she added, "more than once?"

"I'm sure our numbers are elevated today. It's not something we measure. We're after a normal audience, young adults to seniors, lots of baby boomers."

"There you go again with that 'normal' word. I'm sure *Gayline* listeners would successfully argue your opinions aren't fact. Maybe the drop in share you had over the winter was your 'normal' listener base switching to my show."

"Yes, Glover, why did your share drop a half point?" I asked.

"We tried a number of new things during that time. We can do that. We have the luxury of commanding the airwaves during daytime talk. We're constantly making adjustments to appeal to our audience."

"Like having us on your show."

Glover acted as if Marly had said nothing. "We pride ourselves on being dynamic. I'm sure you can relate. Your show was going nowhere until you added Claire."

I sat up straight. "I'm a laugh a minute," I deadpanned. The two chuckled. "Marly and I have good chemistry. We play off one another and it livens up *Gayline*. Everyone seems to like it." I was feeling upbeat.

"Now, Claire, I hear you joke around about the gay lifestyle when you're on the air, but you're married, aren't you?"

I felt like my sense of humor had been slapped from my face. I wasn't sure where to go. "Yes, um, separated." I had to come back strong. "Why do you ask? Glover, are you flirting with me? What will Mrs. Glover say, I mean Mrs. Hayes?"

Marly burst out laughing. "Mrs. Glover. I love it! And all the Glover kids, like the George Foreman family. We've got Glover Hayes Jr., Glover the third, Glover the fourth. Glover, it's so you!"

"My wife is a kind and generous person. We've been happily married almost thirty years. Marly, too bad you'll never know the joy of having a husband. Doesn't that bother you?"

"I've got a partner," Marly announced with pride. "And she's great—a very neat person, irons and folds the trash before throwing it out. And the sex—*wow*! Night before last I had to replace the sheets. Burned a hole right through them."

I took a deep breath and controlled my smile.

"First, you're not married. Second, you and your friend can't have kids naturally. Doesn't that tell you something's sinfully wrong?"

"Actually, she's already got kids, not that it's an issue. I never was the maternal type, but hey, nothing more romantic than me, my partner, and a sterilized turkey baster. We'll have a brood of gobblers."

"See? This is what I'm talking about. This is not natural. You can't sit there and tell me God's plan included turkey basters."

"Ohhh, that ruffles your feathers. I don't know why. You like women. I like women. Tell me, Glover, when did you *choose* to be heterosexual?"

"I bet he was born that way," I added. "Probably genetic."

"Yes, the way God intended," he said.

"Exactly! Me, too. I'm made in God's image. Which brings me to my next point." Marly leaned forward. "If God didn't want gays, why does he keep putting them on this earth? It's obvious God's plan includes diversity."

"A diverse city, like San Diego," I said.

Glover typed into his computer. "Okay, Jimmy says we've got Michael on the line. Go ahead, Michael."

"Hi, Glover. I'm a Log Cabin Republican. I called to remind you some gays have a right-wing perspective. San Diego used to be on the conservative side because of the military, but that's changing fast. The military has a lot of LGBTQ personnel and they do a great job. Too bad the government doesn't fully appreciate their contributions. There's always pushback and harassment. In any other profession, they'd be able to sue for discrimination, and win."

"You're always fighting the morale issue, especially during wartime," Glover said. "Don't Ask, Don't Tell didn't work any better than letting the world know you're a flamer under your uniform. Those people should go into another line of work from the get-go. It's simple. If you know you're gay, don't enlist. Do something else, for heaven's sake. Personally, I'd like to see more gay Republicans active in politics."

"But not gay Democrats?" Marly asked. "San Diego is known for all the gay politicians it cranks out. Speaking of selective service, that limits the field of babes you can try and win favors from."

"Marly, that's a cheap shot I'll ignore. Thanks for your call, Michael. We've got big surprises coming up, and we'll be taking your calls. More of me, the one and only Glover Hayes, along with Marly and Claire from *Gayline*, right here on *The Glover Hayes Show*. Don't go away!"

I took off my cans and avoided looking at Glover. I could not let down my guard during our break. And speaking of big surprises, what happened to our two guests? Why hadn't they arrived? *What will we do if they don't show up?*

Chapter Fifty-two

"Previously, we agreed I would go ahead with my segment," Glover said during the break. Marly and I concurred. "One of your guests, Kim, has arrived. She's in the lobby. If you want to start, I say ladies first."

I breathed a silent sigh of relief. "No," I said. "We'll wait for Trevor. Besides, we're too curious about your quiz."

Glover shrugged. Because he was receiving messages on his computer, he could have advance knowledge about our guests, not that their appearance would give anything away. I could not read him, which was probably a good sign that no one had tipped our hand. With seconds to go, we adjusted our cans and got ready.

Music came up and faded. "We're back," Glover stated with a genuine air of excitement. His professional on-air style was much different than what Marly and I practiced on *Gayline*. He was more formal and certainly over-the-top with his word pacing and ego-driven persona fueled with more volume than necessary. I wondered if he was mild-mannered at home.

"Marly Megalomaniac here from *Gayline* with my partner Claire Voyant, the woman who knows all, sees all, but doesn't tell all."

"For your sake," Glover said, "let's hope she speaks up a little more. As part of our debate, I've prepared a quiz to see how much you really know about

lesbians. You say you're informed. Let's put it to the test. Are you ready, girls?"
"Isn't that sweet? He called us 'girls,'" Marly replied. "Les-be-an-swering. Okay, Claire?"
"Okay!" Of course, I was not ready at all. Everything I knew about being gay was either information I'd heard on *Gayline* or from casual conversation with friends and advertisers, and most of that involved current social events. I doubted I would know any of the answers to his questions and figured Marly would carry us. If he planned to trip us up on trick questions, we would need to fill with wit and humor. I centered the notepad between us and picked up a pen.
"Let's plaaaay, *Gay or Not Gay!*" The sound of heralding trumpets blared through my headphones.
Glover's enthusiasm was infectious. I stiffened with anticipation as if I were a real game show contestant getting ready to guess the answer that would reward me with a long-awaited cruise to Alaska. Mostly, I hoped to come up with a cogent reply, anything to throw points our way.
"Which is it?" Glover continued. "I'll say a name, you tell me 'gay' or 'not gay.' Ready?"
"Ready," we replied in unison.
Glover enunciated each syllable carefully as he spoke the first name. "Martina Navratilova."
"Oh, I know that one," I exclaimed. "Gay. She's gay." A bell tinged.
"Correct! Martina Navratilova is gay."
Maybe I would be of some help after all. I smiled my vote of confidence and Marly gave me two thumbs-up.
"How about Anne Heche?"
"There's an old reference. She's been straight for

a while. Is there a 'bi' category?" Marly asked.

Glover rolled his eyes. "Whatever."

"Great," Marly said. "I'd like to 'bi' a vowel."

"Can't 'bi' me love." I giggled into my mic.

"'Bi' the way—"

"Okay, okay, 'bi.' Let's give her that one," Glover said to Jimmy. The bell tinged.

Glover puffed out his chest. "Hillary Clinton."

"Hillary? Seriously? Now you're using this little game to keep alive the kinds of ancient, supposed put-downs your demographic finds amusing. I'm proud to be gay," Marly said. "But if you want to go down Rumor Road, there are lots of women in that category: Whitney Houston, Dolly Parton, Billie Holiday."

Glover made a disapproving face. "Who would say that about Dolly Parton?"

Marly feigned compassion with a pouty lower lip. "Poor Glover. Did I wreck your fantasies of you and Dolly?"

"Probably made them better," I interjected.

"Is Dolly the girl of *your* dreams?" Glover asked.

"She would be," Marly replied, "but I can't fit her all in!"

Glover returned to his list. Marly and I strayed from the format whenever possible, and Jimmy gave up on the little bell. The next commercial break came up quickly.

I took off my cans and whispered to Marly, "This is easy. He's not being as challenging as I thought he would be."

"Don't be fooled. He's throwing us softballs now, but he'll dig in. You're doing great. Keep it up."

We put our cans on and listened. It was the bottom-of-the-hour news brief. We waited through the commercials, all major advertisers, followed by a morning traffic report. Glover's theme music came up and he introduced us again for the benefit of listeners who just tuned in.

"Before I begin with the second part of the quiz, I know it's impossible to prove that all of the women I'll be asking you about were, or are, indeed lesbians, but they are widely purported to have engaged in homosexual behavior. These women are known for accomplishments in their particular field as well as their, shall we say, affinity toward other women.

"First question. Her first name was Mildred, but everyone called her by a nickname. She excelled at several sports including basketball, baseball, track, and golf. She won two gold medals at the 1932 Summer Olympics and later won the US Open—three times. Who is this well-rounded athlete?"

Clueless, I shot Marly a questioning look.

"Easy-peasy. Babe Didrikson," Marly said with assurance and a hint of boredom.

"Correct! Babe Didrikson." The bell rang with its signature ting. The name was vaguely familiar to me. I was glad Marly knew.

"This woman was Gertrude Stein's companion," Glover stated. "Although her name is connected to a brownie recipe."

"Alice B. Toklas," I said. The bell tinged.

"You girls are too good. Let's heat it up a bit with something a little less obvious. This next young woman organized the French resistance in the fifteenth century."

Marly's eyes bugged out. "What? Fifteenth century!"

"It's Joan of Arc."

"See? Your friend here knows." The bell tinged. "Maybe she knows the next one, too. Amantine Lucile Aurore Dupin," he pronounced eloquently, "was known by her pen name."

"George Sand." I winked and smiled at Marly. She looked utterly confused. I scribbled "writer" on the notepad. Marly raised her eyebrows and shook her head. She was lost. Glover grilled us with tough questions, and to my delight I was able to answer most of them correctly. When we were wrong or couldn't answer at all, an obnoxious buzzer jolted me from my chair. Marly guessed the sports figures correctly, all names I never would have gotten right. Between the two of us we did well, and occasionally spit out an obviously wrong but funny answer. I felt more like we were on one of those witty NPR radio game shows than on AM talk.

Glover announced the break and his theme music reached a crescendo. Jimmy switched to an ad and we were off the air. I checked the clock. Marly and I carefully lifted off our cans. She massaged her fingers through her hair, and for a second I replayed the memory of my hands clutching her dark locks with fervent passion.

"Girlfriend, you were awesome. What do you do, sit around at home reading Wikipedia?"

"I have a liberal arts degree, remember?"

Glover nodded. "I was also very impressed," he said to me with a twinkle in his eye. "Marly, you have a degree too, don't you?"

"Yes, in communications. I went to Cal State. That's what got me started in this crazy biz." She tapped her fingers. "Are they all here yet?"

Glover typed into his computer. He shook his

head. "We're not running overtime if he doesn't come."

Marly sent off a text.

Once back on the air, Jimmy patched through several quick calls. There were questions and affirming comments for Marly and Glover, yet a subtle bias emerged in Glover's favor. For an intern with limited experience, Jimmy was skilled at his job. Superficially, he made it appear as if we were hearing from a balanced cross-section, but of course he had the benefit of pre-screening for content and so far was catering to Glover. The underlying prejudice made me feel increasingly irritated as if chiggers had worked their way underneath my skin. At the break I pulled off my cans, stretched, and scratched myself. Glover gave me a once-over glance and smirked lasciviously. I didn't want him flirting with me and I hoped I hadn't given him the wrong idea earlier. If he thought he could gain an advantage by subtly coming on to me, he was mistaken. That was not the plan.

"Trevor is here," Glover said off-mic.

Marly hummed affirmatively and sent off another text. "We're almost ready for them to join us, but first, we've got a surprise for you." I looked at her impish smile and knew I was in deep. Nothing could save me now.

Chapter Fifty-three

Marly started in after the break. "Glover, in the first segment, everyone got a better idea of what our shows are about—how they're alike and not so alike. Claire and I decided not to come to this showdown armed for bear or try to slam you whenever we had the chance, although it was tempting. We have a reputation for joking it up, but we also do charity work and good deeds—like gay boy scouts! We know you're quite the man about town when you're not on the air, so we put together a bunch of clips I think you'll like."

"Sound clips?" he said.

"Photos actually, on a video."

"Hardly seems appropriate for radio."

"Stay up with the times here, Glover. We put together a short video and I'm going to narrate while it's playing. Actually, two two-minute videos. Go to your computer and turn off the sound. There's a soundtrack, but you can listen to it again later when your ego gets hungry. Go to the KZSD website and click on *Gayline*. The first video link is posted on the top of the page where it says 'Glover Hayes Video, Part One.' You listeners out there, if you're sitting at your computer or are on your phone, click on the link and follow along. The link is also posted on all of our social media sites. This is your life, Glover Hayes!"

She positioned her phone in front of us so she

and I could watch together. In the meantime, Glover turned to his computer, found the page, and Marly signaled for him to click on the link the same time she did. The video loaded and began to play.

"Our video starts out with early photos," Marly said. "Look, here's Glover at around three years old with his legs dangling out of a tire swing—looks like his middle is stuck, but I guess you eventually got out. And now a few school pictures. Great hair, Glover. Did you cut it yourself?"

"Where did you get these?" he asked.

"Your family. They were good about keeping this a surprise. Camp photos. More school pictures through the years. Good thing hair regrows. Wow! Can you say acne? Now the prom. Who would guess you'd wear ruffles? Not too feminine, noooo."

"That's my wife. I mean, she became my wife."

"Moving along...you both look pretty young in these wedding photos. Couldn't wait to get her in bed, you rascal. And what else? Your new baby. Isn't that sweet?"

"You put in a picture of my dog. He's just a pup! Later, I got more of those hounds. Started breeding them."

I glanced at Glover, whose face beamed in the reflected light of his computer screen. Marly narrated between interruptions from Glover, who reveled in the positive attention as the photos played out, chronologically documenting his family life and kids. Career shots and short video clips taken at media events followed. At two minutes, the video stopped after a clip showing him shaking hands with local politicians at the mayor's inauguration.

"All right. That ends Part One. Glover, we'll play

Part Two next. I wanted to keep the videos short so they would load quickly."

"I can't believe you did this! It really is a surprise."

Jimmy fed through a few short calls and Glover fielded the compliments, even though they were directed at Marly. So far everything was going to plan.

"Next caller, Jimmy."

"Don't you believe for one second that Marly is a nice person," the female caller said. "She's got mental problems and wouldn't know the truth if it hit her in the head."

"That voice..." Marly looked stunned.

"You know she has a drunk driving conviction."

Marly turned red. "Stephanie! Why you—"

"Drunk driving, you say?" Glover mused.

My eyes widened and I stared at Marly. I could feel heat coming off her body and I started to feel warm, too. This was not part of the plan. I looked at Jimmy, but his head was down and I couldn't catch his eye.

"Marly, is that true?" Glover's tone, dripping with feigned innocence, indicated he knew the answer.

"That was years ago. I did my community service. I was young and I learned from my mistake."

"Oh, did you?" Stephanie said. "Because after that you still drove crazy, like you were drunk, even though you weren't. But who knows? I was afraid to get into the car with you. You were completely unstable."

"Look who's talking."

"I lived with you, I ought to know. And then, Glover, she didn't shower—for over three months! The whole house reeked. Ewww! I couldn't stand it. I had to break it off and move out. And she still wouldn't leave me alone."

"Wow, talk about separation from reality. The restraining order was against *you!*"

Glover cut in. "Marly, it's hard to know the truth from fiction when you're talking. Earlier you told me you graduated from Cal State, but not according to their records. You didn't graduate, did you?"

"I, I'm just a couple of classes short," Marly sputtered.

"See, she lies," Stephanie said. "Lies, lies, and more lies."

Now I felt one accusation short of another hot flash. I was speechless and looked at Marly for reassurance.

"I may joke around on the air," Marly said, "but my listeners aren't fed a bunch of bull crap and distortions. They know I'm joking around. You serious types are the scary ones. You believe your fake news." Marly shifted her attention away from Glover and looked at me beseechingly, as if to convey she hoped I would believe her.

Music came up and Glover segued to the sign-off. Jimmy put on a commercial and broke in to say our two guests waiting in the lobby would have to come in now or they wouldn't have another chance.

"Great. Fucking pig, jerk-off," Marly muttered. "You set me up. I'll be right back, *asshole!*" She practically knocked over her chair on the way out. She pushed on the door and tried to slam it behind her, but the shock absorber made it close gently as she stormed away down the hall.

I looked at Glover. My jaw clenched tight as I glared at him.

"This is radio," he said lightly. "It's all for entertainment. Don't you know that by now?" My heart pounded in my ears. Was it true about Marly? Did she have a "Loony Lesbie" side to her personality that went beyond the airwaves? Did she still drive drunk? Hadn't my daughter warned me?

Glover broke the silence. "I've been impressed with your performance."

"Who? Me?" There was no one else in the room.

"Yes, you. I think you have special talents. And honestly, I'm not sure if I want to work with you or ask you out." Glover's lip curled into a smile. "I was hoping you'd pick up on my interest. I find you quite attractive. I know I'm being forward, but I grab opportunities when they arise. Merely a friendly drink after work, you understand. What do you say?"

"Really? What about Mrs. Glover and your family values?" I flushed anew.

"Listen, Jimmy's leaving for a summer grad school program and he's not coming back. I don't have to take another intern. I could use someone like you around here."

"Thanks for the job offer, but you're out of your mind."

"Think about your career. *Gayline* isn't for you. I can help you. This is the big time."

I reached for my purse as if I were about to leave. I turned and saw the KQEW receptionist leading Marly and our two guests, a young man and a woman, toward Glover's studio. Glover stood as the three hustled into his office and the receptionist went back to her station. Marly introduced Kim, a tall, fair blonde with cropped hair, no makeup, and a bag flung across her shoulder, and Trevor, a slender black man with a short scruffy beard. His hair was completely covered beneath a bulky red-, green-, and orange-striped knit cap favored by some Rastafarian types I'd seen hanging out by the beach. The two grabbed a couple of folding chairs and sat slightly behind us. This was my first time meeting Kim, too.

Glover gave the pair a once-over. "Who's this? Your security detail?" He guffawed.

"They're just observing," Marly said. Her anger had subsided. "You think I'm pissed off—well, I understand. The show must go on. And despite your nasty attempts to dig up a little dirt on me—"

"Ha! You said it. You're the one who didn't shower." He smacked his hand on his desk in delight.

"As I was saying," she said through clenched teeth. "Despite that, we're going to play the second part of the video."

Glover's eyes narrowed as he took us all in. "Observers, you say. Hmm. Doubtful."

"They may have something to add to the conversation," she said.

I glanced over my shoulder and noticed that although Trevor had managed to grow out a little beard over the past few days, his eyebrows were missing. I didn't want to call attention to our guests, who sat impassively as they had been instructed, so I turned the conversation toward a likely point of diversion.

"Glover, those dogs we saw of yours, I bet they're champions."

Glover immediately brightened. "You bet they are. Bloodhounds of quality pedigree only come from a few respected kennels. They—"

"Fifteen seconds," Jimmy announced. "I'm going to run the sound through the room so you don't need your headsets. Quiet. Mics on in six, five, four..." The music came up and I tried to put my exchange with

Glover behind me. I needed to focus and glanced at the clock to check on the remaining time. Five minutes of airtime remained—right on schedule.

"Glover Hayes here. We're back on *The Glover Hayes Show* with my guests Marly and Claire, and now two of their friends have joined them for much-needed moral support. Maybe they'll break out in song."

"Let's get right to it, Glover," I said. "We loaded up the second link. Everybody, scroll to the very bottom of the *Gayline* website and click on the link that says 'KQEW HIV Prevention.'"

"What kind of a dig is that?" Glover raised his brow at Marly.

"Our bad. It should read: 'Glover Hayes Video, Part Two,' but it was mislabeled. Click it, Glover, and let's get started." He clicked on the link as Marly did on her phone.

Marly narrated. "Here's the rest of the video of you at the mayor's inauguration. Must have been a fun evening, and now...oops!" The video broke off and flashed brightly. A new video scene appeared. "What's this? Somehow we've skipped ahead to the fundraiser you emceed a couple of weeks ago. Okay, well, too late to fix it now. The champagne is flowing. A close-up on the dessert table. Here's you and the mayor, except now you're at the after party. And look at the babes! They're almost wearing something. Who else is here? A councilman, press secretary, a couple of supes, and live music. Nice. We break through the crowd and, gee, that looks like you getting a lap dance from a very attractive Black woman. What a striking young lady. Not your wife, is it?"

"So this is your idea of a joke. It's a fraud,"

Glover stated.

"Kiss, kiss! I've heard you aren't supposed to touch. Naughty, Glover. Put your tongue back in your mouth where it belongs. She's shimmying off your lap. Look at her flip those long braids your way. You're pulling her by the wrist back toward you. Wanted a little more, huh?"

"That's not me. This is a charade! Jimmy, kill it."

"You're writing your cell phone number on a bill and tucking it into her costume. She's holding it up. Oooh, a Ben Franklin! Guess you liked that little dance."

"That's not me, I say. That's a look-alike. Jimmy, turn this off!"

"Here's another scene with some of the same guys on the same night in a hotel suite, and you've got your arm around another lady. Those implants must've cost a fortune. Is this your wife? No!"

"This is utter nonsense! I was never there. It's another one of your lies. Jimmy?"

"Jimmy can't help you, Glover. This is on our website and YouTube channel, and we're reporting live. Look, the guys are migrating into the next room for, what's this? A show! *Two* women, a redhead with curls and a blonde hottie, making out on the bed wearing lacy underthings, and you and the guys are all smiles and laughter. Sexy! I thought you didn't like lesbian action. You said it's not 'normal' as I recall."

"Get this thing off! It's clever editing, that's all it is. Jimmy, do something!"

"That's right, we've edited you diving on the bed. Look out! The redhead with the curly hair is leaving, and it's you and the blonde for some one-on-one action."

"Jimmy! Get this off the air. Use the delay. Kill it!"

"You're waving everybody off. They're out. Door's closed. Darn! Wish we could get the bedroom scene on video."

Outside Glover's studio, employees flitted from cubicle to cubicle all abuzz, while others crowded together around a computer monitor. Out of the corner of my eye, I could see Jimmy looking intently at his computer screen with his arms folded and a smirk on his face.

"Jimmy. Jimmy! Did we lose our connection? I don't have my board in place."

"Gee," Marly said. "Must be the next day. The sun is barely up and you're leaving the hotel with the blonde. And next week, here you two are again at Foxy's Entertainment Lounge where she works."

"It's a lie, and you're an expert liar. I'll sue you!"

The video ended. Kim quickly reached into her bag, and as she put on her curly red wig, Marly switched her phone to record. "Felt real to me at the mayor's after party, when I was doing the horizontal tango with your girlfriend," Kim said as she leaned in toward the mic.

"YOU! What are *you* doing here?" Glover barked at Kim. His eyes bulged, as did the veins in his neck.

"It's the curly redhead from the party," I announced cheerily.

"Don't forget me," Trevor said. He pulled off his knit hat and with a saucy gesture tossed his braided hair extensions over his delicate shoulders. "The hundred bucks is real," he said as he snapped the bill into the mic. "Here's your number. I'll be sure to call you. And there was nothing fake about that 'stiffy' you

gave me. No use pretending—you loooove that gay action!" Trevor laughed.
"OUT!" Glover stood up and thrust his finger at us. A bead of sweat flew off his head. "Out, all of you! Take that video off right now! You'll hear about this." He swept his arm in a grand gesture.
Marly panned her phone around Glover's studio to take in the action. "Woo-hoo! Too late, Glover. You've gone viral."
I grabbed my purse. As we ran out, we could see horror on the stunned faces of some of his co-workers, but also heard laughter and muffled screams coming from various quadrants. Our job was done, the show was over, and my heart felt like it would burst through my chest. I ran out of the building with Marly, Trevor, and Kim. We scattered in different directions and took off in our cars.
I drove about a half a mile and pulled into a parking lot. What had I done? I was in shock over my own behavior. Maybe Glover was right about one thing—my career. What had I gotten myself into? Though I hadn't seen the final version of Glover's video, I was somewhat prepared. I was not prepared to hear from Stephanie. Was Marly really nutso? The Loony Lesbie? Did she drive drunk? Was she a pathological liar? And what did this say about me? This whole episode sprang from one of my ideas, though Marly assured me she had permission to film everything. My thoughts were a jumble and my head tingled. I ran a couple of tissues over my forehead and neck. They shredded and rolled, and I had to look in my rearview mirror to pick off the pieces. When I felt somewhat composed, I drove back to KZSD where we had to set up for Betty's going-away party.

Chapter Fifty-four

I arrived at the KZSD employee lounge to find Marly busy at work pulling colored streamers from a brown paper bag. It was strangely out of character to see her put in a concerted effort on Betty's behalf, or maybe she looked out of place with something resembling a craft item, but in any case, Marly acted blasé, as if decorating were a weekly event. She could have viewed the retirement party as an outright celebration, but the lines around her mouth were heavy.

"Where's the tape?" she asked without greeting me.

I put down my purse and produced the sought item. "I thought we could string these at a diagonal, kind of loop them in and out across the ceiling tile supports."

"Fine. I'll get on the table," she said, "and you can hand me the roll."

It was obvious we wouldn't be talking about the simulcast, or us, which actually made our tasks easier to accomplish. We would have to talk about it eventually, all of it, the good, the bad, and the ugly. And of course Fred would be joining Betty's party. He would have heard the simulcast. Did he know these things about Marly's past? Maybe only Marly and her old girlfriend Stephanie could know for sure. I stopped a moment and sighed. *Everyone* at the station would have heard Stephanie's on-air pronouncements of

Marly's crazy behavior. I felt queasy and embarrassed, as if everyone also knew I had slept with Marly two evenings ago. That was between her and me, and I shuddered to think if that revelation would one day hit the airwaves. I pushed it out of my mind as I handed Marly an opened package of multicolored crepe paper streamers. Whenever the inevitable discussion would take place between Marly and me was of no consequence at the moment, as I had no idea what I would even say to her, or what she might say to me. I guessed she was feeling the same. Fred's reaction to our video/radio stunt might pull us off the air for good if advertiser feedback was negative. My mind spun. I was overwhelmed to the point where I felt emotionally drained, numb, and light-headed.

Just then, our co-worker, Patsy, bounced cheerily into the employee room, her arms full of packages. I wondered what she thought of me, but I could tell by her mood she hadn't heard the show. She'd been at the grocery store. I helped her set up a few deli trays on tables covered with white paper cloths. As she arranged fresh flowers in a vase, she chatted on merrily as if *The Glover Hayes Show* had never happened. If she hadn't heard the show, then maybe others hadn't either. I had never detected much interest from other employees about whether they cared about our show. The last moments of Glover's show had in actuality lasted a minute or two at best. Or, even if they had heard it, perhaps it was a non-event as far as the employees were concerned—just another day in radioland. Fred wouldn't do anything at Betty's going-away party. If we were going to get fired, he'd wait until either the party was over or he heard from the advertisers. I decided not to leap to conclusions and refocus on what I was doing as we had a short window of time to prepare the room.

Patsy and I cleared an area in the middle of the food display for the sheet cake. It was pretty, a sunset and palm tree painted in colored icing with the script "We'll miss you, Betty!" written across the sky.

We finished setting up right at one o'clock, and employees began to trickle in. They served themselves drinks and picked at the food until a sizable crowd had formed. Folks acknowledged Betty's arrival with applause, the signal for two men to pick up large plates and help themselves to real portions. Personally, I could wait. My guts were knotted and the extra pastry I ate at Glover's studio sat high in my stomach. I took a small plate to be polite. Zach sat in the chair next to mine and asked if I'd heard about the three-car pileup on I-5. Marly picked at her food at another table while someone from the ad department prattled on in her ear.

The sound level in the room dropped to a murmur as everyone feasted. Wrapped gifts from other co-workers mounted on a separate table. Fred came in and quietly loaded up a large plate. I stole a few glances his way to gauge his mood. He seemed hungry. I doubted anyone would say anything derogatory with Fred around, but when I heard bursts of laughter from a private conversation, I felt self-conscious.

The party grew louder as people dropped their plates in the trash and milled about the room. Betty made a point to thank me for my effort in the celebration and I heard her make similar comments to Marly before she joined another group. I watched Betty with newfound curiosity as she relished her brief moment in the spotlight.

"Attention, everyone!" Fred stood on a chair and lifted his hands as if he were a lord speaking to his peons. The room quieted in seconds. "We're gathered today to say good-bye to a valued employee. We give thanks because we're fortunate to have had Betty with us for seventeen years. That's longer than I've been here!" Laughter broke out amid applause. "We're happy for Betty even though we'll miss her. She's been loyal, dedicated, and a real asset to our company. I wish I could write a letter of praise for her next employer to tell them about her hard work ethic, her efficiency, and her lively personality, but she's going to be taking a break from the work world by playing tourist around California with her husband. Let's raise our glasses. To Betty!"

Everyone raised their drinks in the air. Betty's assistant began a round of "For She's a Jolly Good Fellow" and we all joined in. The chorus of voices was upbeat and I realized many of our co-workers would genuinely miss her around the station. I felt ashamed for treating her badly and making fun behind her back. She was an easy target, in part because her rivalry with Marly had been predetermined before my arrival, as had my alliances. I decided to make the best of my last opportunity by expressing to her my sincere wish for a fun trip and interesting future.

After the cake had been cut and the gifts opened, I noticed the crowd thinned. It was Friday, and some would leave early if they could. One by one, everyone wandered out with parting good wishes, handshakes, and hugs. A few brushed away tears, including Betty, who with the help of her assistant gathered her gifts and departed. A few stragglers dumped their plates and left.

"Good party," Fred stated when only Marly and I remained. I was afraid to breathe for what he might say next. "Do you have proof of permission to film?" he asked Marly. She nodded. In his typically abrupt manner he turned on his heel and walked out, obviously uninterested in further discussion about Betty's party or our morning on *The Glover Hayes Show*.

Marly seemed worn out. I avoided interaction by gathering paper plates and half-empty plastic glasses. She stood on a table and began removing the festive decorations. We worked in silence until a deliveryman interrupted us.

"Delivery for Marly Mesterhazy," he said. Marly ignored the visitor. I approached him.

"Party's over," I said. "What's in the box?"

"A cake." He set the unobtrusive square white box on a table and turned away.

"Oh, well," I said. "We'll find someone to eat this." The man seemed in a hurry, but that wasn't what bothered me; it was the cord tied around the box. It was thick jute, not your typical thin white string. And no one called Marly by her last name. No one even *knew* her last name. And why was he wearing thick gloves on a warm day to deliver a cake box? Then I realized he looked familiar, a tall, thin man, much older than one would suspect for a person delivering baked goods. "Hey!" I called out.

He looked over his shoulder and then bolted out the door. I stood there frozen in space, knowing something was more than odd; there was something very wrong. Then it hit me. A rush of energy sent an icy blast of shivers up my legs, spine, and out my fingertips. My hair stood on end as if the room had been charged with static electricity. It was a man we'd seen in the photos, one who appeared over and over again in the portfolio Agent Emerson had shared with us some weeks back.

"*IT'S A BOMB! RUN!*"

Marly looked at me as if I were psycho. She stood on the table with a dull look about her, like the food she had eaten had drugged her senses. I grabbed her belt loop and pulled. She made a halfhearted jump off the table, her hand and knee hitting the floor before she scrambled to her feet. We charged for the door. I swung it wide open, pushing Marly ahead of me.

The noise was deafening. Something launched me off my feet and threw me out the doorway. I could feel my body lift off the ground and propel forward, yet I had the sense I was also moving in slow motion, strangely aware of the space around me and at the same time not in control of my body. Shrieking. I could hear it—a high-pitched wail. Was it my own voice? Marly's? Her body beneath mine cushioned my fall. My left wrist hit the floor with a crack as my head scraped along the rough texture of the wall with its countless coats of paint, pulling my hair, ripping my skin, my backside aflame in a prickly heat of a thousand hot needles. My body curled as my bottom rolled over in a somersault, ricocheting off one wall, into another...

Chapter Fifty-five

"Look! Her eyelids are fluttering. Nurse, I think she's waking up."

"I'll get the doctor."

"Claire, can you hear me?"

I saw Ted's blurry form through my eyelashes. He squeezed my hand. It took a few more seconds and a few hard blinks to focus in on him. Tear tracks ran down his cheeks. He looked like hell.

"Why are you crying?" I mumbled weakly.

"Oh, Claire, I've been so worried."

Slowly, I became aware of my surroundings: the metal railings of the bed frame, stiff white sheets, a thin pastel yellow blanket, oversized loops holding up a long, dull pink curtain surrounding the bed and separating it from the rest of the room. The bandages on my head felt like a winter hat and my left wrist was set in a fiberglass cast. I lifted my arm, but the cast felt heavy. I let it drop onto the bed.

"I remember falling," I said. "Is it bad?" I wiggled my swollen fingers.

"It's a clean break. They're concerned you suffered a concussion. You've been fading in and out for a while."

"I think I'm okay, but I feel kinda drugged. Oh, I remember the emergency room."

Moisture welled up in Ted's eyes and pooled until two steady streams poured down each side of his face. "I'm so sorry," he choked. "I didn't do it! You have to believe me; it wasn't me. I never wanted anything bad to happen to you."

What happened? I tried to remember. Someone had pushed me, or no, thrown me down, but I couldn't remember where that was or who would do such a thing. I wanted to sit up, but my body ached horrifically. I could barely move.

"Here, let me help." Ted adjusted the electric bed to raise my upper body. I could feel myself come around a little more. He handed me a cup and I took a sip. The cool water moistened my dry throat. A few drops were enough. I closed my eyes and tried to remember. I saw the scene pass through my mind like a movie.

"It wasn't you," I said. "It was that tall guy." I could see his face. The box. The fibrous cord. The details were coming back to me.

The doctor arrived. While she examined me, Ted went to retrieve Jenny, who had gone to the cafeteria. It was an effort to move and even a simple thing like the blood pressure cuff was almost more than I could take. My head still felt woozy and my ears were ringing, but I was definitely coming to my senses. The doctor asked for my name, the current president, and a few other things. Then she assured me I would be okay. Her recommendation was for me to spend a night in the hospital for observation.

As soon as the doctor left, Agent Emerson walked in and stood beside me.

"Welcome back," she said.

"It's the man in the photo," I said eagerly. "The tall, skinny guy."

"Yes," she replied. "The alleged perpetrator and accomplice are in custody."

The words fell over me in a welcome shower of relief. I felt safe in the hospital. They got the bad guys. Justice would prevail even if there would be challenges in the road ahead.

"Who are they?" I asked.

"The tall, thin man you recognized from the photos is Ivy O'Neal's brother. We've had him under surveillance for a long time."

Hmm, Ivy. I mulled over the connection and wondered if her brother was responsible for a bombing at an abortion clinic I had read about years ago.

"Who's the other guy?"

"Not a guy." Emerson paused as if weighing her words. "I suppose you'll hear soon enough since it's already been on the news. It's Betty."

"What? No! Betty?" If my eyes weren't open before, they were now. I could not wait to hear more.

Agent Emerson continued. "It was her thumbprint we found on the cassette player, but that in itself was rather weak evidence. The man she was protecting is, or was, her lover. He would call in a bomb threat near the end of Marly's show, before lunch, so the two of them could spend extra time together. She broke it off, and I don't think he wanted that. She's already given us a statement and agreed to turn state's evidence in exchange for immunity. It's unlikely she had anything to do with the actual blast. Fortunately, it was meant to be small. The room sustained minor damage considering what could have happened."

Betty. She seemed like such an average type at that invisible age women achieve as they extend well into their middle years, and yet here she was living a secret life. It cast the timing of events in a whole new light, and I wondered if her retirement was somehow connected to it all. Wouldn't Marly be surprised.

"Marly!" Tears flooded my eyes.

"It's okay. She's okay. She's in another room."

"I have to see her." Betty and her criminal cohort were blown out of my thoughts as a more important person came to mind.

"She wants to see you, too—awake."

"Help me. I think I need a wheelchair."

Surely the doctor would not have approved of my getting out of bed, and I was not about to ask for permission. The truth was my sense of urgency was stronger than my realization of how sore I felt. I had to see Marly, and no amount of pain would keep me from her. My body cried out in silent agony as Emerson helped me into a chair she had wheeled in from the hallway. I tried not to let on how difficult it was for me to move. Every muscle in my body had been pummeled, and I discovered bandages wrapped around me in unlikely places. I lowered my head as she wheeled me out the door and down the hall. I didn't want to be discovered and ordered back to bed. We passed half a dozen doorways before she maneuvered me into a room. Marly was sitting up in bed chatting with a visitor.

"Oh, my God. Look who rose from the dead." Marly's voice lacked her usual robust clarity. She pushed a button on a remote control. Her bed hummed as the backrest came up, allowing her to sit taller. "How are you? I'm so glad you're up."

"We'll talk again later," said Agent Emerson, "when it's just us. Excuse me." She walked out of the room.

I wondered if Marly's visitor would take the hint and give us a private moment, too. The woman greeted me by name. She looked familiar, but her voice didn't help me match up who it was. I stared at her, my brain still muddy. I looked harder.

"Lourdes," I said. "Is that you?" My mind raced ahead as she asked about me. I had never heard her say more than a few words. "You look so different, not like I remember." She was beautiful, and as she spoke, I realized the dramatic change.

"I had surgery to fix my underbite," she said. "It's been a long haul, but it was worth it."

"Isn't it amazing? A total knockout," Marly said. "It's like she's a new person."

"I feel like a new person. I go out more now and it's shocking how people treat me differently. It's the same me inside, just a new me outside. But I like it. I like what I see in the mirror."

"Well, yeah!" We all laughed. "And your voice…"

"Can you tell? I speak more clearly. I had a few sessions with a speech pathologist. But enough about me, how are—"

"No," I said. "Your voice…I recognize your voice. It's Yin-Yang. You're Yin-Yang! I recognize your voice." I looked at Marly, who smiled. She looked tired, but not surprised. "It's Yin-Yang," I repeated emphatically. "You know, she calls in to *Gayline* all the time."

Marly and Lourdes laughed.

"Claire, it's good to see you're going to be all right," Marly quipped. "Of course I knew Lourdes was Yin-Yang. I've known all along."

"Are you shittin' me?" I never swore and I'm sure I looked as startled as they did. We all laughed.

The movement caused my sides to ache terribly and my head throbbed.

Lourdes touched her jaw as she explained. "For years, I worked out of my house so people wouldn't have to see me. Insurance wouldn't pay for my surgery because they said it wasn't medically necessary. It took me years to save up enough to pay for it myself. That's why you didn't hear from me for a long time. My jaw was wired shut while I was recuperating. I could only send emails. Then I had to relearn how to talk."

"Lourdes is going to fill in for us while we're out," Marly said. "We're working it out with Fred because I wasn't sure when we'd be back at the station."

The mention of work made me feel weighty. For a moment, I wished I could fall back into the sleepy torpor from which I had emerged, yet the fuse box in my head was tripping light switches back on in rooms I wasn't prepared to see.

"It's pretty late," said Lourdes. "You probably want to visit with each other, so I'll leave you two for now. Anyway, I have to go meet with Fred soon. Let me know how I can help, if there's anything else. Feel better, you two."

"Thanks."

After Lourdes left, I wheeled in close to Marly and took her hand with my good one. I rested my bandaged head lightly on top of her forearm. We sat together in relative quiet save for the busy hospital sounds outside her door. She sighed several times as if she planned on speaking and then decided not to. It seemed like whatever was on her mind must have been important. Rather than give her a rundown on my ailments or bring up all the events we had been through, I waited for her to speak.

"It's true about me and Stephanie," she said finally. "I did that stuff. I'm not going to lie about it."

"It doesn't matter. That was years ago. You're entitled to your life before me."

"I told you I had to do something drastic to get rid of her. The funny thing is that's how I ended up in Studio B—because I wouldn't take a shower." She didn't smile. "No one used that old studio because it wasn't modernized. That was before I ever needed a call screener. And then, I kind of liked being in there. I could spread out and no one messed with my stuff." She paused. "I did eventually shower. Anyway, I knew what I was doing. Stephanie was obsessive and jealous, and I didn't want to be with her. I told her to move out and she wouldn't, she held on tighter. I started to drink too much. After I got a DUI, I knew it was a mistake. I wasn't going to blame my drinking on her, so I cleaned up my act. But I still couldn't get rid of her. She didn't understand it was over or that she had to move out, so I started doing things. I drove like a crazy person. I wouldn't talk to her for days and then I'd go on these psycho rants. I did it on purpose to get her to leave. Maybe that was mean or stupid or immature. I can understand why you'd be disappointed in me."

"It sounds like you acted out of desperation."

"I was desperate. And when she did leave, she stalked me. That's why I had to get a restraining order. Every time I'd turn around, there she was. I woke up one morning and saw her staring at me through the window. It was scary! I'm not saying it was all her fault. I know it takes two.

"If you don't want anything to do with me ever again, I would understand. I've turned your world on end. I wanted to be a good influence in your life, to make your life better. At first, I only wanted a friendly working relationship. I could tell you were going to work out so I took a special interest in you. I believed we could help each other. But the more time I spent with you, and the more fun we had...well, you know. We just click. I was hoping you'd see more of my softer side, to see me as a well-rounded person, because... because I fell in love with you. I thought we were good together. But now look at what's happened. You've gotten caught up in all my craziness. You wouldn't be the first not to be able to deal with it. We were blown up, for Christ's sake!"

"That doesn't happen every day. Besides, you look like you're going to make it. What happened to you?"

"Bruised ribs. One fracture. You landed on me."

"Sorry. I was trying to save you."

"Thanks for trying. Don't you know, I'm beyond being saved. Ask Ivy and her brother."

I exhaled a chuckle. "Oh, it hurts when I laugh."

"Then you don't want to hang around with me."

She was giving me an out. It would be a natural time for me to go back to my caring family, or at the very least my apartment. After I got better, I could get another job. I had skills and a new, stronger outlook. The door was open. I could make a graceful exit and no one would question why I left.

I lifted my head and looked at her uplifted brows, so full of worry. I reached over and combed her hair with my fingers. Her eyes appeared glassy, as if a trail of tears was not far behind.

"I'm cold," I said. "Why are hospitals always so chilly? Move over."

Marly's eyes widened, and then she obeyed by pulling back the covers and shifting her body to the side. She used the remote to lower the bed angle. I pushed up using my good arm and inched sideways onto her bed. We snuggled in together, spooning with my back to her front. I could feel the bandage wrapped around her chest press against my spine. Her breathing was labored, and I felt badly for her, yet when I caught a whiff of her shampoo, my body let go of its tension. I took her hand that rested on my leg and wrapped it close to my heart, and with each breath we relaxed further into our embrace.

"I'll warm you up," she whispered in my ear. "You're right. It is a little cold in here."

I couldn't resist. "How cold is it?"

She gave me a small hug and kissed my neck above the hospital gown. "It's so cold…"

About the author

Zoe Amos started off writing short stories and has increased her word count to full-length fiction. Her work under this pen name is both traditionally and self-published with entries in various lesbian romance and erotica anthologies. In 2013, she published *Superior,* an adventure romance. In 2010, she authored the acclaimed self-help book, *You Don't Ask, You Don't Get,* under the name Janet F. Williams.

A creative career jumper, Zoe's path includes graphics, fine arts, health, radio, avocado farming, high-end automotive and jewelry sales, and sales training. She has spent well over twenty years producing as an award-winning author, writer, editor, and writing coach, and has presented workshops at writers' conferences.

Zoe enjoys living in San Diego County where on any given day she can hike on a beach, hill, mountain, or desert landscape. When not engaged in backyard gardening, she writes the stories she likes to read.

IF YOU LIKED THIS BOOK...

Share a review with your friends or post a review on your favorite site like Amazon, Goodreads, Barnes and Noble, or anywhere you purchased the book. Or perhaps share a posting on your social media sites and help spread the word.

Join the Sapphire Newsletter and keep up with all your favorite authors.

Did we mention you get a free book for joining our team?

sign-up at - www.sapphirebooks.com

Other Sapphire books from Sapphire Authors

The Dragonfly House: An Erotic Romance - ISBN- 978-1-952270-14-7

On the outskirts of a small, picturesque Midwestern town, sits a large, lovely old Victorian house with many occupants. This residence, known simply as The Dragonfly House, is home to Ma'am, the proprietor, along with several young women in her employ. One such woman, Jame, is very popular among the female clientele. One such client, Sarah, fresh from a divorce and looking for a little adventure, as well as some gentle handling, becomes one of Jame's repeat clients. Once Sarah enters the picture, Jame and Ma'am, as well as the brothel, will be forever changed.

The Coffield Chronicles – Hearts Under Siege: Book One – ISBN – 978-1-952270-12-3

The year is 1862. The war between the states has been raging intensely for a year now. The country is in complete and utter turmoil, and brother is fighting brother to the death, dying for what each believed. It seems it's all the townsfolk of New Albany, Indiana can speak of, and Melody Coffield is paying attention. Through a series of heartbreaks and sorrow, she settles on the decision to cut her hair and don men's attire. Going under the alias of Melvin A. Coffield, she leaves her childhood home, the only home she had ever known, and enlists in the United States Army. Chewing tobacco and drinking liquor were ways of men, and she learns quickly how to behave like one. She would soon know the horrors of battle, and what was called the glory of war, through roads that led straight to

Vicksburg, Mississippi. However, her biggest concern was making sure she was not detected by the others. Keeping her secret would not only be challenging, but trying as well. Will she remain in this solitude the rest of her life, never allowing anyone into her heart again? Or will she find love, once more, in a world that was intolerant and unaccepting of who she truly was?

Keeping Secrets – ISBN – 978-1-952270-04-8

What would you do if, after finally finding the woman of your dreams, she suddenly leaves to fight in the Civil War? It's 1863, and Elizabeth Hepscott has resigned herself to a life of monotonous boredom far from the battlefields as the wife of a Missouri rancher. Her fate changes when she travels with her brother to Kentucky to help him join the Union Army. On a whim, she poses as his little brother and is bullied into enlisting, as well. Reluctantly pulled into a new destiny, a lark decision quickly cascades into mortal danger. While Elizabeth's life has made a drastic U-turn, Charlie Schweicher, heiress to a glass-making fortune, is still searching for the only thing money can't buy. A chance encounter drastically changes everything for both of them. Will Charlie find the love she's longed for, or will the war take it all away?

Diva – ISBN – 978-1-952270-10-9

What if…you were offered a part-time job as the personal assistant to someone you have idolized for years? Meg Ellis has just completed the school year as a nurse in the Santa Fe school system. It isn't her first choice of profession, but a medical problem derailed her musical career years ago. The breakup of a bad relationship is still painful. The loving support from her close-knit family and good friends has buoyed her spirits, but longing still lurks below the surface. She can't forget the intoxicating allure of the beautiful diva who haunts her dreams. Nicole Bernard is a rising star in the world of opera, adored by fans around the globe. When Meg learns that Nicole is headlining a new production at the renowned New Mexico outdoor pavilion—and then is asked to accept a job offer to be her personal assistant—she is beside herself. After a short time learning the routine and reining in her hormones, Meg discovers that Nicole's family will be visiting for the opening. Her responsibility to the charismatic singer immediately becomes more difficult when Nicole's young husband Mario shows up and threatens the comfortable rapport between Meg and the prima donna. The two women brace for a roller-coaster interlude composed by fate. Will the warm days and cool nights, the breathtaking scenery, and the romance of the music create summer love? A heartbreaking game? Or something very special?

Made in the USA
Las Vegas, NV
04 March 2021